A Musket in My Hands

by
Sandra Merville Hart

SMITTEN
HISTORICAL ROMANCE
LIGHTHOUSE PUBLISHING OF THE CAROLINAS

A MUSKET IN MY HANDS BY SANDRA MERVILLE HART
Published by Smitten Historical Romance
an imprint of Lighthouse Publishing of the Carolinas
2333 Barton Oaks Dr., Raleigh, NC 27614

ISBN: 978-1-946016-67-6
Copyright © 2018 by Sandra Merville Hart
Cover design by Elaina Lee
Interior design Karthick Srinivasan

Available in print from your local bookstore, online, or from the publisher at:
ShopLPC.com

For more information on this book and the author visit:
https://sandramervillehart.wordpress.com

Brought to you by the creative team at Lighthouse Publishing of the Carolinas
(LPCBooks.com): Eddie Jones, Pegg Thomas, Shonda Savage, Brenda Kay Coulter,
and Stephen Mathisen

Library of Congress Cataloging-in-Publication Data
Hart, Sandra Merville.
A Musket in My Hands/ Sandra Merville Hart 1st ed.

Printed in the United States of America

Previous Smitten Novels
By Sandra Merville Hart
A Stranger on My Land
A Rebel in My House

PRAISE FOR *A MUSKET IN MY HANDS*

I don't always read Civil War novels, because I'm not into graphic battle scenes. Sandra Merville Hart's *A Musket in My Hands* is a wonderful book. The characters grab your heart right from the beginning and they take you through a unique story line right into battles, where I followed willingly. The book isn't battle-driven. It's character driven, and the reader becomes intimately acquainted with these people who had to face things they never dreamed about happening. This is my favorite Civil War novel. I highly recommend it.

~**Lena Nelson Dooley**
Bestselling, multiple-award-winning author of *12 Gifts of Christmas, Esther's Temptation,* and *Great Lakes Lighthouse Brides*

Sandra Hart, author of the acclaimed *A Stranger on My Land* and *A Rebel in My House* has done it again with her third and best novel to date, *A Musket in My Hands*. In this brilliant historical fiction, Sandra has sat against the backdrop of Confederate General John Bell Hood's Tennessee Campaign a study of the little known but genuine phenomenon of women masquerading as men to serve and fight in the opposing armies of the Civil War. An excellent and well-researched read, this is one of the first books I've read to put a touchingly human face on the horrendously bloody Battle of Franklin.

~**Kevin Spencer**
Historian—ON THIS DAY in North Carolina History

What would make two sisters escape the only home they've ever known to join the Confederate Army disguised as men? Prompted by both love and fear, Callie and Louisa are caught up in the War Between the States in a way they never imagined. It soon becomes a nightmare they couldn't possibly foresee.

In *A Musket in My Hands*, author Sandra Merville Hart has penned a thrilling, well-researched novel set in the latter months of the Civil War. Her characters are believable, likeable, and, at times, frustrating in their decisions. But readers will find themselves rooting for the protagonists and anxiously awaiting resolution, not just on the battlefield, but in the battleground of their souls.

Inspiring and exciting, this novel will capture your heart as well as speed up your heartbeat. A historical romance well worth the read!

~Elaine Marie Cooper
Author of *Saratoga Letters*

Through *A Musket in My Hands*, Sandra Merville Hart brings to life the last months of the Confederacy as experienced by two Tennessee sisters who become soldiers for the South. Detailed research contributes to the realism in a tale of courage and strength during a tumultuous time in America's history. I was moved by the despair and deprivation yet inspired by the characters' resolve. A captivating read for historical fiction fans!

~ Sandra Ardoin
Author of the award-winning historical romance *A Reluctant Melody*

A Musket in My Hands shines with Sandra Hart's talent for historical romance. Vivid historical details highlight the romance and adventure, excitement and heartache of those desperate to survive the Civil War, while an endearing collage of characters evaluates their own allegiances to God, country, and their fellow man.

~Carrie Del Pizzo
Del Pizzo's Pen Editing

Though the fig tree does not bud and there are no grapes on the vines, though the olive crop fails and the fields produce no food, though there are no sheep in the pen and no cattle in the stalls, yet I will rejoice in the LORD, *I will be joyful in God my Savior.* Habakkuk 3:17-18 (NIV)

DEDICATION

This book is dedicated with love to
my sweet daughter, Megan.

You've inspired and encouraged me
many times.
What would my life be without you?
God was smiling when He made you, knowing
what joy you'd bring to all who love you.
I am so blessed to call you my daughter.

CHAPTER ONE

Clopping in the yard drew Callie Jennings' hand to her throat. She rushed to the window and lifted the curtain. A moment of relief washed over her. It wasn't Yankees looking for food again, thank the Lord. Pa had returned. He never said much about being a ranger, one of those irregulars who participated in guerrilla warfare for the Confederate States of America. The irregulars cut telegraph wire, pulled up railroad tracks, and worse—so some of the townsfolk said. His mood—and his drinking—depended on the success of their last mission. Would he be the even-tempered pa of her childhood today, or the drink-induced stranger she barely recognized?

Porter Jennings rode his horse into the barn and disappeared from sight. Callie dropped the curtain and hurried to the stove. Frying a batch of corn cakes didn't take long, thank goodness. Pa would have a hot meal waiting when he got done brushing down Midnight. Must have been a hard night's riding to take nigh onto noon to get back.

She didn't like the Yankees all over Tennessee any better than Pa, but she'd heard rumblings about the irregulars catching one or two of the enemies alone and hanging them on a tree. That didn't set well with her. It didn't seem fair, though she kept those thoughts to herself. He wanted to protect his daughters and, being past the draft age of forty-four, this seemed his only choice.

Her shoulders rose and fell with her sigh as lard melted in the skillet. She patted three generous portions of corn batter onto the skillet as the door slammed open.

She cringed.

"Why ain't you working at Mrs. Hobson's today?" Pa tossed his wide-brimmed hat onto a wall hook. "Ezra Culpepper said she has an order."

She glanced at Pa's clenched jaw. His friend knew the town's gossip almost before it happened. "She does. Mrs. Robbins needs a dress. That job won't pay enough for Mrs. Hobson to hire me to help."

"That ain't good enough." The gray streaks in Pa's auburn hair were as wide as the calloused fingers he ran through it. "You need to pull your weight around here."

"Hardly anyone hereabouts has money to pay for seamstress work." Her cheeks burned hotter than the sizzling cakes warranted. Not pull her weight around the house? She was the one who cooked and cleaned and tended the vegetable garden, for all the good that did. Yankees passing through got most of the crop. "She hasn't needed me regularly for two years."

"When the Yanks took over Tennessee." He pounded a fist into his hand.

"The same year Mr. Hobson died at Shiloh."

His brown eyes shifted toward the back window where his cornfields used to be. "Another widow left to raise her children without a pa."

Callie caught her breath as worry for another soldier arose, one she prayed for daily. Best think about that later, when she was alone.

Pa's neck turned scarlet. Time to give him something else to think about. "Are you hungry?" Her stomach rumbled at the appetizing smell. She turned a corn cake with a spatula too quickly. Oil splattered the stove.

"Yep. Starved." He pulled a chair away from a rectangular table in the middle of the large front room and sat. "Pity Jeb Booth can't use both you and your sister at the Mercantile. Louisa's job puts food on the table."

Such as it was. They'd all grown accustomed to getting by on less since the Northern invasion. Callie rubbed her sleeve against her forehead. More than August heat stifled the air in the clapboard home. "Here it is." She placed a plate with two corn cakes and a cup of water in front of him. "We'll have fried tomatoes from the garden for supper tonight." She retrieved her plate with a single cake from the narrow table next to the stove.

"I'll drink whiskey." Pa started eating without saying grace.

This early in the day? Callie swallowed and plonked her plate back on the side table. Ma would be turning over in her grave at the sight of hard liquor in the house. About a lot of things, in fact.

Callie hated Pa's angry mood when he drank.

"Fetch that liquor."

She forced her legs to move toward Pa's bedroom. She suspected his friend, Mr. Culpepper, of having a still. She'd like to give that old man a piece of her mind about supplying Pa with liquor. Any fool could see how drinking affected his personality—much less someone who professed to be a friend. On her knees, she reached under the bed and grabbed the first jar she touched.

The liquid in the jar sloshed up the sides, stirring up a repugnant odor that reminded her of corn and turpentine. Walking slowly, she held it away from her side to give to Pa and then brought her lunch to the table. She bowed her head, asking for strength and guidance along with the blessing for food.

"Any Yanks here while I was gone?" Pa gulped down his water and then poured a generous portion of liquor into his cup.

"Not since last week." She savored a bite of corn cake. This would have to last her until supper.

His lip curled. "You mean when they stole the corn?"

Callie's hand jerked, rattling her wooden plate. She'd worked hard to have extra vegetables to put aside for the winter. Their precious food going to feed Billy Yanks liked to turn her stomach, but it wouldn't do to throw a log onto the fire that burned inside Pa. Thank the Lord for the tomatoes and string beans still on the vines. "Half of it wasn't ripe yet. They left us that—and they paid for what they took." Though not nearly enough.

"Cold-hearted buzzards!" He pounded a fist on the table. The clear liquid in his cup sloshed over the side. "Wasn't enough to take last year's harvest—they had to trample what they left."

She tugged at the high collar of her dress. Pa hadn't been this bothered when Confederate agents confiscated the majority of their crop two years ago. He hadn't had much say in that either, but at least it had fed their own soldiers. And she'd still had a reserve of dried and canned vegetables back then—food long since consumed. "They suspected our loyalty is with the South."

"That it is." Porter took a drink. "They invaded our state, replaced our governor, burned our mills, ate our crops, killed our brave sons—what'd they expect?"

His heart was in the right place, but she hated how he'd changed since the Yankees had attacked cities and towns throughout the state. "They haven't bothered my garden patch—except for buying that corn." She spoke in a soothing voice. "I reckon an acre is beneath their notice."

"And better than twenty-five acres goin' to waste." His Adam's apple bobbed. "I ain't gonna plant a field to feed the Yanks and get nothing from it for my family."

"We've still got vegetables in my garden." She wrung her hands. Bitterness rose up in her throat.

He shoved the last bite into his mouth. "Finish your lunch. I'll start harvesting whatever's close to being ripe."

"I'll dry, pickle, and can the vegetables." Some of the burden slid off her shoulders with Pa sharing the load.

"Then we'll bury it—hide it from those varmints so's we can eat this winter." His shoulders pushed back, he stood.

"Yes, Pa." It seemed the only way to keep their food for themselves. Now that he had a plan, Pa left his cup half empty. She tossed the remains in the grass when he took a basket to the field. He always stayed calmer when not drinking to excess.

How she missed her mother's calming influence over Pa. If only Ma had survived that bout of pneumonia. She grimaced as she washed dishes. Some things couldn't be helped.

Seemed that list grew daily.

A shell from a Yankee thirty-pound parrot gun swooshed over Zachariah Pearson's head. He followed the missile's path toward Atlanta behind him. Shouting—too far away to discern the words—must have alerted citizens to get out of danger. The artillery moved slowly enough that it didn't threaten lives if soldiers and citizens alike kept their wits about them.

The ground under his feet rumbled at the impact. Black smoke billowed against the clear sky.

"No screams." His cousin, Nate McClary, watched for activity in the city. "That's a good sign."

"Most are likely hiding in gopher holes." The town's residents should have taken cover in their hastily-dug cellars. Zach turned to watch the sky near the Yankee line. No need to remind his fellow soldiers that artillery sometimes burst in the air, scattering deadly shrapnel along its path.

"Yanks are just reminding us they're around." Nate took a long drink from his canteen and then swiped water from his bearded chin.

He was right. Since they weren't actively fighting today, other comrades around them wrote letters home and cleaned their muskets, only glancing up to make certain of the projectile's path before continuing on with their tasks.

Zach leaned his back against a concrete building and slid down the hot wall to the ground. "We must hold Atlanta."

"Yep. We will."

"What if we don't?" Zach squinted up at him and pulled his kepi lower over his eyes against the scorching August sun. "You ever think about that?"

"Nope." Nate squatted on his haunches. "What's eatin' you?"

Zach lowered his voice. "Think we can win this thing if this city falls into enemy hands?"

"Better believe it. Remember when we signed up? We thought this thing would be over before we ever saw a Yankee."

"We've been wrong a time or two." He grinned.

Nate chuckled.

"We mustered into the army to protect our property—"

"Our families." Nate's blue gaze set on the horizon to the north.

"The rights granted by the Constitution making each state a sovereign government." Zach shielded his eyes against the bright sun as another shell swooshed toward them.

"Just asking the Northerners to honor our rights." The ground shook under another impact. "But we've talked about this a hundred times. Why bring it up now?"

Zach shrugged. What good would it do to talk about it now? Everything went back to Pa, in his grave these past eight years, and yet Zach still heard that disapproval in his head. Pa had considered Zach a failure, a quitter, an embarrassment to the family.

A career in the army had seemed the best way to prove himself, but even that wasn't turning out right. He excelled at being a soldier, that was true, but he was fighting for a losing cause. He couldn't ignore the truth of that much longer.

He hoped he didn't have to die to prove Pa wrong ... but he would if that's what it took.

"I'm fit to be tied."

Callie looked over her shoulder as her sister slammed the front door. Louisa, with her blue eyes and blonde hair coiled and pinned at her nape, might look like their mother but she hadn't inherited her calm temperament. "What happened?" She concentrated on slicing corn from the cob into their largest wooden bowl.

"If you had a betrothed like Nate McClary, you'd be riled, too." The hem of her blue dress flounced as she turned to lean against the long table where Callie worked.

"What's he done now?" At least Louisa was betrothed. With all the men lost to the Northern Aggression, it was a wonder any of the town's single women were promised to someone. Not that Callie wanted Nate—she had her doubts about the depth of his feelings for her sister. It was his cousin, Zachariah Pearson, whom she longed to see.

"Martha Rose got a letter from her beau, Johnny." She fidgeted with her sleeve. "He says that Nate has a wandering eye for the ladies. Too much for a man who is soon to marry."

"Martha Rose is mad because Johnny hasn't proposed."

Louisa raised her eyebrows.

"Nate proposed. Maybe she's jealous of your good fortune." Callie wiped corn kernels from the knife before picking up the next ear.

"I never thought of that. I am a lucky woman." She glanced over Callie's shoulder. "Aren't you about done drying the corn yet? You've been at it all week."

"I wish I weren't. This is the last of it—all we can spare toward winter's needs. We have to save some food for the next few weeks." Callie peered out the window where Pa bent over a row of beans. "I'll string the beans. Pa wants to bury everything that's dried. Feels good to see him working, even if it's just in my little garden. He's been happier this past week."

"Probably has more to do with him being at home for a whole week." Louisa followed her gaze. "Can't expect that to continue."

"At least he hasn't been drinking too much." She tossed an empty cob into a basket on the floor. She'd boil the cobs later for a flavorful broth. The corn's sweet smell made her stomach rumble.

She'd save a few cups of kernels for supper. "Build up a moderate fire in the oven, will you? These kernels will be ready to go in soon."

Louisa added wood from a bin to embers in the oven. "Do you think he's courting someone while betrothed to me?"

Nate again. He worried Callie. Was he really interested in other women? Or was he simply a flirt? Neither was good as far as she was concerned. "He's committed to marrying you after the war ends." Her beautiful sister could do a lot better than a man who acted as if he were the most important person in the world. But Louisa loved him. "Does that sound like he'd be courting another lady?"

Louisa gave an unladylike snort. "She might not be a lady."

The knife in Callie's hand paused against the corn cob. "You mean … you think he's taken up with a camp follower?"

"He better not have." Her blue eyes snapped. "He'd be more likely to visit a bawdy house. He says he has a hard time waiting for wedding bells."

Callie gasped. "Louisa Jennings, respectable women don't mention those places. And Nate has no call to be telling you such things."

Her chin dropped to her chest.

"Louisa?" Her fingers smashed the kernels on the cob. "Don't tell me … you didn't …"

"No, we didn't." Arms crossed close to her chest, Louisa averted her eyes. "But he said since we were getting married it didn't matter about waiting."

"It matters." Callie picked up a new ear of corn and applied the knife in short, quick strokes. For the thousandth time, she wished her mother were here to guide her tempestuous daughter. "Remember what Mama told us. Fornication is wrong. God wants us to remain pure until marriage. What if you don't marry him after all? We're to remain true to our husband."

"What about the man?" She pressed a fist to her mouth.

"He's supposed to do the same. Being a man doesn't change anything. He'd better be true to you." Her body tensed at the sheen of tears in her sister's eyes. Her opinion of Nate, never very high, plummeted. "You're not married yet. It's not too late to change your mind, cancel the whole thing—"

"No. I want to see if he's true to me first." Her chin jutted out as she shook her head.

"That's sensible. Folks are all the time gossiping. Starts no end of trouble." Callie gestured toward the table with a toss of her head. "Prepare the dripping pan for me. The flour-sack paper is on the table." Frowning, she glanced at Louisa's stormy expression. "Johnny's pretty reliable, but Martha Rose tends toward exaggeration. You can ask her to write him again for details."

"No, that's not enough." Louisa smoothed the paper over the pan. "I've got to see for myself."

Callie rolled her eyes. "How are you going to do that? Aren't they still in Georgia?"

"Johnny's letter was from Atlanta."

"That's what I thought. You can't go to Atlanta with all the fighting going on." She poured the corn over the paper and spread it evenly. "Besides, even if Nate acted shamefully, he'd be a fool to act that way while you're around."

Louisa's shoulders slumped. "Then how will I know?"

"Zach won't betray his cousin. There's no reason for me to ask him in my next letter." Callie peeked at her sister out of the corner of her eye. She must learn to control the breathless quality in her voice when mentioning Zach's name.

"Hmm." Louisa studied her sister's expression. "Seems to me you're sweet on one Zachariah Pearson. He writes to you enough. Why has he never courted you?"

Good question. She'd given him plenty of opportunities. "I don't know. I'd just turned seventeen when he mustered in at Camp Trenton. Perhaps he thought me too young."

"Maybe. But you're twenty now—he can't say that any longer."

"That's true." A desire to see the man she hoped to someday marry welled up inside her. The men had been in the Atlanta area for a few weeks. That major Southern city had to stand. Zach, as a soldier, had an important job. And that's all he thought about, too. She shoved the pan into the oven. "For all the good it will do me."

"You don't have red hair for nothing, Sister."

"Auburn." Callie rounded on her. "My hair is auburn, just like Pa's."

"You're right. Those wavy locks are auburn." She held up her hands, palms forward. "Except no one can tell your hair is curly the way you keep it twirled into a tight bun on top of your head."

She wiped the table. Her sister's wavy blonde hair was coiled and pinned at her nape. Perhaps Louisa was right, but she wanted a different look than her beautiful sister. Callie couldn't compete. "Weren't we discussing Nate?"

The animation on Louisa's face died. "I have to know if he's loyal to me."

Callie squeezed her shoulder. "I don't know if you can be certain. His comrades are the only ones who really know." Maybe he'd changed since proposing to her sister. She sighed. Though she couldn't say why, somehow she believed Martha Rose.

The back door opened. "Here's a bushel of beans." Pa set the dusty basket on the table. The earthy smell of fresh vegetables entered with him. "Once you get that corn ready for drying, start stringing these. Gonna have another bushel today and then more in about three days." He glanced at the mantle clock. "You're home early, Louisa."

"There weren't any customers. Mr. Booth sent me home." She picked a leaf off a bean.

Pa grunted. "Reason enough to prepare for winter. There's two flour sacks of corn buried by the barn ... not near enough. Since you're here, help your sister get these beans strung." He poured them on the table and strode outside with the empty basket.

"Wash the beans while I finish the corn." Callie tilted her head.

"We can talk later." They'd have to discover the truth about Nate's fidelity. Was it worth asking Zach? Would he tell the truth if it meant betraying his cousin?

Callie stirred bubbling vegetable soup for supper two days later, its savory steam tickling her nose. The pleasant scents of dried parsley, marjoram, and basil she'd added to the broth filled the kitchen. Perhaps Louisa might have something to add to their meal when she got home. It had been weeks since she'd received her pay, but a slab of bacon, a can of peaches, or a couple of potatoes certainly stretched the little they had.

Pa had walked to town after lunch. If he had another mission, he'd come back for Midnight. He kept their horse rested in between trips, hiding him in the woods if Federals were near.

Word around town was that things weren't going well for the Army of Tennessee in Atlanta. The news increased her prayers for her brave soldier. If only Zach considered himself her soldier. It seemed the twenty-two-year-old had married the army. He'd taken to soldiering in a way he never had to working on his uncle's horse farm.

"It's so hot today." Louisa trudged in, leaving the front door open. "Not much better in here." She dropped a paper sack on the table. "Five pounds of corn meal this time. My pay for the whole week."

Callie ran her hand over the coarse sack. "This is good. We were almost out of meal."

Louisa peered out the back window. "Where's Pa?"

"In town."

"Good, then we can talk. I figured out what I want to do about Nate."

"Oh?" Not much could be done from Cageville, to Callie's way of thinking. "What's that?" She stored the meal on a shelf.

Booted feet struck the porch. Pa wobbled through the door. The smell of liquor entered with him. "Need coffee." He swiped his forehead with a handkerchief. "Riding out tonight."

Callie exchanged a wary glance with Louisa. "We don't have any coffee beans, Pa, but I can make rye coffee. I put back some rye that I boiled and dried."

"Pack it." He grimaced. "Looks like we'll be gone a while. I'll take a sack of corn, too."

"I'll pack it for you." Callie kept her tone even. "Supper is ready."

"Good." He went outside, leaving the backdoor open.

The well crank creaked from the backyard. Water gushed from the spout.

"Don't say anything to anger him." Callie ladled soup into a bowl, gazing out the window at Pa.

"Hate it when he drinks." Louisa, pouring water into glasses from a pitcher, stole a glance outside. "Maybe eating will sober him."

Pa returned as she and Louisa sat on either side of the dining table. Sitting on the end, he began to eat.

She raised an eyebrow at Louisa. They both bowed their head for a silent blessing. "How long will you be gone, Pa?" Callie blew on a steaming spoonful of vegetable soup.

"Three weeks or better." He tilted his head at her. "Gonna be a wedding when we get back."

She blinked. Was Pa courting someone in town? "Who's getting married?"

"You are."

The casual announcement jolted her. "I'm not betrothed to anyone."

"Happens that you are." He shoveled in a dripping mouthful. "Worked it out today."

She met Louisa's wide-eyed gaze. *Tread lightly.* "I don't know what you mean."

"Talked to Ezra Culpepper. You need a husband. He's willing."
He kept his attention on his meal.

Louisa's eyes widened as she drew a shaky breath.

Pa's drunken state made this a bad time for a discussion, but
if he expected a wedding when he returned, Callie couldn't stay
silent. Mr. Culpepper was at least thirty years her senior. The very
thought of her … with him … "Please thank Mr. Culpepper for his
kind offer, but I'll be refusing."

Pa slammed his fist on the table. "You don't have a choice,
little missy. You've a score of years now and no suitor in sight. I'm
struggling to feed you. Them Yankees are to blame, not you. But it
ain't gonna make no difference. Why, your sister's a year younger
than you, and she's betrothed. Picked her a good, solid Southern
soldier. If you'd have done that, you wouldn't need to marry Ezra."

Callie's mouth went dry. "We're scraping by, Pa. With Louisa's
job and my vegetable garden—"

"Scraping by ain't good enough. Ezra's got land. Money put
away where the Yanks won't find it—some of it in gold. Food
buried all around his property." He gripped the table. "You'll be
taken care of, better than I can do."

"I've been writing to Zach Pearson." She fanned her face with
her hand. "I'm not interested in Mr. Culpepper. He's a nice man …
I reckon … but I aim to marry Zach someday."

"He didn't ask you, did he?" His eyes narrowed.

She lowered her gaze to her soup, all appetite gone.

"I know he didn't. You know why?" Sweat broke out on his
forehead.

She shook her head.

"Because I asked him."

Callie gasped. "You asked …?" Words died in her throat. Pa
approached Zach on her behalf?

"Back in March when he and Nate were here on furlough."
He took a long gulp of water. "Nate proposed. Zach won't marry
until this war is decided—one way or the other. Said he had a bad

feeling about what was coming and refused to leave you a widow."

Callie's heart shrank. Pa offered her hand in marriage without her knowledge … and Zach refused.

Louisa leaped to her feet. "You're the reason Nate proposed to me? He told me he loved me." Splotches of red tinged her cheeks.

"Likely he does. I just planted the thought like I was planting a row of beans." He drank the last bit of water. "Where's my whiskey?"

"It's all gone." Callie forced the words through stiff lips. Zach didn't want to marry her. Heart pounding, she struggled to tamp down her despair at Zach's refusal and her rising anger that Pa promised her hand without consulting her.

He thought a minute. "That's why I moseyed into town."

She rubbed shaking hands over her temples. This was a nightmare. That was the only explanation. She'd awaken and find it was all a bad dream.

Pa's gaze slid away from Callie's face. "Don't take on so. A man's willing to marry you. Everything will be all right."

Her breath came in shallow gasps. Nothing would be all right ever again.

In a daze, Callie cleaned the dishes and then readied food and clothes for Pa's trip.

Dusk fell, and Callie prayed that time and food had sobered Pa. The best—and only—opportunity to confront him was as he led his horse from the barn. Louisa handed him a bulging sack. He looped it over his neck.

"Pa, I don't aim to marry Mr. Culpepper."

"You're getting as stubborn as your sister." He mounted Midnight. "I already agreed. We shook hands." He patted the horse's neck without looking at Callie. "He'll be good to you—I'll see to that. The man wants sons."

"Then let him ask the Widow Baker—"

"Already did. She turned him down."

Callie clutched her throat. "Pa, I can't marry him."

"You can and you will." He sat tall in the saddle. "Can't you see this is the best I can do for you?" He scowled.

Callie shrank away from him. "No, Pa. It's not what I want."

"I about died last time we all went out." He took off his slouch hat and shoved a finger through a hole. "Another inch and I'd be dead."

Callie's gasp mingled with her sister's.

"If something happens to me, Ezra will take care of you and your sister until Nate gets home. He's agreed to it."

The blood drained from Callie's face.

"I don't want to hear no more about it." He nudged the horse toward town.

Callie swayed. She grasped a low hanging tree limb for support. This couldn't be happening. Yet Pa rode toward town without a backward glance. Marriage to a man old enough to be her pa had no place in her dreams. Or her future. But what could she do? She had no money, no family except Pa and Louisa.

"Can't believe he told Nate to propose." Louisa's chin tilted toward the upper branches of the mighty oak they stood under.

Callie pressed her lips together. Her sister tended toward selfishness, but this was ridiculous. Had she not heard what Pa was forcing her to do?

She sighed. At least Nate had listened when Pa offered Louisa's hand. They were betrothed. Not Zach. How could she face him again? Her father had made her an object of pity. And now he wanted her to marry his friend, Mr. Culpepper. The town cemetery held more than its share of young men—cut down too soon by Northern bullets, Northern shells. With the rest off fighting, she should wait for the soldiers to march home just like the other women waited for their men. Perhaps there was still hope that Zach would offer for her then.

"I thought it was my kisses that convinced Nate to propose." Louisa gave her a side glance. "He always seemed to want more."

She gasped. "Louisa! What did you do?" Zach had never kissed her. Two years ahead of her at school, he'd never seemed to forget the gap in their ages.

"Nothing. I told you." Her gaze returned to the dust cloud left by Pa. "But I know how we can save you from becoming Mrs. Culpepper *and* figure out if Nate has a straying eye."

"How?" A chill shot through Callie. That gleam in her sister's eyes usually meant trouble.

CHAPTER TWO

Lovejoy's Station, Georgia, September 5, 1864

Word reached Zach down the line that the Yankees were returning to Jonesboro. The battle was over. Federal General Sherman hadn't ordered his troops to attack again. Zach sank deeper into the ditch that had guarded him for three days. Removing his kepi, he swiped at his brow. He and his Southern comrades hadn't been able to push the Northern soldiers out of Jonesboro four days ago. Instead the Army of Tennessee retreated during the night along the Macon and Western Railroad southward to Lovejoy's Station.

Sherman's men had followed

Zach picked at the dirt under his fingernails from digging entrenchments against the strong Yankee attack that came on September second. After the loss of Atlanta, beating the Federals back had been a hard fight, but Billy Yanks were finally leaving.

His musket stank of gunpowder from the battle—he'd clean it later. He stacked it in the circle of arms of his regiment, the First Tennessee, and then rested with his back against the peeling bark of an old log. Other fellows nearby stayed behind the earthworks to write letters home or take a nap.

A whiff of coffee boiling on a fire awoke his senses. Someone probably found coffee beans in an abandoned knapsack. Wishing he'd been the lucky recipient, he stared at the field in front of the earthworks. Trampled underbrush and splintered trees told only part of the story. They still needed to bury the dead that lay there. He sighed. It might have been worse if the Yankees had pressed the battle further.

Like they had at Atlanta. His jaw tensed. Yankees now controlled the destroyed city. The Army of Tennessee had been engaged almost continuously for six weeks. Cheatham's Corps—his corps—had lost a lot of good men since July. And what had that accomplished? They still had to leave that critical Georgian city in Northern control.

The loss knocked the air out of him.

"Why so glum?" Nate plopped beside him. "They're leaving us the field this time."

"Oh, I don't know." Tucking his arm around one raised knee, Zach gave his brash relative a side glance. "Could be the six weeks of hard fighting we just endured. All for nothing."

"Bit of bad luck losing our stronghold in Atlanta." Nate's eyes narrowed. "Did you hear the latest?"

"About Atlanta?"

Nate nodded.

"Doubt it. Been trying to keep my mind on the task at hand." He steeled himself for more bad news. "Do I want to know?"

"Nope. It's bad. We had so many supplies and ammunition in Atlanta that we couldn't take everything when abandoning the city. General Hood left detachments to destroy it, so it didn't fall into enemy hands."

A weight descended on Zach's chest. "How much?"

Nate sucked in a breath and blew it out. "They blew up a score and eight carloads of ammunition and a cannon foundry. All that equipment in the Western and Atlantic roundhouse was blown up too."

Zach whistled. "That's a loss we can't afford." How could the Army of Tennessee recover? First the vital city fell, then to leave behind ammunition sorely needed by their army. It liked to turn his stomach. What a waste.

"Had to abandon rail cars, locomotives, siege guns." Nate scowled. "And we're about to get hungrier. Large stores of food were left behind."

"That's a blow." Zach rubbed his flat belly. "Ain't had a satisfying meal since spring."

"The commissary doors were opened to hungry citizens."

"Only good thing to come of all this." The townspeople hadn't deserved those terrible weeks of terror. Deprivation. Shells dropping on city streets. The citizens now had food, but it came at a high cost.

"The last really good meal I ate was at the Jennings' house back in March." Nate ran a blade of grass through his fingers.

"Callie made chicken stew and rice pudding." His gaze shifted to the north. Tennessee. "Doesn't sound like much. She'd have made a larger meal back in the old days before the war, but it tasted like … like heaven at the time."

"You're sweet on Callie. It's plain to see she cares for you. Why haven't you courted her?"

"She was only sixteen when the Northern Aggression started." Zach rested his chin against his knee. "And barely seventeen when we mustered in."

"She's my age. And you're only two years her senior." Nate took a swing at Zach's arm. "You act and talk like you're already an old man."

"I had in mind to court her when she got older. If she'd have me." Pinching the bridge of his nose, he closed his eyes. He'd seen too much death to believe himself immune to enemy bullets. If not for that, he'd court Callie. He already knew her pa approved of him. "War changed all that."

"Why? When Mr. Jennings mentioned getting betrothed to Louisa, seemed like as good a time as any to me." He grinned. "Now there's a sassy woman. Prettiest girl around."

"She knows it too." Zach liked the confident beauty just fine, but it was Callie's auburn braids and big brown eyes that haunted his dreams. "If you like her so much, why do you still chase other women?"

Nate brushed down his gray coat, raising a dust cloud. "Can I help it if loyal Southern ladies want to express their appreciation to us lonely soldiers with bounty from their table and a kiss or two?"

"Yes, you can." His cousin had been complimented on his good looks just often enough that he believed it. Nate usually managed to keep his beard cropped close to his chin. Ladies responded to his flirtatious smile as much as the combination of blue eyes and brown hair. "Your betrothed trusts in your fidelity. Stop acting the fool with local women you'll never see again."

Nate laughed. "What Louisa don't know won't hurt her. She won't mind. And there's plenty of years ahead for us to get leg-shackled and respectable. These battles are brutal. I intend to have all the fun I can along the way."

"You had no call to propose with that attitude." Zach clenched his jaw. Louisa loved his ne'er-do-well cousin and, unless he missed his guess, possessed a jealous streak. "And you've certainly no right to lead these maidens on with kisses. You ought to be ashamed."

Nate's smile slipped. "You worry too much. And you're not even leg-shackled to anyone. Can't figure what's eating on you." He scratched his head and looked around. "I'm on forage detail later. Some of the fellas plan on trying to find a family who will offer us a meal tonight. Want to come?"

"I haven't been ordered on foraging detail." The offer tempted him. A home-cooked meal was secondary to being welcomed around a family's table. But if Nate flirted with young women in the house, Zach would feel like he betrayed both Louisa and Callie just to be in the same room. "No, I'll stick around here unless ordered to help. How do you get all the best jobs?"

"You know why." Nate flashed a grin. "I'm buddies with some bachelor officers. They invite me along because I'm not bashful about talking to women."

Nothing Zach said got through to his cousin. Why did he try?

"Yanks are gone." Rob Tyler, a comrade from the First Tennessee, strode up to them carrying a shovel. "Time to bury our dead."

Zach tugged his hat lower over his eyes and stood, hating the stench that rose from the field. Burying their dead … the worst part of any battle.

"Pa's been gone two weeks, Callie. It's already September. We have to make plans to sew us some soldier's clothing and join up with our army." Louisa extracted two plates from the cupboard. "Pa may be back in a week."

"Don't start on that again." Her sister had talked of little else since Pa left. Callie brushed back wisps of hair with the back of her hand before flipping a sweet-smelling slice of tomato breaded in cornmeal. It sizzled in the hot skillet. Louisa had come home yesterday from work—without pay—with instructions to stay home for a week or so. "This is your craziest idea yet. We can't pretend to be men and muster into the army."

"Other women have. The newspapers reported that women in uniform have been arrested. We won't get caught." Her smile widened. "I figure we'll just find the army and join up there. I'm thinking there won't be as many questions that way."

Callie rubbed her throbbing temples. This argument was getting old. "I don't want to be arrested. Or sent home in disgrace. Or worse yet, discovered by our soldiers and thought to be women of loose morals."

"We'll join up with our fellows in the First Tennessee. If anyone discovers us, our friends will help us." Louisa's eyes had a faraway look. "You know they need every man they can get since Atlanta fell."

"We're not men, Louisa."

"We can dress like them. We'll cut each other's hair." Her finger brushed the thick bun at her nape. Her eyes dimmed. "You can sew us men's clothing."

"With what? I don't have any fabric."

"I do. Mrs. Booth gave me fabric for my pay the past two weeks. Cotton for blouses and wool for coats and trousers. I hid them under the hay in the barn until you were ready to listen to me. You know it's a great idea."

Callie shook her head. Her sister had been making plans. "How will we hide the fact that we're women?"

"Loose clothing. I think that strategically placed padding sewn onto our drawers will suffice." She shrugged. "Other women figured it out. We can too. And remember that Pa's going to force you to marry Mr. Culpepper when he returns."

"Maybe not." Callie studied the stubborn tilt of her sister's face. She usually let things go quicker than this. "I put up three more cans of tomatoes and filled another sack with dried beans since he's been gone. Have to bury them today so they don't get stolen."

"How much more is left in the garden?" Water sloshed out of a bucket as Louisa hefted it toward two empty glasses.

"Can't be much more—beings it's the second week of September. We're still getting tomatoes and beans. And the apples are about ripe. We'll stretch it as far as we can. Pa's worried about feeding all three of us. Last winter was hard, too, but he didn't say anything then about forcing me to marry." A scorching smell prompted her to flip the tomatoes again. "Wonder if he's scared of dying or if he knows something he's not telling us."

"That bullet came mighty close to taking Pa from us." Louisa avoided her eyes. "Brushes with death can change a man's thinking."

"Reckon that's true enough. Yankees seem to be everywhere— or I reckon they come by often enough that it just seems like it the past two years. We've been lucky this month." A fly circled the skillet. Callie shooed it away before dividing the fried tomatoes onto two plates. "I've noticed that soldiers treat you better if you're nice to them."

"Hard to be kind when they're stealing our food."

She raised her eyebrows and nodded.

Louisa asked the blessing.

Callie stared at the food that barely filled a third of her plate. "We haven't talked about the most important reason we can't join the army."

"What's that?" Louisa took a dainty bite of tomato.

"Could … could you shoot someone?" Her heart skipped a beat at the mere mention of raising a musket at a Federal soldier.

She scooted her chair closer to the table, looking everywhere but at Callie. "It won't come to that."

"How do you know?" Callie toyed with her food. "If we don soldier's garb and muster into the army, we'll be expected to shoot at the enemy."

"We only have Pa's old musket that he keeps here for us to hunt with." Louisa glanced at her out of the corner of her eye. "Or to use for protection. Reckon we'll have to share. You could shoot someone who's trying to harm you, couldn't you?"

"I don't know." Tennessee was a dangerous place to live since the state fell. A threat to their safety could arise at any time. "I might just as soon die as kill someone."

"What if they were hurting me?" She leaned closer. "What if they aimed to kill me? Will you shoot then?"

Sweat broke out on Callie's forehead. "I'd stop them."

"But will you shoot?"

Callie tugged at her collar. "I'd never let anyone hurt my sister."

"I'd kill anyone who was hurting you or Pa." Louisa tightened her fists. "Or Nate. That's why I can fight for my beloved South. Not to keep slavery alive as most of them Northerners believe. Nate's not fighting so some plantation owner can own slaves. Zach's not fighting for that." She shook her head. "No, they fight because our country is under attack."

"Killing's wrong." The thought of her sister pointing a weapon at anyone stole Callie's breath.

"So is starving to death because Yankees destroyed our livelihood or stole our food." Louisa stabbed a piece of tomato with her fork. "This little bit don't fill our bellies. It just keeps us alive one more day."

Callie stared at Louisa. There was more behind her desire to join the army than spying on her betrothed. "How long have you felt this way?"

Scarlet stained her cheeks. "Been pondering it ever since that fella came into the store talking about those women soldiers. Then Martha Rose talked about Johnny's letter. I have a bad feeling about Nate. She might be right. I should have married him in March. Then he'd keep his promise to remain faithful to me."

Callie gazed out the back window at their beloved fields, overgrown with weeds from neglect. "I'm sick to death of this war. We're starving. Our neighbors are no better off. We live in fear of what's coming next. Pa's changed so I hardly recognize him sometimes. I hate to think about what he does on his missions."

"Remember that whatever he does is to protect his daughters. The South is under attack." Louisa swatted at a persistent fly. "Soldiers aren't camping in town, but groups of them ride through too often to suit me. Why, either of us might be assaulted on the mile's walk to town."

Callie sighed. "I just wish we had family who lived in the deep South. Or maybe in New York. Anywhere but Tennessee."

"Pa's the only family we have left." Louisa's gaze fell. "And no friends who don't live in Tennessee. Can't think of anywhere that's safe from the Federal soldiers in our state."

The clopping of horses' hooves bolted them from their chairs. Many horses were never good news—either Federal cavalry or bandit gangs approached.

"Hide the tomatoes." Callie grabbed the burlap sack of beans beside the stove. There wasn't time to hide them behind the fireboard in the fireplace. Where? Her shawl hung from a wall hook. She snatched the garment away and hung the bag. Then she replaced it with the shawl as shouts came from the yard.

Louisa held two red tomatoes in her hand as booted steps struck the porch.

A half dozen blue-clad soldiers entered without knocking. More held the horses in the yard. "We're on a foraging expedition for our army."

"You've already taken more than we can spare." Callie crept toward Louisa, who tossed her head back.

"Then two more tomatoes aren't going to matter." The leader advanced into the room without a trace of a smile.

"That will be one dollar." If soldiers took their food, Callie reasoned they could pay for it.

"One dollar? No." He reached for the tomatoes.

Louisa squeezed the vegetables. Seeds dripped through her fingers.

The back of the man's neck turned the color of the smashed tomatoes. His hand worked into a fist.

"Sam?" A man spoke from the back of the group. A rifle rested against his shoulder. "No need to wait around. We can get something from the fields."

Stomach churning, Callie rushed between them. "My apologies. We barely have enough food to eat as it is."

"Should have thought of that before she destroyed those tomatoes." His eyes bored down into hers. He glanced over his shoulder. "Take what's left in the fields."

The men scattered with their leader following.

She held Louisa's sticky hand as some twenty men made short work of stripping every green tomato and bean from the vines. They trampled the plants as they went, whether on purpose or merely careless, it was hard to tell. The result was the same.

Half the men moved to the ripening fruit of five apple trees. Every piece of fruit—ripe or not—went into bulging burlap sacks.

Her whole body shook as she watched the soldiers destroy their livelihood. These men didn't care if they starved to death. She lifted her chin. This was the reason Pa refused to plant crops again. Large acreage certainly drew more attention than her small plot. She had counted on the garden being too small to warrant attention.

Their cows and chickens had long since been eaten. This travesty sealed her family's fate. Her heart sank at the loss of the apples. She'd only dried enough to fill one ten-pound sack, preferring to wait until the fruit ripened to pick them at the peak of their flavor. The family's only salvation against starvation this winter was the war's end … unless the South started winning again and drove the Yankees back North and the railcars could haul food into Tennessee again.

The soldiers mounted their horses. There was no offer to pay for the food, no apology. Callie's legs quivered at the wreckage of her garden.

For the two years the Northern Army had taken over much of her state, she had tried to keep up her courage. She had been glad when the slaves were emancipated, but there was plenty to be angry about.

Like this.

She met Louisa's snapping eyes.

Louisa put her hands on her hips. "You ready to join our soldiers now?"

Callie sewed for four days—long hours well into the night to ready uniforms for both of them. She thanked God that she had quit her job at the mercantile when the war started. Helping Mrs. Hobson create uniforms for their brave young men had taught Callie how to cut and sew the coats, increasing her skills. Who'd have guessed she'd use those skills to clothe two more soldiers—women this time?

She'd found enough fabric so that each of them could have an extra blouse. Four one-button, over-the-head style blouses were done, completed while Louisa finished dyeing the wool material to a charcoal gray, choosing a darker shade because repeated washings faded the color to butternut. She had soaked the wool in strong tea and then soaked it in vinegar, water, and a bit of salt to set the stain.

Sunset had come and gone an hour ago. Callie rubbed the back of her neck. "My fingers ache from pressing the needle through the wool. Even with the thimble." She yawned. "Reminds me of those weeks that I worked with Mrs. Hobson back in the summer of sixty-one."

"Back when we thought we'd be done fighting by Christmas." Louisa leaned closer to the candlelight. "I'm tired, too. Sewing padding onto our drawers is about as much fun as learning 'rithmetic back in school."

"The first coat is almost done." Callie yawned again. "I'd quit for the night except it took the better part of a day to get this one done."

Louisa jerked her head toward the fabric laid out on the table. "Next one's cut and ready for your needle and thread. I'll finish these tonight and start on the trousers in the morning. I don't possess your skill, but time's a wastin'. After the sewing's done comes the thing that gives me the most qualms."

"Cutting our hair?" Callie glanced at her sister's downcast face. She dreaded that part too, but her sister considered her long blonde hair her crowning beauty. "We can still change our minds. Pa's not pushing you to marry—"

"I'm worried that he'll write to Nate. Ask him to marry me on his next furlough."

"That's fine with you, isn't it?" She frowned. "If you two marry, I can live with you until the war ends, right?"

"Nate likes soldierin'." Her brow furrowed. "He told me there won't be a wedding until the war ends, so don't even ask him. He said Zach feels the same way."

"About being a soldier?"

Louisa nodded. "He's good at it. Reckon it runs in the family. Zach's grandfather fought in the Revolution—on our side, not England's."

Zach had proven himself as a soldier. He had confided that his officers sometimes gave him increased responsibilities, especially with training and drilling. He enjoyed that and figured they might promote him from being a rank and file soldier to being an officer someday.

Callie's heart swelled with love and pride just remembering the glow in his eyes when he talked about his ambitions. He'd been her friend these past eight years, since he'd arrived at his uncle's—Nate's father's—house after his parents died. Callie wanted more than friendship. At least Zach didn't write to any of the other unspoken-for women in town. She knew because she'd asked them.

Louisa rubbed her eyes. "Nate likes the adventure of seeing new places. If Pa pushed him to marry me now, he'd probably end the engagement."

Callie couldn't disagree. From where she stood, Louisa held onto Nate by a thread. The man was an even bigger flirt than her sister, or than she had been before accepting Nate. "Then why are we joining Nate's regiment?"

"He's my man." She pulled her needle so hard the thread snapped.

"But if he's not true to you—"

"Then he will be."

Chilled, Callie sank against her chair. That's not the kind of relationship *she* wanted. "You're beautiful. If Nate can't see what a treasure he has, let him go and find someone else."

Her chin lifted. "You're a good one to be advising me about marriage. You ain't never even entertained a beau."

Heat rose in Callie's cheeks. It was true. Zach had never asked to court her, and she had never paid attention to anyone else after he'd stolen her affections.

"I'm sorry." Louisa touched Callie's hand. "I didn't mean it."

"I know." The apology didn't erase the hurt or the loneliness. She longed to see Zach as much as Louisa wanted to see Nate. "There's something else worrying me."

"What's that?" Louisa tugged on the padding she'd just sewn.

It held in place.

"We've already talked about speaking in low-pitched voices, but we'll also have to walk like men."

"We'll practice."

"A man's stride is different from a woman's, so that's important." Callie bit her lip. "Another thing to remember is not to look at Nate flirtatiously. He'll notice … and so will other men. Remember, you are pretending to be a man." Louisa's slow smile did nothing to appease Callie's fears.

"Oh, never fear, I'll wait to reveal my identity. For just the right moment." Her eyes gleamed. "First, I'll give Nate a chance to prove that he's faithful."

"You will be a soldier first. You will carry our only musket." The thought of raising a weapon to anyone caused her heart to pound.

"I still think that's a mistake. You're the better shot. You get more rabbits than I do."

"That's because you aren't quiet enough. You scare them off." Callie's fingers shook as she stitched. "Are you certain that you've never mentioned Ma's maiden name to Nate?"

"We always had other things to talk about."

"Then I reckon our new names will work out fine."

"I'm Lou Shaw, and you're my brother, Calvin Shaw." Louisa gave a crisp nod. "I like it."

Callie held up the coat. "This one's done. I'll sew two more hours tonight to get a good start on the second one. I want to be long gone before Pa returns."

CHAPTER THREE

Lovejoy's Station, Saturday, September 10, 1864

A woman with a burlap sack over her shoulder dragged another sack on the dirt road, raising a cloud of dust behind her.

"Let me carry that for you, ma'am." Zach reached for the strings of a burlap sack from a woman old enough to be his mother.

Her bonnet hid her face until she raised puffy eyes to meet his. "Take the one from my shoulder—it's heavier and contains all our food, thanks to Hood opening the commissary in Atlanta."

Zach tossed the bag that weighed as much as a small child over his shoulder.

"Much obliged. Fed my family right proper for the first time in weeks." She jerked a shoulder at a brood of children lagging behind her. They carried boxes and bags. "Then those Northern scalawags took over our city after Hood left. General Sherman ordered us out. Where does he expect us to go?"

Zach ground his teeth. He'd just returned to Lovejoy's Station after helping an Atlanta family move to Lafayette. That family owned a wagon to tote their possessions, but no horse. They'd eaten the horse during the battle that prevented supplies coming into the city. Zach pulled the wagon to Lafayette with the help of twelve-year-old twin boys. He'd done his best to talk them out of enlisting. Their anger about losing their home to a bunch of Yankees had burned too hot to quench with words. "Do you have family, friends in Georgia?"

"My husband's sister lives this side of McDonough." She brushed a wisp of brown hair from her forehead. "Don't know how excited she'll be to see us. She don't like children."

"Tell her what you've endured." His heart went out to her. "I doubt she will turn us away."

"Us?" Her gaze flew to his.

"Hood's allowing the army to help folks move." Aiding these displaced families allowed him and his comrades to do something positive for their fellow citizens, though the soldiers reviled Sherman and his army all the more for causing additional suffering. These folks had been through enough. He nodded at the half-dozen school-aged children staring at him. "As much as we are able." His smile died at passing buggies and carriages, so loaded with trunks, barrels, and bags that the owners had to walk. "I'm Zachariah Pearson, of the First Tennessee. I, along with my cousin Nate McClary, will help your family get safely to McDonough."

"I'm Mrs. Anderson, and these are my children. We sure do appreciate the escort, don't we?" The woman's posture straightened as she looked over her shoulder at her offspring.

A chorus of "Thank you, mister" accompanied nods. No smiles. Their lips didn't seem to remember how to smile.

"Did you hear?" Nate strolled over with filled canteens. "Georgia's Governor Brown recalled his state's militia to look after their own interests. Probably need to after all that's happened. Where we going next?"

"McDonough." Zach introduced Nate to Mrs. Anderson. "We'll take our haversacks, canteens, and weapons, and leave the rest of our belongings here just like last time."

"Here, little lady." Nate walked over to a girl toting a box a foot wider than her thin frame. "Let me take that from you. You and sister can take turns with her box."

The little girl of perhaps ten flapped her arms.

Nate tucked the box under one arm. "Did your arms go to sleep on you?"

She shaded her eyes with one hand and looked up at him with a nod.

"Ain't no wonder." Nate grinned. "What do you have in here—five skillets?"

"Them's our dishes, sir." Her brother squinted up at Nate in the bright afternoon sunshine.

A bit of the burden fell off Zach's shoulders. His cousin might be a flirt, but he was good with children. Nate might even coax a smile or two out of them on this ten-mile journey.

Callie dared not wait any longer, so this was their last night at home. The sun had set. Candles lit the large, barren main room of their home. The curtains were drawn.

It was well past the three weeks Pa said he'd be gone. Though her anger lingered at him for forcing her to marry, she whispered a prayer for his safety while gathering the scissors and a bowl.

Louisa came in from the bedroom. "Our knapsacks are packed with our soldier uniforms."

"Good. We'll leave before dawn. I've already packed the food."

"What's in it?" Louisa opened a ten-pound flour sack beside the door.

"Lots of dried corn. Some meal and dried string beans. Ma's smallest skillet." Callie pulled out a chair. "It's time, Louisa. We have to cut each other's hair."

She drew her hands to her throat. "How are you going to cut it?"

"I've been cutting Pa's hair since Ma died." She held up a bowl. "I'll do yours the same way."

Louisa clutched her hair, already freed of its pins. "Nate loves my long hair."

Callie studied her. Should she rely on her sister's vanity to save them from their foolhardy plans? Though where else they could go was beyond her. "I guess it's decided then." She placed the scissors on the dining table. "We stay here."

"You can't stay."

True. Callie lowered her head. At least Louisa had someone who loved her.

"And I won't let you leave alone. I need to see Nate. Confront him if he's done wrong." Picking up the bowl, Louisa placed it on her head. "I'll go first. It will grow back." She sat with her back to Callie. "Do it quickly before I lose my nerve."

Callie drew a deep breath. She snipped a section closest to Louisa's face. Two feet of wavy blond hair fell to the floor. It shimmered in the lantern light. "Oh, Louisa, I'm sorry. I just hate to do this."

She squealed. "What did you do?"

"Nothing. It's … your beautiful hair."

"Thank you." Louisa's shoulders relaxed. "You don't often say things like that. Reckon you don't want to feed my vanity."

"You've already got plenty enough for both of us." Callie gave a shaky laugh. "Ready for me to continue?"

"Can't stop now."

Callie snipped again. "I'm glad we went to church one more time. Who knows when we will worship with our neighbors again." Would the folks at church be so welcoming if they knew their plans? Pretending to be something she wasn't went against the truth she'd been taught since she was a wee child. Was God angry with her?

"When the war's over, that's when. How does it look so far?"

"Hard to say." *Like Ma with Pa's hairstyle.* Her heart sank— she'd look even less appealing like this. "You know what Pa's hair looks like when I'm done."

Louisa gasped. "I hadn't thought of that."

"If we could afford to go to a barber, he'd fix our hair in the latest style." Callie's scissors chased her sister's fine hair around. The blonde locks were twice as thick as Pa's.

"If we had money for such luxuries as that," Louisa scoffed, "there'd be no need to join the army. Except to find Nate and hold his feet to the fire."

"True. Now hold still. It's hard enough to cut your hair when you're not moving." More hair floated to the floor. "We have to start our journey dressed as women, so we'll wear our bonnets all the time until we don soldiers' garb."

"Do you know where the Army of Tennessee is?"

"Somewhere south of Atlanta is what I heard."

"Martha Rose told me the Yankees went in and took over Atlanta. Then they kicked out the citizens."

Callie pursed her lips. She snipped again.

"The Northern general transported those that wanted to go south down to Rough and Ready, which Martha Rose says isn't far from Atlanta." Louisa tapped her foot. "Women, old men, children, babies—that Yankee General Sherman had no compassion for anyone."

"Sounds like the man has no heart." Since the Northern soldiers came through and destroyed their crops a second time, she'd lost her forgiving mood. Their family, their neighbors—the whole state, probably—had been subjected to hunger and disrespect since the soldiers came. It was high time they were sent back home.

"Agreed. I'm glad we'll aid the Southern Cause."

"Are you really?" Callie cut carefully around Louisa's ears.

"Yes. Aren't you?"

Callie removed the bowl. She stifled a gasp. Blond hair was two inches above Louisa's brown eyebrows yet covered her ears. It was longer at her nape at an inch above her collar. The manly hairstyle certainly helped their cause of masquerading as men. No woman Callie knew wore her hair this way. "Better look in the mirror before you decide."

Louisa rushed to their shared bedroom where the only mirror hung on the wall. She shrieked. "My beautiful hair." Her moans reverberated to the main room.

Sighing, Callie swept up the hair.

The moans stopped. Louisa returned, a steely glint in her eyes.

"Your turn."

Callie tossed the hair into the fireplace. The embers flared up and a stench filled the room. "I know. You'll enjoy this." She didn't hold much stock on the color of her hair, but she'd received occasional compliments. She cringed inwardly to lose it.

"Why, yes, I believe I will." Her eyes gleamed. "Especially after looking in the mirror and inspecting your handiwork."

"Now, Louisa." Callie picked up the bowl with hands that jerked. "I was as careful as I could be."

"I know you were." Louisa smiled. "I'll be careful, too."

Callie took a deep breath. "Reckon we'd better get this over with."

No sooner had she sat than an auburn section tumbled to the floor.

"Not much fun, is it?" Louisa began to hum "Dixie."

"No."

The patriotic song resonated in Louisa's rich alto tones. The volume decreased as she continued to hum yet increased in feeling, stirring Callie's loyalty. Their reasons for joining up might not be pure and noble, but no doubt they'd be able to do their country a good turn as soldiers.

Somehow.

Zach shooed a buzzing bee away from a peach he munched on as he sat near the platform awaiting his regiment's turn to board the train. His army was moving to Palmetto, but at least he needn't march in the hot sun to get there. At his side, Nate napped like so many others. A dog barked in the distance. He swiped at his brow before taking his last bite of the over-ripe fruit. It wasn't filling, but it was something in his belly. Fight when you had to, rest when you could, and eat whatever was close to hand to supplement meager rations. That was life in the army.

He shook his head to recall his fantasies about soldiering. It had been Nate's idea to muster in. They'd dreamed of adventure … the new country they'd explore. He'd even feared the war's ending before they left Camp Trenton.

Boy, had they been wrong.

The surprising thing was that Zach liked being a soldier. He seemed to have found his calling in life.

Pa had despaired of him ever sticking with any occupation, but his soldiering instincts were good. They'd proven true time and again. He'd stay in the army when the war ended.

Yet he'd seen enough death and dying. And enough of seeing his country devastated, family businesses destroyed, mills burned to the ground. Those scalawags had forced citizens from their Atlanta homes.

Just when he tried to release his anger and forgive the enemy for the atrocities they committed, they did something else. There'd be no forgiveness until the whole thing ended. If he was strong enough then to let the heartache go.

He reached into his knapsack. His fingers caressed Callie's latest letter. She always knew what to say to ease his soul. Reading a funny anecdote about her sister, something her pa said, or what book and chapter the pastor preached on—all these grounded him to home.

And Callie. How he missed her. He sighed. Seemed likely to be a while before the next furlough.

What would she be doing now? Baking bread maybe. The yeasty smell would linger in her hair—that auburn mass that she tried to hide with those pins he'd been tempted to pull out a dozen times.

Zach had been tempted to propose. Though he'd never courted her, they'd been friends long enough for him to know his heart. His chest ached as he gazed at the northern horizon toward Tennessee. Soldiers were vulnerable to dying young. And with the number of fighting men seriously depleted, his turn might be coming up.

Dead or wounded soldiers weren't the only ones his army lost. He rubbed his hands over his face. The desertions were the ones that stuck in his craw. His parents, gone eight years now, had badgered him to finish a task, something he'd struggled with as a child. His heart wasn't in the work of the farm, and he'd quickly lost interest in it, disappointing his Pa. Callie and the folks back home relied on soldiers like him. His officers relied on him and his comrades. He'd not disappoint them and shirk his duty.

A whistle blew in the distance.

"That our train?" Nate stirred and sat up.

"Hard to say if there will be room on this one." Zach studied the lounging crowd of men in front of them. "Maybe. Your canteen full?"

Nate shook the wooden canteen resting against his side. Water sloshed. "Yep. Did you hear where we're going this time?"

"Palmetto. Still in Georgia for a while longer." Zach caught a red maple leaf as it floated to the ground, like that autumn day back at school with Callie at his side. Life had been so carefree in those long-ago days. "Reckon Hood's already there."

"I don't trust him."

"Lower your voice." Zach coughed as black engine smoke wafted over. "He's got command of the Army of Tennessee now, much as we'd like to see Uncle Joe come back." General Sam Hood was no General Joseph E. Johnston and that was a fact.

"Things might not have gone so sour in Atlanta if Uncle Joe had stayed." His happy-go-lucky cousin didn't spend much time in contemplation. Maybe one of his officer friends had put a burr in his stockings about Hood.

"We'll never know." Zach glanced at the comrades closest to them. No one looked their way, but that didn't mean they weren't listening. "Everyone takes some getting used to. Give Hood a chance."

They gathered their belongings and fell into line for the cars.

"Let's put in a request for winter quarters to be away from the snow this year." Nate punched Zach's arm.

"I'd do that if I thought it'd do any good. Better speak to Hood yourself. You have more influence than me." He mounted the first high step onto the car and waited for those in front of him to move ahead.

"Good idea." Nate laughed. "I'd like a new adventure—away from the snow, sleet, and ice."

"It's the third week of September. We've got time before we have to worry about snow." He sighed. The way things looked, he was going to spend his fourth winter away from home, defending a country he loved.

CHAPTER FOUR

Leaves crunched on Callie's left. She grabbed Louisa's hand, and together they scurried behind a bush.

"What is it?" Louisa whispered, tucking her skirt behind the branches.

"Heard something." Her heartbeat quickening, Callie peered across the wooded path that ran parallel to a southerly road. They had been following it all day, hiding once when a few soldiers dressed in blue rode past. Even dressed as women, they had no desire to talk with Northern soldiers. "Someone's here."

A crow cawed overhead, its wings flapping.

Callie kept an avid gaze on the area where the sound first came. They'd abandoned the main roads for forest trails whenever possible in the ten days they'd walked. They had to be getting close to Mississippi by now.

"Who's there?"

Callie gasped. "It's a boy. Can't be much harm in answering."

Louisa shrugged.

"We're two sisters from Ca—up near Humboldt."

A boy with unkempt blond hair stepped from behind a tree holding a lead rope for a cow. He couldn't be more than twelve. "Are you Yankee sympathizers?"

Callie and Louisa joined him on the path.

"Not us." Louisa studied his smudged face. "Are you?"

"After having to hide our last cow so's they won't steal her? What do you think?" His blue eyes darted from the left to the right before settling on them. "They got all the rest. My ma and sister are like to starve."

Callie gave an understanding nod. "Yankees took all our crops. Barely enough food hidden to get one person through winter. That's why we had to leave." Well, one reason anyway, but the boy didn't need to know the other.

He brushed his hair away from his forehead. "Where ya goin'?"

Callie and Louisa exchanged a glance. Having avoided all strangers, they hadn't been asked that question.

"My betrothed is a soldier in the Army of Tennessee." Louisa touched the burlap sack resting on her shoulder. "We're taking him some food."

Licking his lips, he stared at the sack. "Yeah, it's shameful our soldiers ain't eating any better than we are. He'll appreciate the grub."

"Where are we?" Callie had never been more than ten miles from home. Heading south was all she knew to do.

"Tennessee." He peered over her shoulder. "About two miles from Mississippi. That way's south, if you follow this path." He turned to his right. "The Tennessee River is off to the east. Reckon you can follow it to the south if you want. Leastways you won't have to cross it." He grinned. "That's good, 'cuz you'd need a raft or something."

Following the river might be a good idea—if the Southern army were near it, which they weren't. "You heard where Hood's army is right now?"

The light dimmed from his eyes. "Atlanta fell."

"We know. Our hearts broke at the terrible news." Callie squeezed his shoulder. "Our boys then went to Lovejoy Station. We received letters from there."

"You got a beau in the army too, miss?"

Her spirits sagged. How she longed for Zach to speak of the admiration she sometimes saw in his eyes. But Pa had practically pushed Callie on him—and he refused. Hard to misinterpret that rejection. "No." Her gaze dropped to a root jutting above the ground. "Just a friend."

He shrugged. "Our neighbor got a letter yesterday from their son. He's at Palmetto. That's along the Atlanta and West Point Railroad."

Callie frowned. "Is that in Georgia?" The Tennessee River curved north through Tennessee near the Mississippi and Alabama line. The river was too wide to cross unless they found a ferry, so they'd best avoid it though they still had to traipse across Alabama to get to Georgia.

"Yep." His cow tossed its head, and he patted its neck. "But armies move around a lot this time of year. That's what I like. They get to see the country." His bright gaze settled on the horizon. "Ma made me promise not to join up with them 'til I turn thirteen next year."

"Best wait a little longer. You'll be that much taller and stronger for waiting an extra year," Louisa said.

"Maybe." He plunged a fist into his pocket. "I ain't gonna miss all the fun of whupping the Yankees and that's a fact."

Callie sighed. Zach's tales told a different story, but they weren't going to change this boy's mind. "You think we should follow the river?"

He nodded. "Leastways for a while. It heads back up into Tennessee 'round Chattanooga. Don't go there. It'll be Christmas before you meet up with your soldiers if you go that far."

Christmas? Callie blinked back tears. What had made them think they could walk across three states to join the Army of Tennessee? Ludicrous. "But we've come so far already."

"There's the railroad if you've got money." He tapped the lead rope on his chin. "Naw. I keep forgettin' that the Yankees control the railroads too."

Louisa's eyes darted in Callie's direction and then refocused on the boy. "Do you know about the railroads?"

"Yep. The Memphis and Charleston Railroad goes through northern Alabama and into Tennessee again, probably near

Chattanooga, but the Yanks control that area real good. If you figure a way to ride the train, maybe get off at Decatur."

Callie raised her eyebrows. "How do you know all this?"

"My uncle worked for the railroad before he joined the Cause. Always figured I'd follow his path." He lifted his chin. "The Mobile and Ohio Railroad goes south past Tupelo. Head west to catch that. I ain't sure how that connects over toward Georgia."

Callie's head spun at all the information.

"Ticket sellers at the depot could tell you the best route, iffen they was still there. Tupelo's the long way, though. Don't know as I'd head that far south. Tracks have probably been torn up along the way—maybe any way you go."

Louisa gasped. "Tracks torn up? By the Yankees?"

He nodded. "Reckon both sides take part in that one. You can maybe go 'til the tracks end and then walk. Or you can walk the whole way. Don't make me no never mind. I got chores." He tugged on the rope and sauntered away.

"Thanks for your help," Callie spoke to his retreating back. He and his cow were soon hidden by autumn foliage. She turned to her sister. "What should we do?"

Louisa patted her short curls. "Maybe I can sweet talk someone into letting us ride on the Memphis and Charleston line to Decatur, Alabama."

Zach's sore feet attested to the army being on the move again. After crossing the Chattahoochee River on a pontoon bridge a few miles west of Palmetto, he squelched through mud and rain toward the Western and Atlantic Railroad, which they reached on the third of October. Tired of the muddy march, Zach whooped and hollered with his comrades when ordered to tear up the tracks—once a major route for providing supplies to their army—now in enemy hands. Destroying the supply line for the Yankees who had taken over Atlanta made the miserable march worth the effort.

Sweat slid down Zach's face as he pushed on a fence rail with Nate and several comrades to pry up an iron rail.

"The first one's always the hardest." Scarlet stained Nate's face.

Zach grunted. "Ain't that the truth."

"It's loose." Jonesy, a wiry yet strong comrade in their regiment called back the encouraging news.

The iron popped up. Zach pumped his fist in the air amidst the cheers. While some worked on the next rail section, Zach and Nate joined others pulling up wooden ties.

"Feels good to tear up what they took from us." Zach tossed a wooden tie on a growing stack in the roadbed.

Nate grinned. "Don't it, though?"

Spence, a tall, broad-shouldered soldier beside Nate, tossed a rotting tie on the pile. "The Yanks have robbed us of too much. See how they like losing tracks."

"Amen to that." Zach stood nearly six feet tall, but he had to reach up to clap the good-natured man on the shoulder, and then joined in the laughter that didn't drown out a few Confederate yells.

Once the stack of ties was a man's height, Jonesy lit the pile.

"Let's make one of Mrs. Lincoln's Hairpins." Nate grinned.

"Thought you'd never ask." Zach picked up one end of an iron rail, and Nate took the other. They balanced the rail over the top of the flaming pile. Spence and Jonesy set another rail beside theirs.

The center section soon glowed red hot. "Reckon it's ready?" Nate quirked an eyebrow at Zach.

"Only one way to find out." Zach removed his jacket and wrapped it over his hand. Nate followed suit. They picked up the rail and carried it to a telegraph pole. Placing the glowing center next to the pole, Zach walked his end toward Nate, curving the rail as he went. Nate did the same until the ends overlapped.

Laughing, Nate slapped his coat over his knee. "Yep, looks like Mrs. Lincoln's Hairpin to me."

"Good work, Cousin."

"You too, Cuz." Nate grinned as Jonesy and Spence wrapped a rail around the same pole. "That was fun—let's do it again."

"Fine by me." Zach whistled "Dixie" as he returned for another rail. Nate and others joined in. When a few voices began to sing, *"Oh, I wish I was in the land of cotton,"* Zach looked around the group.

These were the men he ate with, marched with, and went to battle with. His chest puffed out. They were fine men, the best he'd ever known. If his country had to be at war, these brave soldiers were the ones he wanted at his side.

Toward evening, the cousins collapsed under a tree.

"Looks like a tornado struck the countryside." After taking a long drink, Zach upturned his canteen over his head.

"Yep." Nate leaned back against the trunk with a grin. "Maybe that scalawag Sherman will think twice about kicking Southern families out of their homes."

"I'd love to see those Yankees' faces when they find this mess."

"You and me both. Got my second wind. Wanna give them another hairpin to look at?"

Rising to his feet, Zach laughed. "Let's get to it."

After the better part of a day, Callie had finally convinced her sister not to use her feminine wiles to secure them seats on the train. Nothing good could come of flirting with Northern soldiers. Instead of being noticed, they needed to remain unseen. They'd stayed with a poor farmer's family last night. They'd been welcomed into the home and the warmth of the fire, but there was no food to spare. Callie assured them a shelter from the rain was plenty though everyone knew in prewar days such treatment would have been almost an insult. Instead she had been grateful for the safety of their home.

"Where are we?" Leaning one hand on a swaying sapling, Louisa peered down the desolate country road.

"Somewhere in Mississippi is all I know." Callie rubbed her lower back. "We're following the railroad tracks to the next depot, just like we talked about."

"How was I supposed to know we'd walk three hours this afternoon before finding the next town?" Louisa grimaced. "Can't we rest a minute? My feet hurt."

"I want to get there before dark. We have to keep moving. Daylight will be gone in an hour."

"So will my patience."

Callie sighed as Louisa fell into step beside her again. "The next town probably won't be big enough to warrant a lot of Yankees nosing around."

"That's the only good thing about being from a place like Cageville." Louisa tucked a strand of blond hair under her bonnet. "Hope it *is* small. That gives our plan the best possibility of success."

"Let's find the depot quickly." She frowned. Their plan to stowaway on the train was risky—especially with Confederate uniforms hidden in their knapsacks.

"No telling how often trains arrive and depart with a war going on."

Callie wondered if Pa faced this type of danger on his missions—or even if he'd come home safely from the last one. Her heart wrenched to think of him coming home, possibly wounded, to an empty cabin—save for the letter they'd left. She rubbed her fingers across her forehead—she couldn't think about that now or she'd lose her nerve. Boarding that train shortened their walk by days—depending on where they had to get off. "It's worth the risk." She spotted a creek. "Let's wash in that creek and fill our canteens."

"Good idea. Hard to say when the next opportunity will come." Louisa sprinted toward the ankle-deep water. "Oh, it's freezing. Let's hurry."

Callie rolled her eyes—that's what she'd been urging all day.

A wolf howled. Chill bumps covered Callie's arm as she and her sister crept into a small town about suppertime. A horse neighed from a stable. No appetizing smells wafted from the dozen or so homes they passed though smoke rose from chimneys. Times must be as difficult for folks in Mississippi as they were in Tennessee.

Bullet-ridden homes and buildings gave mute testimony to a past battle, even in the gloom of twilight. Callie pressed her lips together. When had the battle occurred? It seemed likely the Yankees won since they hadn't seen Confederates in the area.

Heart heavy, Callie shuddered at the price Southern citizens had paid in this war, making countless sacrifices that never seemed to make any difference.

There was no sign of soldiers as they followed the railroad tracks to a small depot. A locomotive with five cars sat at the station. The train had seen better days, but the sight of it warmed Callie's heart. They'd finally found a place to board the train.

Footsteps.

She clutched the burlap bag holding the last bits of dried corn as she peered over her shoulder at a woman about her age scurrying toward them.

Reaching them, the woman clasped Callie's arm as if they were old friends. "Walk with me as if you know me in case the soldiers see you."

Louisa inched closer, and they matched the stranger's rapid pace.

"I'm Lily Swanson. There are six Yankees in town, all dining at my mother's table." She opened the door of a white clapboard home and followed them into a sparse front room. "These men are often here and will know you are strangers to Iuka."

"I'm Callie Jennings." Her gaze darted to her sister. "And this is my sister, Louisa Jennings."

"Soon to be Mrs. Nathan McClary." She lifted her chin a fraction.

Callie rolled her eyes. As if that mattered now.

"A pleasure." Lily inclined her head. "If you don't mind plain speaking …"

Callie shook her head.

"Then what is your business in Iuka?"

A blunt question indeed. Callie fingered the sleeve at her wrist. Could they trust her?

"We've come to take the train east." Louisa blurted out. "My betrothed is in the army. We are on our way to see him."

Lily raised her eyebrows. "Hood's Army?"

"Yes."

"They are moving northward. According to the Yankees, they may be headed toward Dalton or into Alabama." Her brow puckered. "Trains are closed to passengers. Did you plan to steal onto the train?"

Callie nodded. Louisa had already told Lily as much as she needed to know to help them—if she was so inclined.

"The train leaves at four in the morning. Hide in the last car tonight. Their final destination is Tuscumbia. Make certain you get off before then to avoid detection. You will be questioned if you are discovered."

Callie's breath caught in her throat. "How will we know when to disembark?"

"It's doubtful the locomotive will stop at every depot." Lily tapped two fingers against her lips. "Disembark at a stop before sunrise for safety's sake. Wherever that is, you will be closer to your beau. Wait just a moment."

She hurried through a door. Callie met Louisa's wide-eyed gaze. Neither spoke.

The door opened. "Here are four boiled eggs and a loaf of bread for your journey. It's all I can spare."

Tears rose in Callie's eyes at Lily's kindness. "Thank you for the food. You don't know what this means." She stored them with their dwindling supply of dried corn.

"I can guess." Lily smiled for the first time. "I had need of kindness not so long ago, and someone helped me." The smile disappeared. "Go back to the train and get onto the last car. If the door is open, don't shut it. If anyone questions you while in town, tell them you are my cousins from Tennessee. We may be related for all I know. We never exchanged family information."

A tear rolled down Callie's cheek. "Thank you."

"No need to thank me. You're not on the train yet." She tilted her chin. "Go now. I will wait five minutes and return to my mother's home. That should be time enough for you to find your way. The soldiers have already loaded the cars. Be quiet as a mouse when they come around. Don't fall asleep."

"Bless you." Callie peeked out the window. No one on the street.

She led the way back to the train. They walked on the grass until reaching the last car. Thankfully, the door was open. Closed-in places made her want to claw her way out. She pulled herself up and reached to give Louisa a helping hand.

Straw lined the car partially filled with barrels and boxes. Callie wrinkled her nose. It smelled like a stable. They stepped carefully on the straw and settled themselves in the back corner. The straw cushioned the floor. Shivering, Callie couldn't see her sister's face in the darkness. Staring at the car's opening, she clasped Louisa's shaking hand.

What had they gotten themselves into?

CHAPTER FIVE

ale voices outside the car woke Callie. How long had she slept? Smoke from the locomotive's engine wafted inside. She touched Louisa's arm. "Shh."

"Do we need the colonel's horse on this car?" A young man stuck his head inside the open door. "It's not here yet."

Unable to see anything but his silhouette, she stiffened. It was pitch black inside.

"Naw. He don't need it this time. Everything's in here." A different man's voice. "He'll be back on Saturday."

It was Wednesday, the fifth of October unless Callie had miscalculated on her days while traveling. Restlessness stirred inside her. They had to reach Hood's army.

"Should we shut this door?"

Please don't, Callie pleaded silently.

"Leave it open. Maybe get some of that smell out of there. There's only one stop between here and Tuscumbia this time."

Callie appreciated the information. Exiting at the next stop was their best opportunity.

"Did you check everything?"

Louisa clutched her arm, fingernails digging into Callie's flesh. She held her breath.

"Yep. Checked it earlier. It's ready."

Callie cringed. When had the Yankee checked this car? Before their arrival at suppertime? Or while they'd slept? Either way, it seemed God had been watching over them. They'd escaped detection.

So far.

The whistle blew. She loosened Louisa's grip. Wheels squeaked. Callie's body went limp, so great was her relief. This train was taking them closer to Zach and the Southern army—and fewer miles to walk.

A rush of wind blew straw into her face. They were underway and picking up speed.

She leaned over to whisper in Louisa's ear. "We'll have to get off whenever it stops."

"If we're quiet, we should be able to sneak off and hide somewhere until the train takes off again."

Only darker shapes, possibly trees, were visible from Callie's spot. "Every mile this train takes us is one less mile to walk."

Louisa sighed. "Amen to that."

"Have you been praying?"

"I've hardly stopped since we stepped into that bullet-ridden town."

"Me, too. Thank you for coming with me." Callie's shoulders relaxed. They were in this together. "Gather your things. Let's move up to the door so we can jump out right when it stops."

They crept forward. Smoke blew into Callie's face when the train rounded bends, but otherwise, the cool air enlivened all her senses. The fresh scent of pine occasionally overpowered the odor of horses that clung to the car. The locomotive chugged along quicker than a horse's gallop for what must have been an hour.

It was still dark when the brakes squealed. The train slowed. A whistle blew. Callie stuck her head outside for a quick glance. The only lights ahead were the signal lamps. "We can do this," she whispered. "Let's not wait for a complete stop. Everything secured over your shoulders?"

"Yes."

The squealing grew louder. The train slowed to a crawl. "Now!"

Callie fell onto a grassy slope. The whistle blew again as Louisa dropped beside her. "Let's hide."

Bent double, they ran behind a clump of bushes. Car doors squeaked open ahead. A conductor held a lantern aloft for two men in blue uniforms. Their beards hid their faces. "We're the only ones departing here, my good man. The colonel wants to be on his way as quickly as possible."

"Very good, sir." The conductor lowered the lantern and stepped inside after the men had climbed down two long steps. A whistle blew twice, and then the train chugged away.

Callie tensed as the men walked toward them.

"They will be in Tuscumbia in ten minutes." He puffed on a cigar. "Nell should have breakfast ready for us."

"Can't be ready too soon for me. My breadbasket is telling me it's time to eat."

"Hey, what's this?" They paused at a spot near the tracks.

Yards from the sisters' hiding place.

Callie clutched Louisa's hand and prayed.

"Straw." One man bent. "Reckon this was where the last car stopped. Where the horses ride—when we have them."

"Wind probably blew it out. Let's get to my sister's house."

The first man straightened. "Sooner we get there, the sooner we can eat."

His companion clapped him on the back. "Hope it's biscuits and gravy."

Biscuits? Flour had been hard to come by for months back home. Her stomach grumbled at the mention of breakfast. She'd pull out Lily's gift of eggs as soon as they were safe.

The men sauntered off. The sisters waited until their footsteps died away.

"Let's get out of here." Callie grabbed her sister's hand.

They scrambled around the houses and bushes until they found a path. "Which way?" Louisa whispered.

The sky lightened to the east. "Head toward the rising sun for now. Then we'll walk southeast. Quickly."

The sisters hurried from the sleepy town and didn't slow until the sun had fully risen.

"Captain said between all our divisions, we've torn up twenty-four miles of tracks from Marietta and Allatoona." Nate bit into his meager breakfast of one corn muffin.

"That's good." Zach's spirits rose despite his aching body. Tearing up track was hard work. He'd slept well enough, he supposed. At least no Northern bullets awoke him from a deep sleep last night.

"I'll say." Nate took a long drink from his canteen. "After the summer we had, this feels good, like we accomplished something important."

Zach tossed his canteen strap over his head without answering. The loss of Atlanta still rankled. He dismissed it from his mind as much as possible because the thought of it made him want to quit. And he couldn't do that. No matter what, he wouldn't prove Pa right.

"French's Division had to retreat from a fight at Allatoona." Nate shoved the rest of his muffin into his mouth.

"You learn a lot roaming about camp, don't you?"

"Pays to make friends with the officers." Nate's grin died. "We lost a lot of men in that one. Even worse, we had captured a Yankee storehouse. In retreat, French had to leave the rations behind and ordered them destroyed."

Zach turned his head away. That hurt. He couldn't remember the last time he'd eaten and been satisfied. Callie's face sprang to mind. Yes, he could. It was during their March furlough when she cooked for them. How he missed her.

"You eat already? We're back on the march today."

Having packed his belongings, Zach already knew this. "Know where we're going?"

"West is all I know. Toward Alabama. Reckon we'll have to see when we get there."

"How far do you figure we've walked since leaving the train?" Louisa kicked at a stone on the muddy road.

"Let's see." Callie trudged through the wide, open field without a farmhouse in sight—just a friendly little brook running beside the road. "We slept in an abandoned home our first night in Alabama, in the forest the next two nights, and in a field under a maple tree to escape last night's rain." She sniffed. "The rain freshens the air but makes the nights miserable."

"That's where we slept, not how far we've walked."

"I don't know. Better than fifteen miles every day. That's a far piece."

"That's why I'm so tired." Louisa's eyes widened. "Isn't this Sunday? We should be resting. Even God rested from creating the earth on Sunday."

"Church." Callie sighed. "We should be in church today."

"But there are no steeples or crosses in sight."

"You think decent folks want two women wearing dirty clothes to come smear up their pews?" Callie brushed at a smudge of mud on her skirt. "I'd be ashamed to step inside looking like this." Not to mention being ashamed at their deception. What must God think of them?

Louisa put her hands on her hips. "I don't see why. Folks know there's a war going on. They couldn't hardly forget it. And we're still decent—just a little dirty. Even if we weren't decent people, God wouldn't turn us away."

Callie's cheeks burned. "You're right. About all of it. I want to find a church today. I miss our home, our friends. I'm hungry. All that's left in the food sack is dried corn." They ate one meal a day to stretch it. Had they been wrong to leave Cageville? Louisa would still have a roof over her head this winter. And Callie would be married by now. She shuddered. No, this was better.

"Let's wash the worst of the dirt from our clothes and take a bath in that creek." Louisa searched her face. "Then, if we find a church, we won't feel bad about attending."

"Yes, let's do that. A bath always soothes me, though it will have to be a quick one in this chill."

Louisa grinned. "That's the spirit. I see a copse of trees ahead for privacy."

"Thanks, Louisa. What would I do without you?" Callie pulled her in for a hug.

"Don't worry—you'll never need to find out."

The sisters slipped into a church four hours later and sat on the last pew during prayer. It was a long prayer in which the gray-bearded minister pleaded for an end to the hostilities. He asked for God's protective hand over their soldiers and solace for the grieving. His voice broke then. Several women sobbed.

Then he prayed, "Lord, hear the cry of our hearts because we have no words to express our pain."

Two women moved across the aisle to sit with a woman wearing mourning black who wept brokenheartedly. Her sobs reverberated throughout the small church. One friend sat beside her. The other placed a hand on the weeping woman's shoulder from the pew behind.

Tears rolled down Callie's cheeks as she again bowed in prayer. It wasn't difficult to imagine the woman's loss … perhaps a husband or a son. A dozen faces of friends gone too young rose in her mind. Zach's original regiment, the Twenty-Seventh Tennessee, had lost so many men that those remaining were now part of the First Tennessee. Bitterness spurted up like bile. This dratted war had taken the best the South had to give … and demanded more.

How long, Lord? How long will this continue? Can't you stop the death, the dying, the destruction? Too many have died or lost their sons, fathers, brothers, uncles, cousins. Too many have lost their farms, their businesses, their livelihood. How can we recover unless You sustain us?

"Let's stand and sing our closing hymn, "Amazing Grace.""

Callie swiped at her cheeks, wondering where her handkerchief was. Then she remembered. They left their feminine, embroidered handkerchiefs at home, exchanging them for extras from their father's supply as part of their deceit to join the army. Soldiers' clothing lay hidden in her knapsack. The pretense weighed on her spirit. Was God angry with her and Louisa for the deception they planned?

She stood. Tears clogged her throat, making it impossible to sing, yet Louisa's beautiful voice rose above the rest.

Amazing grace! How sweet the sound
That saved a wretch like me!
I once was lost, but now am found;
Was blind, but now I see.

When the last notes died away, folks turned to look at them.

The minister left the pulpit and walked down the aisle. "We welcome you to First Baptist Church. You are strangers to us. Are you just passing through?"

In control of her emotions once more, Callie nodded. "We are journeying to my sister's betrothed in Hood's army."

"Ah." His gaze shifted to Louisa. "The army is on the move in Georgia. You've a long journey ahead unless they move into our state." He studied their faces. "My wife has made a pot of vegetable soup for dinner. You're welcome to join us before you resume your travels."

Louisa's eyes glowed. "We'd be grateful to accept."

As Callie sipped the deliciously hot soup, watered down though it was, Pastor Donovan asked them about the soldiers they were visiting. Louisa's eyes shone as she described her dashing beau.

"And how about you?" Mrs. Donovan, perhaps ten years younger than her husband, turned a bright blue gaze on her. "I feel like we already know Mr. Nathan McClary. Are you also betrothed to one of our brave soldiers?"

Callie gaze fell. "No. I have ... a friend, Zachariah Pearson. He is Nate's cousin." She wrung her hands. "Do you have friends or family in the army?"

Tears filled Mrs. Donovan's eyes and spilled over.

Color drained from the pastor's face. His gaze darted to his wife.

Callie exchanged a startled look with her sister. She had imagined them to be a childless couple. "I am sorry if ... I regret speaking out of turn—"

"No, my dear." The pastor stared at the empty bowl in front of him. "You could not have known." He drew a deep breath. "Our only son, Miles—"

"Just sixteen-years-old," Mrs. Donovan burst out.

He covered his wife's hand with his calloused one. "Died at Shiloh, Tennessee. There's not a day that goes by ..."

"I hate this war!" Mrs. Donovan held a lacy handkerchief to her nose. "It's robbed us ... our neighbors ... of too much."

Sorrow for the couple tightened Callie's throat. "We're so sorry. The war has taken our best from us."

"That it has." Pastor Donovan nodded.

She exchanged a glance with Louisa. "Please allow us to clean the dishes before we leave."

"The help is most welcome." He smiled graciously. "But why not stay for evening services? We have a bedroom where you may spend the night, get a fresh start in the morning."

Mrs. Donovan swiped her cheeks with the handkerchief. "You can boil your clothing this afternoon, if you've a mind to. There is plenty of lye soap to clean them. I normally don't offer such a thing on Sunday, but war changes the way we do things. And, of course, you are welcome to boil water for a bath if you choose."

"Thank you." Callie couldn't wait for the chance to be clean again. "We accept." A hot bath was an unexpected gift. Sleeping under a roof in a bed sounded like heaven.

Louisa gave them all a radiant smile.

CHAPTER SIX

Zach shifted his musket from one aching shoulder to the other. It had been a busy week with the Yankee garrison's surrender at Dalton and tearing up more railroad tracks. His body ached from all that hard work. "Where do you think we're going this time?"

Nate shrugged. "Don't know. I hope it ain't far. Hope we stay put at the next place longer than it takes to pitch a tent."

"Agreed." A rest of a week or better might be just what soldiers craved, but Zach doubted they'd get it. He couldn't figure out what General Hood had planned. They'd headed west and then north and then northeast and then south and now west again ... Zach ran a hand through his hair. Were they running from the Union army? Searching for supplies? All he knew for sure was that they were somewhere in Alabama.

"Got me a hankering for some home cooking." Nate grinned.

Home cooking would be wonderful if only his cousin didn't mean to seek female companionship. "You don't even know where we're going."

"No. But there's bound to be a town nearby. At least a farmhouse or two."

"Remember that Louisa waits for you at home."

"That's right. Louisa waits for me some two hundred miles from here—maybe more." He tossed his cousin a grin. "She'll never know if I smile at a pretty girl."

Zach's jaw tightened. "Make certain that's all you do, and Louisa may not care."

"Why of course that's all I'll do, Cuz." Nate clapped him on the shoulder. "You worry more than any woman I know."

He gave his cousin a sidelong glance. "Act like you've got a good woman back home. Be true to her. She loves you."

"She does." His gaze dropped to the muddy path. "And I love her best."

Zach rolled his aching shoulders. He was too tired and hungry to argue any further. He resolved to keep his eye on Nate for Louisa and Callie's sake but let the matter lie for now.

He glanced at the gray skies. Unless he missed his guess, they'd soon be marching in the rain.

"It's chilly, and I'm tired of sleeping outside." Louisa pouted.

Brown leaves crunched under their shoes as they trudged across the bleak Alabama countryside.

Callie raised her eyebrows. "Soldiers don't sleep in fancy hotels and fine homes. Didn't you listen to Zach and Nate describe being out in all kinds of weather?"

She folded her arms. "Well, I don't have to like that part of it."

"No, you don't. Sheltering from the rain under trees or in an abandoned barn will soon stop." She frowned at the gray skies. "Soldiers have to obey orders and keep marching in the rain and snow. We'll have to get used to it."

"Snow?" Louisa shuddered. "That's not part of the bargain. I'll discover that Nate's being faithful to me and reveal my identity long before winter."

"We can't let anyone know who we are." Callie's heartbeat quickened. "We'll be two women in an army of men. Some soldiers may not be as upstanding as others. They might not treat us as ladies. For safety's sake, we have to keep up the pretense."

"I'll remember." Louisa grimaced. "When should we don our uniforms?"

"I've been thinking about that." Callie peered at empty fields ahead. With no houses in sight, they were all alone. "I don't know where our soldiers are, but the next town on this road is Gadsden, according to that boy we met last night. Maybe we'll find them easier if we dress as soldiers."

"It's time." Louisa nodded. "Let's bury our frocks tonight."

Zach was glad to stop marching. They were to set up camp in Gadsden, Alabama. He was too bushed to care where they were as he and the others went about the familiar tasks of setting up camp.

The fellows that carried tents on their backs erected them. Zach chose not to carry his side of the A-tent that he shared with Nate. Both of them stored the heavy canvas in one of the long line of wagons that followed the troops. Those were far behind, so he'd sleep under the cloudy skies without the shelter. No matter. He was used to it.

He arranged dead leaves into piles as a soft cushion against the cold grass. As he spread his gray blanket in a clearing surrounded by tall trees, some already leafless, his comrades lit campfires. Smoke rose only to dissipate over their heads. A corn cake sizzled on a skillet, its grainy aroma wafting over to fuel Zach's hunger. He finished his task before joining his friends around the fire.

When the bugler played taps, there was no sign of Nate. Perhaps he had picket duty tonight. Zach hated to stand picket after long marches.

He fell onto his blanket and cocooned himself inside its warmth. It had been a long day.

"You're walking like you're still wearing a skirt." Callie frowned as her sister pranced around the campfire in gray breeches.

"You're a fine one to talk. You're not much better."

"Widen your stride a bit like we practiced at home." Callie demonstrated and giggled at the strange step.

"No giggling." Louisa laughed even as she admonished. "That will give us away. Practice a masculine laugh." She gave a deep, low-pitched laugh.

Callie fell, laughing, onto the chilly grass.

Louisa practiced walking to an elm tree and then returned. "At least we don't have to get accustomed to new shoes along with everything else." She sighed. "I've never been so happy that Pa couldn't afford to buy us the fancy styles or even black leather boots. These brogans look enough like the men's shoes that no one will notice."

"That's a blessing." Callie pushed herself to her feet, marveling at the ease of rising in trousers—without the hindrance of a skirt and petticoats. "When we meet up with the army, let's watch the other soldiers and emulate them. Think of how Nate walks and practice his gait."

They walked back and forth in their strange garb in the darkness, hidden by a small wood.

"Don't pat your lips daintily after eating. Men swipe their mouths with a napkin," Callie said.

"If they use one at all," Louisa grumbled. "I don't think soldiers have the luxury of napkins."

"That's probably true. Then use the back of your hand—or your sleeve."

"My sleeve?" Louisa shook her head. "This is going to be harder than I thought."

"A thousand little things can give us away." Staring at their small fire, Callie frowned. "Be on your guard at all times."

"Remind me why we wanted to do this?"

Callie put her hands on her hips. "Because I'd be Mrs. Culpepper by now if I'd stayed. Because I have no place to go. And because you want to spy on Nate."

"Right." Louisa's eyes narrowed as she circled the fire. "It's worth it."

"And it was your idea in the first place." Callie continued walking with an unfamiliar, widened stride.

"It was a good idea." Louisa perched on a log.

"Don't do that."

"What?"

"You sat down slowly and daintily. Men don't do that."

Louisa rested her chin in her hands. "This ain't going to be easy. We'll have to think about everything we do."

"Exactly." Callie sat beside her and then stood again. Her thoughts strayed to the man she most longed to see. "We'll ask to join the First Tennessee, but I don't know how these things work."

"They'd better put us with Nate's regiment." Louisa's eyes hardened. "That's the reason I came."

"I know. Say a prayer that we find them."

"I will."

What if they didn't find the right regiment? Callie's gaze darted to the road. They simply had to find them. "Zach won't recognize me, but you will have to be careful around Nate. I've seen the way you watch him. Don't look at him often. You're pretending to be a man. The other soldiers will find that odd."

"You think you don't watch Zach?" Louisa's lips tightened. "You can hardly keep your eyes off him."

Callie blinked. Were her feelings really that transparent? "Sorry. I didn't know." She turned her face away. Her feelings for Zach scarcely mattered when he felt only friendship for her. "We can nudge each other when we see the other one doing something wrong."

"Will do."

"We don't shave." More than the chill of the mid-October night raised chill bumps on her arms. "We don't have Adam's apples either."

"Keep your coat buttoned all the way to your chin." Louisa pushed up her collar. "And we'll claim a younger age to explain the lack of facial hair. I'll be fifteen. You can still be a year older."

"Good idea." Callie studied her. "You may be too pretty to hide that you are a female. The haircut disguises you but if you start giving Nate that special look—"

"I won't."

"Louisa, you must not flirt." Callie met her sister's gaze in the flickering firelight. "Not by words or actions or looks."

"I won't."

"You might do it without thinking." Callie held her gaze. "Promise me. Flirting will completely give us away."

"I promise." Louisa looked away. "Cal, I think we'd better start calling each other by our new names."

"Right, Lou. That will take some getting used to." Callie sat on the log and peered toward the road some yards to their right. "I wonder where Hood's army is."

"We can ask someone in the morning. Hope they're not far." Louisa removed her shoe and rubbed her feet. "I'm tired of walking."

"Let's bury our dresses and then get some sleep. From now on everything we say and do, even in private, has to be in pretense of being brothers ready to join the army." Suddenly feeling very alone, Callie searched the woods around them. "Never know who's listening."

CHAPTER SEVEN

Picket duty again. Zach really didn't mind guarding their camp, but he hated standing picket after long marches.

Spence was another one of the six from the First Tennessee who followed Corporal Ben Morefield back to the line where they were to relieve others. "Think we'll be in Gadsden long?"

"Hard to say." Zach shrugged. "You heard anything?"

Spence squinted into the sunrise directly ahead. "Just not to get too comfortable."

Zach grunted. "My aching feet are glad for one less day of marching."

"Ain't that the truth? My feet aren't the only part of me that aches." Spence rubbed his back with the hand not supporting his musket. "At least we got to eat breakfast before coming out here."

"Yep."

The pair fell silent as they reached the men they came to relieve. Several feet apart, Zach and his comrades stood under the cover of trees and underbrush that hid them from the road twenty feet away while affording them a great view of foot traffic and wagons.

Zach's attention wandered to Callie. He hadn't heard from her for over a month. Her last letter had reached him at Palmetto. True, they'd been on the march, skirmishing, and tearing up track with little rest since then, but at least one letter should have found its way to him by now.

His eyes darted at movement. A squirrel. If only there was an opportunity to hunt the little fellow. The possibility of squirrel meat and dried corn cooked in a soup made his mouth water. He'd fried a corn cake for breakfast. His belly rumbled.

Best turn his mind to something else.

Callie's last letter had a different tone from the others, almost like she'd distanced herself from him. At first, he'd decided she merely meant to grumble—not that she didn't have plenty to complain about. She'd written that Yankees took the last of their crop. He tried to figure out just what troubled him about her letter and decided that she was simply angry with Yankees—just like the rest of the Southerners.

Plenty enough to be angry about since her family had no more money than most folks to purchase food.

Movement on the road. "Spence, you see that?"

"Yep. Two of our own."

"Why are they heading toward town?" Zach peered at the downcast faces. They carried knapsacks, blankets, canteens, and only one musket between them. Hadn't they been to camp yet?

"Let's ask them."

"Probably got lost on the march." Zach, keeping his gaze on the pair, followed Spence to the road.

Twigs snapped under heavy footsteps in the woods beside the road. Yankees? A picked-over garden to Callie's left and handful of houses beside the road ahead didn't offer an immediate hiding place. She took a step back from the noise on her right, well aware that the gray uniforms she and her sister now wore made them targets for capture … or gunfire.

"You fellas lose your way?" A tall man in gray burst onto the road with a musket resting on his shoulder.

She exchanged a glance with Louisa. "No, we aim to muster into Hood's army." She widened her stance, mimicking the soldier's attitude. "Have we found it?"

"That you have." He grinned. "What about that, Zach? Fresh

recruits. Let's take these boys for our regiment."

Callie's gaze flew to the soldier behind him. Zach? Her heart pounded as her eyes drank in the lines of exhaustion on his face. And when had he last shaved? The close-cropped dark beard actually enhanced his green eyes against thick brown hair that touched his collar.

"Always glad to see new men join up. Do you have experience?" Zach asked.

"Hunting rabbits and such." Callie lowered her head. He didn't recognize her. That was important for maintaining their masquerade, but it hurt. She'd roughened her voice to disguise it. Of course, he'd see through the disguise if she were important to him.

"My brother's too modest to brag." Louisa shifted their only musket to her shoulder. "He's provided far more squirrels and rabbits for our supper than he'd let on."

"Shooting at Yankees is a lot different than shooting squirrels—as you'll soon find." The broad-shouldered man extended his hand. "I'm Robert Spencer. Folks call me Spence."

"Call ... Calvin Shaw." Callie's hand was engulfed by his. She blinked at her first handshake. She'd almost reached for her skirts to curtsey when the introduction started. "And this is my brother, Louis."

Spence shook Louisa's hand. "Pleasure to meet up with brave men. This here's Zachariah Pearson."

"Call me Zach." He shook Louisa's hand and then Callie's.

She stared at his strong hand. The brief contact was the only time he'd held her hand. Ever. "It's a pleasure, Zach. We answer to Cal and Lou."

"Shaw, you say? Don't recall knowing any Shaws." His brow wrinkled. "Something about you all seems familiar. Where'd you say you were from?"

Callie glanced at Louisa.

"Tennessee." Louisa deepened her tone. "Up near Jackson."

"Jackson?" Zach raised his eyebrows. "Anywhere close to Cageville?"

Callie ran a finger underneath her coat's high collar and then stopped. The collar needed to stay in place to hide the fact that she didn't have an Adam's apple.

"Where?" Louisa's brow furrowed.

Callie held her breath.

"No matter. The town's so small it hardly warrants a place on a map." Zach waved his hand dismissively. "Most folks ain't heard of it. But at least you'll fit in fine with our regiment. We'll ask to put you in our company. We need all the good men we can get."

Callie nodded. That's exactly where she and Louisa wanted to be. "Much obliged."

"Do you have a musket?" Spence's eyes darted in both directions on the road.

"Just the one." Callie nodded her head toward it. Her pa's old black slouch hat shifted. Her hidden stitches to make it fit snugly hadn't worked as well as she'd hoped. She tugged it down over her ears until it also hid part of her eyes.

The men exchanged a glance. "Maybe Sarge can get hold of one of the muskets we took off the Yankee prisoners back in Georgia." Spence turned and waved for them to follow. "You fellas are raw recruits. You'll need trainin'. Let's get back to the picket line. Our relief should be coming soon."

"Think Sarge will ask me to run 'em through the drills like he did last time?" Zach gestured for the new men to follow Spence and then brought up the rear.

Spence shrugged. "Dunno. But I've heard we ain't going to be here long. Might be on the march again as early as tomorrow."

A march? Tomorrow? Callie didn't know much about drilling and even less about following military orders.

"Word is that we're headed to Tennessee." A bearded man in a group ahead spoke with authority. He stood a little apart from about a dozen men with muskets resting against their shoulders, the barrels pointed toward the top of the trees.

Zach whipped off his hat, yelling some type of coyote yelp with the rest of the men until silenced by the officer.

"Sorry, corporal." Spence's hand curled around his musket. "We'll be happy to be home again after all our wanderings."

"Understood. I'm happy about that myself. But we stand on the picket line where we guard our troops. There will be time for whoopin' and hollerin' when you get back to camp." The corporal peered at Callie and Louisa. "Who are these?"

"New Recruits. Cal and Lou Shaw." Zach stepped forward. "Brothers from up near Jackson so they'll be with us."

The corporal rubbed his whiskered jaw. "You fellas got any experience?"

"We can shoot." Callie put as much bravado into her tone as she could muster.

"Know how to Load in Nine Times?"

"Load … what?" Was that a marching order? A drill? Callie shifted from one foot to the other and back again.

A man in back snickered.

"That's enough, Harve. They have to learn just like we did." The corporal grimaced. "Zach, you're relieved of picket duty. I'll get someone to cover your next shift. Sarge is out with a forage detail, and I'm busy with picket detail, so you'll need to start training the Shaw brothers. I'll be there when I can. We have one day to ready them. Maybe two."

Zach's eyes widened.

"I'll send Sam and Jonesy over to you later to help with drills."

Callie read Zach's expression easily. His nervousness transferred to her. Did he worry about being given so little time to train them? How long did it normally take? She glanced at Louisa, who peered around the trees toward movement ahead. Of course. Since Nate wasn't among the men standing near, her sister searched for him.

Finding Nate could wait. The enormity of all they must learn to become soldiers descended over her like a waterfall.

Oh, Lord, what have we done?

Zach followed the rigid back of Corporal Morefield to camp. Spence, who reminisced about his home near Columbia to the brothers, lagged behind with the rest of the men on temporary break from picket duty.

Axes cracking against wood drew his gaze northward where dozens chopped downed timber for firewood. Men toting shovels strode to the outskirts of camp. A tin cup warming on burning embers caught Zach's eye. It looked like coffee but smelled like roasted walnuts. Not much he wouldn't give for a good, hot cup of the beverage he hadn't tasted in months.

Ben halted near the picket rope where hundreds of horses ate clumps of grass or nudged others away for their chance at a nibble. "The Shaws look awful young." He half-turned to watch their progress some twenty paces behind them. "I'll warrant their faces won't have need of a razor for another year or two."

"I'll wager you're right." Zach studied the brothers. Something strange about the way Calvin Shaw walked. Maybe a horse kicked him in his growing years. The pair nudged at his memory. Had he met them somewhere? Maybe. He'd met many folks in his three years with the army—a lifetime of them. More likely they resembled someone. "That's probably why they didn't join up before ... too young."

"And green. They've still got all their teeth so ripping open the cartridges won't present no problems. Train them hard. Start with basic orders. I'll send a bugler to you, so they learn the calls. Teach 'em how to load a musket. I'll be there by then to either monitor your training or take over. Work fast. Set aside today for drills. We'll hope to renew efforts tomorrow. I'll get my hands on another musket, cartridge boxes, and ammunition while you get them settled. Then I'll see about drawing three days of rations for them." The corporal set off at a fast clip toward the officers' tents.

The bugler played Watering Call. Rank and file soldiers approached the horses behind Zach. He walked to the end of the line to avoid the men who'd lead the horses and mules to streams for a long drink.

His gut twisted to remember the last man—a mere boy really—he'd trained for an afternoon. The next day's fighting ended that young man's life.

Could he have done more … said something else that could have saved that boy's life? He'd never know.

His jaw clenched as the brothers drew closer. One or two days at most weren't nearly enough time to train new soldiers. Zach could almost do the drills in his sleep. He'd helped train dozens of recruits in the spring and taken the lead several times since when the drill sergeant was occupied. They'd lost a lot of men during the summer, thinning out those who'd been around since the early days. Everyone had practiced daily drills back then … when not in danger of engaging.

If training raw recruits—which he enjoyed—had to be accomplished in a day, he'd drill them hard. A day might be the best the army could do.

"Spence said you'd show us where to keep our belongings." Lou's eyes darted in every direction.

"That I will." He set off to his right. The brothers fell into step beside him. "Our company bedded down last night about a hundred yards this way."

"This way?" Cal's brow furrowed as they passed bedrolls, knapsacks, and stacked muskets. "But where are the tents?"

"Our tents are on the wagons that follow us—usually so far behind that they don't get to us until the next day or the day after. Sometimes longer." At Cal's frown, he clapped him on the back.

The boy winced.

Touchy fellow. "It's too much trouble to put up tents while on the march. We don't bother with them unless it's raining."

Cal exchanged a wide-eyed look with his brother. "We'd prefer a tent."

Zach shook his head. "You're in the army—not visiting some fancy hotel. Things happen that ain't always to a soldier's preference. Besides, it's a pleasure to sleep under the stars … when the weather's nice." He stopped in front of his knapsack and bedroll. "You can put your belongings next to ours. That is, mine and my cousin's things. His name is Nate McCleary."

Lou's gaze riveted on him. "Oh? Where is your cousin?"

"He's on forage detail." Something about the boy's piercing gaze made him uneasy. He rubbed his whiskered chin. Just raw recruits … young ones at that. "How old are you fellows?"

They looked at each other. "I'm fifteen," Lou answered. "Calvin is sixteen."

He nodded. Still wet behind the ears. "Our corporal—your new corporal, Ben Morefield—is scrounging up a weapon for you. When he gets back, I'll teach you as many drills as time allows. I'll work you hard today." His mind's eye recalled another face about their age, the boy he'd failed. "What you learn has the power to save your life."

Cal swallowed, the high neck of his coat hiding the bob of his Adam's apple.

"You have a few minutes to eat or answer nature's call. Sinks are to the rear of camp. Rest while you can."

Cal's gaze flew to the woods.

Understandable. Lots of soldiers preferred privacy. He'd give them time to take in what they'd learned so far. It was about to get a lot worse.

These boys didn't know what they were in for.

CHAPTER EIGHT

Callie's fingers shook as she signed the document to enter the army. Her voice wobbled as she repeated the oath of muster. Afterward, she met Louisa's glazed eyes. It was really happening. They were soldiers.

The corporal had located a musket for Callie, which she accepted as if it were a copperhead snake. She and Louisa followed Zach to a field outside of camp, far enough away that the noisy activities of camp didn't distract Callie. Though glad not to be holding a heavy weapon for the first part of the training, she blinked at Zach's stony face. When had he become such a relentless taskmaster? Standing next to Louisa—on the same line, as he called it—she evidently needed instructions on how to stand.

Her heels were already on the same line with her feet turned out, knees straight, with her body erect.

"Incline your body forward." Zach demonstrated.

Callie leaned forward a bit, trying to keep her back straight.

"That's fine, men, but keep your shoulders square and equal."

Gritting her teeth, she complied.

"Your arms fall naturally at your side."

Nothing natural about this stance, Callie longed to observe aloud but didn't dare.

"Those elbows should be near your body."

Easy enough—except when leaning forward with her shoulders square and heels touching at right angles.

"Like this, Calvin."

She looked up. Zach had managed to stand just so and still look relaxed. Keeping the rest of her body in line, she tried again.

"Good." His eyes darted from her to Louisa. "Turn your palms a bit to the front. Your little finger will be behind the seam of your pantaloons."

This was supposed to be a comfortable way to stand? Callie complied, knowing she'd hear Louisa grumble once they were alone.

Zach demonstrated the position of the head. "Gaze straight to the ground fifteen paces ahead of you."

She was supposed to look at the ground while leaning forward, shoulders square? She dropped her gaze. Finally, one command actually worked.

"You move stiffly, but that's to be expected. We'll practice this position again, but time is short."

He rubbed his chin, a well-remembered mannerism that turned the corners of Callie's mouth upward. Though Zach had always been clean-shaven back home, she didn't mind his dark beard, since he'd made an effort to keep it cropped close to his face. He was a handsome stranger dressed in his uniform, but she preferred him clean-shaven in his red-striped flannel shirt, blue pantaloons, and black coat that he'd worn while working on his uncle's horse farm.

Those horses were long gone. Both armies got a share of them from what Callie had heard. Zach had never talked about it.

"We'll do a few basic drills, and then I'll teach you to load a musket."

At least she knew how to load and fire a musket. That should be the easiest part.

"I will demonstrate the Right Face command." He raised his right foot and made a quarter turn. "Now. Right Face."

Callie lifted her right foot and turned with her left foot still facing front. Louisa fared little better.

"Ah. Looks simple, doesn't it? I'll demonstrate again." He made another quarter turn in what appeared to one sweeping motion. "Do it with me. Raise your right foot. Not that high.

Only slightly." His gaze fastened on their feet. "Turn on your left heel while raising your toe a bit. Then put your right heel beside the left."

Louisa toppled to the side.

"Concentrate, Lou. Your mind is wandering."

Callie sympathized with her. This was harder to learn than she had imagined. But then Louisa was probably still searching the area for Nate.

"Let's do that again, men. It gets easier with practice."

Next, Zach taught them the About Face command that was even more challenging. Then he explained the Direct Step, March, Halt, and Double-Quick Step for the next hour.

Callie's head spun. She'd never remember all this.

Zach wiped his forehead with a handkerchief. Not that it was a hot day. The weather was pleasantly mild for October twentieth. No, the cause for his discomfort was that these soldiers were rawer than a green onion just pulled from the ground. None of the commands came naturally to them. Corporal Morefield said he'd send a couple of fellows to help demonstrate loading. Zach narrowed his eyes. The Shaw brothers might be a lost cause.

Weeds rustled behind him. He raised his rifle as he turned. At the sight of comrades in gray, he lowered his weapon.

"Just me and Sam." Jonesy raised the hand not holding his musket in a calming gesture. "Corporal Morefield will work with us this afternoon."

"He sent us to help you train the recruits." Sam Watkins, a fellow soldier in the First Tennessee, peered past Zach at the newcomers. "They need to learn to Load in Nine Times."

A weight tumbled from Zach's shoulders. These two were as steady as anyone could ask—though with a mischievous streak. He introduced them to the Shaw brothers.

Sam questioned them about acquaintances they might have in common even though he lived in Columbia, not Jackson. They didn't know any of the families mentioned yet the simple conversation relaxed the brothers. They hadn't grinned once in Zach's company. Recalling his first days at Camp Trenton, he swallowed his frustration. Drills were a lot to remember.

He picked up Cal's musket and carried it over to him. "To load, you first have to know how to shoulder arms. Bend your right arm slightly." When Cal complied, Zach placed the musket, almost vertical, in his right hand with the barrel resting in the hollow of his shoulder and pointing to the sky. He adjusted Cal's thumb and forefinger to embrace the guard and closed the remaining fingers around it. He did the same thing for Lou and then stepped back with a frown.

"Doing it yourself looks like this." Jonesy rested his musket against his shoulder in two motions.

Sam followed suit.

The brothers studied the placement of their hands and then tried again.

Zach studied the brothers. "Much better, but don't lower that right shoulder."

Lou lifted his shoulder.

"That's it." The veterans were an asset. Jonesy and Sam still faced the brothers. He'd use their expertise. "We will teach you to Load in Nine Times. It's called that because there are nine steps to loading a musket. You'll practice this repeatedly today. First, Jonesy will load on my command. The target is on the tree behind you, Jonesy."

He glanced over his shoulder where Zach had nailed a blue uniform to a tree. "Nice."

"Load." Zach raised his voice.

Jonesy lowered the musket until the butt rested between his feet. He held it in his left hand while his right hand unfastened the cartridge box at his waist.

"Handle cartridge."

Jonesy extracted a cartridge and brought it to his mouth.

"Tear cartridge." The brothers' attention was riveted on Jonesy's movements. Good. Most southern boys knew how to shoot. They might do well at this.

Jonesy tore the cartridge paper with his teeth.

"Charge cartridge."

Jonesy poured powder down the barrel. He placed the ball in the muzzle.

Cal's hand imitated the same motion.

"Draw rammer."

He removed the ramrod from the pipes and held it aloft.

"Ram cartridge." Zach studied the brothers from the corner of his eye, noting that Cal's eyes widened with each command.

Jonesy inserted the rammer into the muzzle, pressing the cartridge home. When finished he placed the ramrod back into the pipes.

"Return rammer."

He slid the ramrod into its seated position.

"Prime."

He raised the muzzle to eye level with the lock above the waist. He half-cocked the weapon then retrieved a percussion cap from his cap pouch and placed it on the cone.

"Ready."

The musket was fully cocked using the right thumb.

"Aim."

Cal's body tensed as Jonesy brought the butt of the musket to his shoulder. He turned and took aim.

"Fire."

His forefinger pressed the trigger. A hole appeared on the shoulder of the target.

Cal flinched.

Zach frowned at this sign of squeamishness. The boy would have to get over that reaction.

Sam whistled. "Can't you do no better than that? That soldier ain't even shooting at you."

Jonesy lowered his weapon. "Maybe you'd best show me how it's done."

"I aim to." Sam grinned at Zach. "My turn?"

Despite his misgivings about Cal's reaction to the shooting, he chuckled. The competition between friends lightened his mood. "Your turn." He stared at the brothers. "Pay close attention. All four of you will be following the orders next time. Don't worry. Before long you'll be loading three times a minute. Maybe faster."

Callie's body went cold. This was the part she most dreaded. Shooting rabbits for supper—that was one thing. Aiming at a target of a man's clothing … that almost seemed as if she'd be shooting the man, something her heart wouldn't allow her to do. Murder was wrong. Her heartbeat quickened to recall Ma's weekly Bible reading and Pastor Brown's sermons. Her pretense at being a soldier already put her on God's bad side. She didn't need to add to it.

Zach knew she could never hurt anyone. He'd never ask her to go through with this, if he knew her identity.

But that was the crux of the matter. He didn't know. And she couldn't tell him. She had to stay in the army. She had no place else to go.

She managed to nod. Loading a weapon was something she'd done a hundred times though not like this. "I'm watching." Her voice squeaked. Louisa nudged her. She altered her voice to a lower tone. "I'll pay attention."

"Good." Zach's gaze darted from Callie to Louisa and back again before he turned to Sam. "Ready?"

"Ready as I'll ever be." Sam grinned.

Callie decided she liked this fellow. If her ma had birthed a son, she imagined he'd be like Sam.

Then her smile died as Zach gave the Load in Nine Times orders to Sam. There was so much for soldiers to remember.

Sam guffawed when his shot landed in the middle of the target.

She smiled when Jonesy extended his hand to Sam good-naturedly and then she glanced at Zach to share the moment with him. His jaw slackened as he stared straight into her eyes.

She lowered her gaze. "I'd be happy with either one of those shots." She maintained a roughened quality to her voice. Did she have a feminine smile?

A bugler blew a different tune in the distance. What now?

"Time to eat." Sam gave Jonesy a punch. "You boys coming?"

"You fellas go on. We'll be along." Zach's nostrils flared. "I'll need you again this afternoon if the corporal can spare you."

Sam nodded. "Fine by me."

Zach stared at Callie until their comrades' footsteps died away. "Cal and Lou." He folded his arms. "Well, ladies? Care to tell me whose fool idea this was?"

CHAPTER NINE

Callie sucked in her breath. Did Zach recognize them or just realize they were women?

Louisa blinked and then gave a tiny shake of her head. "Ladies? What are you talking about?"

"This is serious business." Three strides brought him inches from Callie's face. "You think I'd not recognize that smile anywhere, Callie Jennings?"

Her smile? Callie's heart quickened. He liked her smile. But that didn't mean anything. He'd rejected her. "I ... no. I didn't believe you'd recognize me when wearing a soldier's garb."

"Is this a joke for you two? An adventure?" He folded his arms across his chest. "Louisa, this was your idea, wasn't it?" His eyes bored into hers. "It's not funny. You ladies know that soldiers die in battle."

Callie took a step back. She'd never seen him this angry. Well, maybe with Nate but not with her. "We know."

"Then why?" He stepped closer, his green eyes snapping. "Donning that uniform—pretending to be a soldier—can get you captured ... or killed. I'm surprised at you, Callie. You usually have more sense than your sister."

Louisa glared at him.

"Why didn't you talk her out of it?"

Callie wrapped her arms as close to her chest as the extra padding allowed. "Because I have no other place to go."

"No place to go? The Yankees burned your house?"

"No." Her voice came out in a whisper. "But they took too

much from us. There's not enough food stored to feed all three of us this winter and no money to buy more."

Zach frowned. "What are you saying?"

"It's Pa." She covered her face with her hands and then forced her hands to her side with a furtive glance at the surrounding woods. "He decided I'm to marry his friend, Ezra Culpepper. Mr. Culpepper has been able to hide food … money … so he's not in want as we are. I'd not go hungry with him."

"Ezra Culpepper?" Zach blanched above his beard. "That man has to be three decades older than you." His brows lowered as he searched her face. "Why didn't you refuse?"

"I did." Her tone sharpened. "I've no desire to marry him."

"Pa didn't give her a chance to refuse. He planned to see the preacher when he and Mr. Culpepper got back."

He straightened. "Back from where?"

Callie shook her head at Louisa. "He didn't say."

His gaze shifted to the horizon as if seeing something far away.

"We never ask," Louisa reached for Callie's hand, "because I don't think we want to know."

"Don't do that!" Zach said.

"What?"

"Hold her hand."

Callie dropped her sister's hand, gaze darting to the tree line. Was someone she didn't see spying on them? She brought her attention back to Zach.

"You're masquerading as soldiers. Have you ever seen two brothers holding hands? There are thousands of soldiers in camp. Unless you are answering nature's call," his face turned crimson, "someone will likely be near enough to catch your feminine mistakes. You two will be found out before the week's done." His green eyes darkened. "You're women. You think and act like women. You'll never make it as soldiers."

"Yes, we will, Zach Pearson." Callie stepped up until the toe of her brogans brushed against his shoes that were almost a mirror image of hers. "Because we have no choice. Pa will come around to my way of thinking when this war's ended. Right now, it's the whiskey talking. He wasn't like this when he was sober. With all the Yankees have put us through …"

"Yep. Saw that when I was home." His serious gaze held hers.

"Things will get better someday. I have to hold on to that." Her heart ached for her pa's sadness, his burden. How she longed to lean into Zach, feel his arms around her—if only in comfort. She stepped back, recalling his rejection. The only thing to be glad about was he didn't know that Pa told her of his refusal to marry her. "Pa will stop drinking after all this is over. He can't live with what he's doing. That's why he's pushing us away."

His arms reached for her and then dropped to his side. "Didn't you have other family to go to? An aunt? A cousin?"

Rejected again. "No one." She took another step back. "But Louisa and I will be good soldiers. Wait and see."

His chin dropped to his chest. He peered at her with dull eyes before looking at Louisa. "You are betrothed to my cousin. Your pa won't force you to marry against your will. What's your reason for mustering into the army?"

"My reasons are plenty, Zach Pearson. Not the least of which is seeing to my sister's safety." She gave Callie a bracing smile. "Maybe I don't appreciate Yankees coming in and stealing our crops. Stomping on the plants they leave behind so we can't glean any morsels from them. Maybe I don't like hiding in the woods when I hear horses galloping up behind me on my walk to town, afraid of what strangers will say and do. And maybe I don't like to see my sister do without—work as hard as our ma ever did—with no thanks from Pa."

His gaze darted to Callie and back again. "Somehow I think your presence here has more to do with my cousin."

Louisa's gaze fastened on the woods toward camp. "Maybe it does … maybe it doesn't. My reasons are my own. But don't tell Nate who we are. You recognized Callie from her smile, from the friendly way she looks at you. I won't make the same mistake."

His cheeks flushed. "Maybe not, but this foolishness brings danger. Battles are brutal. Comrades fall dead right beside you and you wonder why they died and not you. Then you realize you can't think about it—just keep doing your job. I'd not wish that experience on an enemy much less …" His troubled gaze lingered on Callie. "I can't allow you to stay."

Callie wrung her hands. "I've no place to go."

"We're not leaving. We've already mustered in." Louisa crossed her arms. "Stiffen that backbone, Callie. You're a soldier now."

"I am a soldier." She straightened her shoulders. She had to be stronger and braver than she'd ever been to get through this. "All I read in the newspaper—and all I heard from neighbors—is how our army needs more soldiers. Here we are."

He sighed. "Truth is, the army'd probably release you today without punishment. Don your dresses and no one will recognize you. We'll figure something out."

"We buried our dresses and petticoats." Callie's face flamed to mention the undergarments. There was no help for it—he had to know there was no going back.

"Why'd you do a fool thing like that?" He widened his stance.

"No room in our knapsacks." Callie's gaze dropped to a tiny rip in Zach's left shoe. "Besides, we won't need dresses 'til the war ends. How long do you think that will be?"

"I fear …" His gaze shifted to the trees behind her. "I'm not a prophet, Callie, but things are about to get really tough for our army. I feel it deep in my bones." His shoulders slumped. "You picked a terrible time for these shenanigans. I don't know how you'd get back home safely now. Word is that the Yankees are near. We've had several skirmishes since Atlanta fell, so I've no reason to doubt it."

Callie held her breath.

He rubbed the back of his neck. "You're putting your lives in peril. Can't you see that?" Callie eyed her defiant sister. Louisa wasn't ready to give up. She wasn't either—not when her heart told her she was strong enough. "We're aware of the danger. But did you consider that maybe we're meant to be here?"

"Not for a second."

Callie ignored his mulish expression. "We prayed that we'd find the First Tennessee the first day. We met up with you right away. What does that tell you?"

"That God's relying on me to send you home." He glared at her.

Callie glared back. "If I'd have known you'd be this unreasonable, I'd have asked for a different regiment."

"This isn't getting us anywhere." He gave an exasperated sigh. "We'd better go see about getting you girls—"

"Men." Louisa arched her eyebrows at him.

"Men some rations." He stumbled over the words. "Watch yourselves. This discussion isn't over."

They headed across the field. "Don't tell anyone who we are, Zach. Not even Nate."

"Why not Nate? She's his betrothed."

His stride widened. Callie could barely keep up.

"Don't fret. I'll tell him when the time is right." Louisa's smile was secretive.

He kicked a stump. "I've no doubt you will surprise him as much as Callie surprised me."

As Zach led the way back to camp, it seemed as if the earth shook under the impact of a dozen twelve-pounder Napoleons. Only there was no artillery fire. His steps wobbled at his discovery. Here he'd worried for Callie's safety with small groups of Yankees all over Tennessee. Porter Jennings had watched over his daughters with a protective eye all their lives—Zach had assumed he'd never stop. Now he had the sneaking suspicion that Porter was an irregular, and that gave him mixed feelings. The Confederate Armies needed all the help they could get. As far as Zach could see, their situation grew worse. The loss of Atlanta cut deeply. He was grateful for citizens who served the Confederacy as rangers. They operated in secret, returning to civilian life as if nothing happened when not on a mission. But the things Zach heard that they sometimes did to Yankee soldiers ate away at a man's soul.

Little wonder that Porter had taken to hard drinking.

Corporal Morefield strode over with small sacks tucked under one arm as soon as the silent trio approached their section of camp. "You men don't have a haversack between you. The sutlers didn't have any either."

"We've been carrying our food in that old flour sack." Callie pointed an earth-toned sack among her possessions. "That will do us for now."

The corporal frowned. "If you can figure a way to strap it around your shoulder, I don't mind. You'll share rations with your brother until we come upon haversacks for you. I'll ask around. It's good that you are wearing gray trousers and coats, so we didn't have to concern ourselves with clothes. Here's some meal, brown sugar, dried corn, candles, and lye soap."

"Much obliged." She clasped the sacks close.

Zach had half expected her to complain about the meager supplies. A huge breath escaped him to see Callie's gratitude. Even Louisa's face relaxed into a small smile at the sight of food. These ladies must have been starving when they arrived.

"Eat quickly, men. We'll drill this afternoon." Corporal Morefield turned to Zach. "I got held up. How'd it go?"

Zach explained the few commands he'd introduced. The brothers hadn't yet practiced the loading so ably demonstrated by Jonesy and Sam.

Crossing his arms, the corporal surveyed the Shaws. "Get them loading after lunch. Work with them until I get there to put them through the drills. Johnny will be there to demonstrate the bugle tunes for the most important commands. Work 'em hard." He clapped Zach on the shoulder. "They'll have to be ready."

After he strode away, Zach was torn between anger that the sisters put themselves in this impossible position and compassion for the pinched look on Callie's face. "You must be hungry. I'll show you how to make sagamite. Won't take long to cook ... and it's a satisfying meal."

"Sagamite?" Callie's voice came in her normal pitch.

He frowned with a slight shake of his head. "Right. Mix corn meal and brown sugar into a little cake and then fry it. I'll show you how much to use."

"We mostly just guess at it." Spence sat around a small fire with Jonesy, Sam, and several others. "Makes every meal an adventure."

The other fellows laughed. Zach chuckled at the irony of the comment. Hadn't been a lot of variety in their rations for a long time.

Callie gave a tentative grin. "We'll not complain. We've been mostly eating dried corn."

Zach breathed a little easier to hear the gruff quality back in her tone.

"Been there." Jonesy grinned while moving a tin cup from a small fire. "We already ate. Use our fire to cook your meal." He introduced the folks that the Shaws hadn't met yet.

Zach's stomach clenched at the curiosity in his comrades' eyes, though there was nothing out of the ordinary in their interest. If they knew the new recruits were women ...

Alert for their feminine lapses, he set about making his lunch. The girls had their own meal sizzling in a skillet. He'd have to warn them about displaying their culinary talents ... along with other womanly accomplishments.

He'd never seen such pain in Callie's eyes as when revealing her father's plans for her. Though he'd protect them from detection as best he could, his breathing turned erratic at the thought of them dying in battle. His heartbeat only returned to normal because they'd give themselves away before a week was up, even with his advice.

His ears perked up when the conversation with the newcomers grew personal. The sisters gave scanty details in response to questions about their family. Their mother died before the war. The Yankees had taken a large portion of their crop. Their pa took to drinking. Then Louisa turned the tables by asking the others about their families.

Zach paid little attention to his comrades' answers. Instead he watched their faces while he wolfed down a sweet corn cake. Spence leaned his back against a stump as he spoke of his wife, Charlotte, waiting for him in their home near Columbia. Jonesy raised his knees, resting his crossed wrists on top. The others were equally relaxed, displaying no more than natural curiosity about the newcomers.

Some of the tension left Zach's shoulders. The ladies had passed the first test. No one suspected them of being other than boys struggling to learn soldiering skills quickly.

His gaze traveled to Callie's auburn hair. After he left for war, she'd discarded her braids and pinned her hair on top of her head. He'd often wondered what that beautiful hair looked like when released from its pins, but he'd never imagined it cut short. Auburn curls almost reached her shoulder.

He took a long drink from his canteen. They were too beautiful to pose as men, even wearing soldiers' garb. How did his comrades miss it? How had he?

Because they weren't expecting women soldiers. Plain and simple. If it hadn't been for Callie's smile …

The smile he dreamed about almost nightly. The girl he most longed to see sat five paces away. He'd wanted to see her—though not like this. Callie had no idea of the danger lurking ahead. The terrible battles where men hit by shells and shrapnel lost limbs—sometimes at your side. Sights that never receded from memory.

He feared that she'd learn all too well. If the sisters stayed. His blood boiled at Porter Jennings. His daughters fled the safety of their home—during a war—because their father was forcing Callie to marry an old man. He rubbed the back of his neck. Porter's intentions might be good. Zach wanted to think the best of him. He liked the man. He used to like the man.

What if Zach had agreed to marry Callie back in March? Could he have saved her from this fate even if they didn't marry until the war's end? Porter's reason for pushing Callie at Mr. Culpepper had been lack of food. He'd still have to find a way to feed her until she married Zach—if he'd proposed in the spring.

Tying her to a soldier who'd decided to remain in the army as his life's work hadn't seemed right. Military life suited him. His direct officers often demanded more of him. He liked the additional responsibility. Usually. If he chose soldiering as a profession, he'd be gone for months, maybe years, at a time. That was no life for a wife waiting back home.

The corporal escorted another group of soldiers to the picket line to relieve those already there, intruding on Zach's thoughts.

Louisa joined in the conversation and finished her meal. All the while her gaze wandered around camp. Her lack of attention might indicate a boy's curiosity, but Zach knew differently.

Nate hadn't returned from foraging. Depending on their success, the expeditions could take hours or even days. He might not return until tomorrow if they had to go far afield to find food to feed a large number of soldiers.

What if Nate didn't recognize Louisa? Should Zach go against the sisters' wishes and tell him about the masquerade?

Crumbs tumbled down his coat as he shoved the last bite of sagamite into his mouth. Lots to ponder. "Cal and Lou, you have ten minutes to clean up and join me back in the field."

He shoved his worry aside. There was a job to do.

CHAPTER TEN

"Where's Nate?" Louisa tugged on Callie's arm in the gathering dusk.

"I don't know." Callie lagged behind Zach, Corporal Morefield, Johnny—the bugler—and the other relatively new soldiers who'd been training with them all afternoon. Some of the tension of meeting Martha Rose's beau diminished when Johnny paid them little attention. Zach's anger when discovering their identity had rocked her fragile confidence. He might have acted a little bit happy to see her, even if he regarded her as nothing more than a friend.

Callie's arms ached from holding a musket *just so* all day. She shivered in the chill as her stomach reminded her that lunch had been hours ago. Ready for a moment's privacy in the surrounding woods, she didn't much care where Nate was at the moment. "I've been in this field just as long as you have."

"Help me find him."

"We can't go looking for Nate. We're not even supposed to know him." She grabbed her sister's hand to halt her.

"Stop that." Louisa snatched her hand away. "Remember Zach's warning?"

"Sorry. But act rationally. Nate will seek out his cousin when he's not busy. You'll see him them. Remember not to give him a special look."

"Like you did with Zach?" Louisa shot back. "You're the reason he discovered us."

"I know—and I'm sorry." The crickets' song drew Callie back into a degree of normalcy. "He promised to keep our secret."

"No, he didn't."

"Of course he did." Callie tugged at her high collar. Thinking back, he actually hadn't made that promise. "You're right. But he won't bring trouble on us. You know that."

"He might take it into his head to tell Nate—far worse to my way of thinking." Louisa shifted her musket to her other shoulder.

No doubt that was the worst thing that could happen in Louisa's view. "Look, Louisa—"

"Lou."

"You're right again. Lou. I promise to remember." She pressed two fingers into her throbbing temple. "We have to get our hands on a tent."

"Zach said we couldn't have one."

"The alternative is sleeping next to a bunch of strange men."

Louisa paled. "I hadn't considered that. I only want to sleep beside Nate—"

Callie gasped.

"Don't worry ... I meant only after we're married." She sighed. "Think we can ask the corporal directly? He seems helpful."

"I think we have to try. Come on—the others are out of sight. Nature's calling. Let's make a quick stop in the trees before heading back."

"Right behind you, sis—brother."

Zach convinced his corporal to let him walk back to the wagons to retrieve a tent for the new recruits. He knew this wasn't going to work when on the march again. Wagons lagged too far behind, especially on muddy roads. At least the girls had a tent for a night or two.

He must make them see this was the end of their privacy.

Their pretense of living as men made it impossible for him to do things for them like erect their tent. That went against the grain.

He was no ladies' man like his cousin, but he balked at making them set up their own camp. This whole thing was wrong. Callie had placed him in an intolerable position.

The welcome scent of hundreds of small fires that lit his edge of camp greeted him when he strode back under starry skies with two pieces of cotton drill slung over his shoulder. Callie and Louisa—no, he reckoned he'd better start calling them Cal and Lou even in his thoughts—cooked something resembling corn fritters in a small skillet sitting on burning embers.

Zach deposited the canvas on the grass near the fire. "Cal and Lou, you have a tent for tonight. And maybe tomorrow night. You'll be responsible for putting it up and taking it down before our next march."

"Thanks." Cal's eyes softened before she bent over the fire again. "Want a couple of corn fritters? Well, not exactly corn fritters. I don't have flour, so I used cornmeal instead with a helping of soaked corn."

His mouth watered at the appetizing aroma of corn fritters—no burnt smell as so often happened when he cooked. "Much obliged. Reckon you learned something about cooking with losing your Ma so young." He'd forgotten to warn her about that. Hopefully, the fellows nearby heard his comment and wouldn't think any more about it. "I'll give you a portion of my cornmeal to make up for eating your rations."

Her brown eyes met his briefly as she nodded.

Did she understand his warning? She was an intelligent woman, something he prized about her. And his admiration had grown even more that day. He'd pushed her hard, and she'd stayed right with him.

"I know they're young, Zach, but don't coddle 'em too much." Jonesy looked up from a letter he was writing close to the firelight. "It ain't even raining tonight."

Heat rose in Zach's cheeks. He'd warned the girls to be careful—he'd have to be on his guard, too. Jonesy was one of the men who wrote in his journal—daily, if he got the chance. He might mention the new recruits. "They're new."

"Yep. Reckon them making your supper is a fair exchange for your trouble." The scratching of his pencil against paper ended the conversation.

Zach dug his plate out of his knapsack and returned to the fire. "Anyone seen Nate?"

Louisa stiffened at the chorus of "Naw," and "Not me," as she dropped two corn fritters on Zach's plate.

He nudged a fritter with his finger. Too hot to eat. "Reckon he's still out foraging."

"Maybe not. I saw Sarge before supper." Spence stood up, the strap of his canteen hooked over his hand. "Going after water. Anyone need some?"

A dozen men handed him their canteen. Zach, Cal, and Lou included theirs.

"Here." Jonesy put down his pencil and reached for the canteens. "I feel like a walk. I'll go with you to the creek."

"I have to wash my cup."

"Me, too."

A half-dozen comrades joined them as they disappeared into the darkness.

Zach glanced at Louisa's raised eyebrows. Little wonder she was curious about Nate's whereabouts. He wondered about it himself. Nate's foraging detail probably reaped an invitation to supper with a family in town. Maybe others in the foraging party had been invited. He gulped down a bite of fritter. Tasty.

"Where do you think he went?" Lou whispered.

"Dunno." It was good that she'd remembered to lower the tone of her voice to mimic a male pitch even in her distress. "I'm certain he's safe."

"But we made him supper. Should we save it for him?"

He shook his head. "No need."

Lou exchanged a glance with Cal. "I'll save two fritters. If he doesn't want them, my brother and me will eat it for breakfast."

"Now you're talking." If Nate was eating a hot supper with an area family, he'd best keep his mouth shut about it. Everyone around here was hungry for a home-cooked meal. The corn fritters were delicious but didn't compare with fried chicken or mashed potatoes … or even rice soup. "Let's clean the dishes and then get that tent up. The bugler will soon blow attention and then assembly when we'll form a line for the day's final roll call."

"Nate should be here by roll call?" Lou's gaze riveted to his face.

"Should be." If only Nate would recognize his betrothed instantly. Then Zach wouldn't have the heartache of choosing between his loyalties to his cousin and betraying Callie's faith in him. He shrank from the trust in her brown eyes. He didn't deserve it when all he wanted was to get her to safety.

A weight the size of a cannon descended on his chest. No matter which choice he made, someone he cared for would be hurt.

Callie had never put up a tent in her life. Once the two pieces of heavy cotton drill were buttoned together, it lay in a heap.

Zach picked up the end of a rope. "Fellas, I'll teach you how to use this rope to create a ridgepole."

She'd learned enough for one day. Why couldn't he just do it for her like the old Zach would? Because she was Cal, not Callie, and she'd landed herself in a passel of trouble. All her own doing. Expecting Zach to get her out of it was childish. And she would not be childish.

"These are tied to your muskets. Nothing could be easier." Zach looked at each of them. "Lou, get your musket. Cal, use my musket since yours doesn't have a bayonet. I'll try to get you one. But don't worry. We haven't used bayonets lately."

Callie gulped. She had no need of the sharp attachment but

couldn't say so with scores of men within earshot.

"Though they make nice candleholders." He grinned and pointed to Jonesy. A lit candle nestled in the round part with the pointed end shoved into the earth.

Handy. Maybe she did want a bayonet. She scanned the group closest to her. Some talked, some cleaned their muskets, some brushed their teeth with charcoal tooth powder, some played cards, while others wrote letters home. One man shaved. Though none appeared to pay attention to them, she had to heed Zach's warning to constantly guard her words and actions.

One thing she was sure of, there was no possibility of her using a bayonet on another person even if ordered to do so. A girl had her limits on how far she could be pushed.

Zach extracted a musket from a nearby stack. "This one's mine. Fix your bayonet like this, Lou." He shoved it into place.

Louisa fiddled with it until the steel slid into the groove. She grinned at him in the firelight.

"Good. Set it on the ground. The rope stretches between the trigger guards of the two muskets." He secured the rope on the trigger guard. "Lou, hold this here while we set up the other side." He lifted the tent, chest high, with the hand holding the rope. "Cal, run the rope where the shelter halves are buttoned together."

Callie was only a couple of inches over five feet and had to duck her head under the canvas to lead the rope to the other side, holding up the canvas around her.

Zach followed her with his musket. "I'll hold it while you tie the rope."

She held her breath as his sleeve brushed against her. He stood so close that he must hear her heart beat, so loudly did it pound. Her fingers fumbled with the rope at their position two inches from the trigger.

"Like this." His voice deepened to a husky whisper as his hand covered hers.

She jerked her head away as his breath warmed her cheek.

"You've had a long day of learning. You're doing fine." His hand slid to the rope.

He stood so close as he tied the rope that all she had to do was lift her face to his for the kiss she'd dreamed of. What was she thinking? There were dozens of men within earshot.

She backed away too quickly. She gasped as her foot caught on the canvas. He caught her before she fell, one arm pulling her close against his fast-beating heart.

"Thank you." Keeping her head lowered, it took all her willpower to take a step back. "Sorry. I'm so clumsy."

"These tents take a little getting used to." His voice was not quite steady as he let go of her arm. Candlelight outside flickered on his face, revealing a dazed look in his green eyes. "Do you want to tie the last knot?"

Her fingers brushed against his as she accepted the rope. Music floated across the field. She paused to listen to the individual instruments. Banjoes, fiddles, fifes, bugles, and drums played "Bonnie Blue Flag." Her gaze flew to Zach as she secured the rope. "What a treat to hear songs in camp."

"That never gets old. The regimental bands play for us most nights we're not marching. Now we have to stake down that corner."

The whole tent went up in far less time and easier than Callie imagined. Why did soldiers not bother with it?

The band played "Dixie" while she and Louisa stored their meager possessions inside the tent. Zach told them to listen for the bugler's orders for roll call. Then he strode away.

Louisa sat outside the tent, her gaze darting all around them.

Someone nearby whistled along with the band.

Louisa stuck her head in the tent. "That's Nate. I'd recognize his walk anywhere. He's coming this way. What should I do?"

"If he sees you, Lou Shaw, introduce yourself." Callie clasped her hands together. No doubt her sister longed to launch herself into Nate's arms—with disastrous outcome. "Remember who you are," she whispered.

Louisa smoothed her hair.

"Don't do that," she hissed in a whisper. "You want to give us away?"

Louisa's hands fell to her side. Footsteps approached. She extended her hands to the fire's warmth.

"Are you a new recruit?"

Callie joined her sister as Nate stopped beside Louisa.

"Just mustered in today. Lou Shaw's the name." Speaking gruffly, she nodded to Callie. "This is my brother, Cal."

"Nate McClary." He shook hands first with Louisa and then Callie. "Always happy to see new recruits muster in." He gestured at their tent. "Must be you boys ain't used to sleeping outside. Give it time."

The band played the opening line of "Home Sweet Home."

"What did you fellas do today?" Nate dropped his knapsack and canteen on the ground.

"Learned some drills from Corporal Morefield and a few others." Louisa stepped into the shadows as she looked up at him. "Zachariah Pearson taught us how to Load in Nine Times."

"Good old Zach." He grinned. "Proud to say he'd make a good officer. He's my cousin."

"He mentioned having a cousin."

Though Louisa's head turned partially away, Callie figured she peered at Nate from the corner of her eye. It must eat away at her to carry on a conversation with her betrothed without announcing herself.

"I'm the guilty man. Reckon we're about as close to being brothers as you can get without sharing the same ma and pa." The sorrowful tune continued in the background. "That song always takes me back to my family's horse farm in Tennessee. 'Course there ain't no horses or mules there now. What our government left behind for us the Yankees got. It's done ruined us, that's for sure." He shook his head as if his thoughts were far away. "Cageville's my home. You all ever hear of it?"

"Your cousin mentioned it." Louisa's words came in a rush. "We also hail from Tennessee. Near Jackson."

True enough. Though neither Callie nor her sister had ever been to Jackson—or even stepped foot outside of their beloved Tennessee before last month. Her body tensed. *Don't say anything to give us away, Louisa.*

The bugler blared a short tune. Callie had heard so many today that it was difficult to distinguish them. "Is that another order?"

"That's 'Attention.' Means we need to line up for roll call." He glanced from Callie to Louisa's profile. "You boys with us?"

"Yes." Louisa turned. Her face remained in the shadows. "We're with you all the way."

"Happy to hear it." Nate tipped his hat. "I expect no less." A grim expression lit his face as he turned. Another bugle song. "Let's go, boys."

Callie's heartbeat quickened as they followed Nate to men assembling near lantern light thirty paces from their tent. Men continued conversations as their feet shuffled in the grass. What did one do at roll call? At least it was too dark for folks to see them make mistakes. She sighed. One more thing to learn.

Zach joined them. "Nice that you made it in time for roll call tonight, cousin."

Nate patted his stomach with a grin. "It's a tough job—"

Zach's gaze shot to Louisa as he shook his head. "I see you've met our new recruits."

"Yep. We need all the good men we can get."

"Ain't it the truth?" Corporal Morefield strode up. "You boys worked hard today. I'm right proud of you. I'll introduce you to our company before we start." He strode to a line of soldiers. "Looks like we're ready."

Ignoring a fluttery feeling in her stomach, Callie tried to lengthen her stride to match Zach's as she and Louisa followed the cousins to a group of men standing in a line that faced the corporal.

The corporal set his lantern on the ground. "Men, I'm happy to announce that we've added two new recruits to our company—Calvin Shaw and Lou Shaw. The brothers hail from Jackson, Tennessee."

The soldiers whooped and hollered as Callie tensed. *Near Jackson* is what they'd said. Hopefully none of these fellows lived in Jackson.

"We'll soon be on the march again—no orders yet—so the Shaws have a lot to learn real fast." Corporal Morefield nodded to them. "I'm certain everyone here is willing to help you boys. Now for roll call. Abbott."

"He—re!" Someone down the line on Callie's left answered with an uplifted cadence in his voice.

"Callahan."

"Here." This man spoke in what might be an exaggerated bass tone.

She smiled at the individual ways each soldier answered to "Dixon, Farmer, Jones." It appeared to be almost a game that played out among several groups within earshot. Some almost shouted their response.

"McClary."

"He—uh!" Nate's voice raised proudly.

"Pearson."

"He—uh!" Zach's response mirrored his cousin's.

"Calvin Shaw."

Callie sucked in her breath. She must remember to speak in a masculine tone. "Here."

Evidently she succeeded because the corporal didn't raise his eyes from his black journal. "Lou Shaw."

"Here."

Callie's shoulders relaxed to hear Louisa's deeper tones. In a day filled with new tasks, speaking in male tones was one more lesson learned.

There were only a few names after theirs. Several men introduced themselves afterward, shaking their hand or clapping them on the back. Callie winced when one man struck harder than others but smiled at the genuine welcome in their voices. The corporal had moved away with his lantern, so darkness hid their faces.

Zach waited alone for them a few paces away. "We now have about half of an hour before taps. Then it's light's out for everyone."

"Where's Nate?" Louisa peered ahead.

"Preparing for bed … as you need to do. Everyone sleeps fully-clothed—many with their shoes on. That's mostly for warmth, but Yankees are following us. They've woken us up rarin' for a fight before."

Callie gulped. Danger was that close?

"Don't fret. That's why we all take turns standing guard. Pickets will wake us shooting and hollering if there's a need. I doubt that will happen tonight." Zach left them when they reached their tent.

Her senses heightened, Callie trudged for another visit to the woods with her sister. The thought of sleeping in the midst of thousands of men and no women made her dizzy. These men hadn't seen their wives or sweethearts for months. Some soldiers might be of questionable character—the type who'd take advantage of a woman. The enormity of what they'd done slammed into her like a cold rain. They must not be discovered.

Zach had to keep their secret.

The sisters readied themselves for bed back in the tent. Callie wondered if Louisa realized the potential perils of the choice they'd made. She didn't dare speak about it with so many men surrounding them.

The bugler played the first few notes of taps. Callie wrapped the wool blanket she'd brought from home around her tired body as she settled on the cold ground. The mournful tune brought thoughts of her father. What did Pa think about the note they left explaining that Callie wanted to marry a man she loved—nothing against Ezra Culpepper. She hoped he understood.

She sighed and snuggled deeper under the blanket. At least Pa didn't have to watch them starve to death this winter. That's what had pushed him to do what he'd done.

A tear traced her cheek. In the days before the war, she'd been close to Pa. Then Ma died, and the war started, and Yankees came … and Pa changed. She knew he loved her and Louisa. Yankees coming South hadn't changed his love for his daughters.

She wiped her wet cheeks. He must be worried about them.

Callie couldn't write to tell him and other townsfolk where they were. If she wrote Pa, there was no telling what temper he'd be in when he received the news. Drunk or not, he might tear off after them, find the army, and reveal their identity. When she weighed easing his mind over the possibility of him finding her and forcing her to marry Mr. Culpepper, she decided not to risk it.

Pa hadn't been like that when Ma was alive. It was the drinking that had changed him. No, the *war* had changed him … led him to find whatever solace there was in hard liquor. Not much consolation to be found in that jar, if the deepening creases in his forehead and tormented eyes were any indication.

The last bugle notes died away.

She turned her back on her sister's even breathing. Louisa was already sleeping? How did she turn off the turmoil in her mind so quickly?

Callie wished she could do the same. Pa fretted over them, that was certain. She wished he wouldn't worry overmuch but knew he would. Despite everything, she knew he loved them and had acted out of love.

A drummer tapped on his drum then all was silent except for the familiar hum of crickets. What were the soldiers around her thinking about?

Lights extinguished. Burning embers from a nearby fire kept Callie from total darkness. She shivered as much from loneliness as from the chill of the autumn night.

Zach slept on the other side of the tent. What did he think about when all was quiet? Not her—at least, not the way she wanted.

He'd been angry ... scared when he recognized her. There had been that moment when he saved her from tripping over the canvas. He'd pulled her close enough that she felt his heart beat against her cheek. Did his feelings for her go deeper than friendship?

Or did his thoughts turn to some other woman?

Her breath quickened. What did it matter who he loved if that woman wasn't her?

Gentle snoring came from the left. Not so gentle snores rent the air from somewhere to her right. Others soon joined in until a regular symphony of grunts, groans, and snores drowned out the crickets. How was a body supposed to sleep here?

So this was a soldier's life.

What had she and Louisa been thinking?

CHAPTER ELEVEN

Two days later, a band played a rousing rendition of "When Johnny Comes Marching Home" as Callie marched next to her sister with two other soldiers in a line. Nate had said they were marching toward Guntersville. She wondered how he knew when the corporal hadn't divulged that information. Zach told them the destination didn't much matter—they had to follow orders. He had reminded them with a grin that their journey eventually led to Tennessee. The route they took scarcely mattered to him.

She figured he was right. Dust clouds raised by hundreds trampling on the road ahead caused her to sneeze. She tried to match her stride to the soldiers next to Louisa. The quick pace wasn't as much a problem as the length of each step, several inches longer than her normal stride. They marched behind rows of soldiers, four abreast, with countless rows behind them. The soldier behind her brushed against her heel when her pace slowed.

With all the miles they'd walked to find the army, she hadn't figured marching to be a problem. How wrong she'd been. Matching her stride to other men required all her focus. It didn't help that Louisa also struggled to keep up. A woman's dainty steps didn't suffice in this situation. The effort wore her out. After two almost sleepless nights, she was ready to rest.

Zach and Nate marched two rows behind them. Nate had disappeared an hour before supper last evening with Sergeant Ogle and several officers. She had met the gruff sergeant after breakfast yesterday. The family man with three decades under his belt had bragged on her and Louisa for joining up to help whip the Yankees. Callie, unwilling to draw his attention to her any more than necessary, simply nodded her thanks.

Louisa had expressed her worry over Nate missing another meal when they cleaned their dishes in a creek. "I'll bet they have him out on foraging detail again. Nate told me that they often choose him to go because he's good at finding food."

Better at sweet-talking the Southern ladies out of their food, more like, but she had kept this thought to herself. "I'd rather hunt for food than swing an axe for hours."

Louisa shuddered. "My shoulders ache from wood detail ... and my hands are raw. Think the corporal assigned us to that task because we're new?"

"Doubtful." Cold water stung the open blisters on her hand. She'd chopped wood plenty of times when Pa wasn't around, but not for hours—and she had never chopped away at trees still standing. Not much give in that hard wood. "We weren't the only ones out there."

"I reckon." Then, with barely a pause, she spoke again. "Where do you suppose Nate is? Think he'll be back before roll call?"

"Keep your concern to yourself, Loui—Lou." Spotting another soldier washing dishes several paces downstream, she lowered her voice. "Never know who might be listening."

Nate had arrived right before roll call. He'd rejected Louisa's offer of a corn cake. Watching her sister drop the food into their sack, Callie'd wondered what he'd eaten that he hadn't been hungry. Had he cooked a meal while away? His satisfied grin had given her a sinking feeling that a local family invited him and other foragers to supper.

Perhaps one with a pretty daughter.

Her fingers tightened around her musket as she marched in the chilly morning air. If Nate mistreated her sister, he'd get a tongue-lashing from Callie. Depend on it. And if Nate was being untrue, he'd better hope that Pa didn't catch wind of it.

She tripped over a tree root.

"Mind your step!" The soldier behind her barked. The man hadn't bothered to introduce himself when they set off. A few soldiers displayed little patience for recruits. Too bad that one walked directly behind her.

"My apologies." She spoke only loud enough to be heard by those near. She lowered her head, staring at the road, sloppy from overuse by thousands of feet.

"Show the boy a bit o' grace, Harve." Zach's voice raised a fraction louder than normal. "I seem to remember that you didn't take to marching until after that first winter."

"Got no time for shenanigans," Harve said. "Everybody's got to pull their weight. Ain't here to coddle the young'uns."

Heat rose in Callie's cheeks. Her shoulders ached from wood detail. Her mind reeled from all the orders she'd learned that she'd never remember. As for Loading in Nine Times, she'd just have to watch Zach or someone else when loading her musket. Her mouth pinched in a mighty effort to remain silent. She gave Louisa a warning glance.

"At least he's here." Zach's tone sharpened. "Not like the fellas who stayed at home either too lazy or too scared to fight."

Exactly. She was here—even though they'd not want her if they knew she was a woman. She pondered Zach's defense. He didn't want her here either, but he seemed more concerned for her safety than critical of her skills. He must care about her, at least a little. Recalling his protective arm around her that first evening, she lowered her face toward the ground. It wouldn't do for anyone to see her blush.

The band played the first bars of "Dixie." A few whistled along.

"I wish I was in Dixie." Somewhere up ahead a rich tenor sang out. "Hooray! Hooray!"

Other voices joined in. She smiled at the lightened mood. These men were her heroes. How she wished she could tell them.

Zach lost sight of Callie and Louisa after the march. No doubt they required privacy after a hard day. There was plenty of activity with folks milling around him, hunting for downed limbs and building fires to cook their meager supper since they weren't receiving fresh rations tonight.

"Glad we stopped for the night." Jonesy stacked his musket in a circle of weapons. "My feet are sore."

"Don't get too comfortable." Spence cracked a small limb over his knee and placed it on a small fire. "We set off again in the morning."

Zach took a step forward to warm his hands on the blaze. His shoe slid on a smooth object. A stone? He picked it up. An acorn.

He lit a candle to inspect the tall tree over him. An oak. Good. Roasted acorns made a delicious cup of coffee. He gathered a handful of acorns by candlelight and dropped them in his haversack. Then he added another handful to his sack a little guiltily. Once he showed his find, his comrades would clear the area of acorns within ten minutes. Better collect a few for the girls.

The girls. He had to stop thinking about them that way. For now, they were Cal and Lou. He hadn't told Nate their secret ... yet. The sisters had their own reasons for hiding their identity from his cousin. Zach just hoped Nate behaved himself. Not much chance to meet ladies on the march. Then he grinned. But Zach had met Callie *before* the march.

Her smile had given her away, though he didn't understand how he hadn't known her instantly since she occupied the lion's share of his thoughts. But who could blame him? She wore a soldier's uniform. Someone had chopped off her glorious red hair—auburn. One of the few times she'd been angry with him was when he'd described her hair as red. No need to make that mistake again.

He'd dreamed about seeing her hair freed of braids or hairpins. His heart sank that the first time he'd ever seen her hair down had been after it was shorn. While she wore a soldier's garb, no less. His blood boiled at the danger she'd placed herself in, but his anger stemmed from fear for her life.

Her squeamishness about shooting at a shirt on a tree disturbed him. She wouldn't be able to aim a musket at a Yankee and pull the trigger. A chill went up his back at the probable outcome. She had to overcome that or die—if she saw battle. He'd do everything he could to protect her from the need to raise that musket to protect herself.

Callie and Louisa could be persuaded to volunteer to refill canteens for the company before a battle. Taking their sweet time about performing the task might save them from fighting unless it lasted for hours or days.

He sighed. That might work the first time, but the fellows would notice their absence. Some, like Harve, might call them yellow. As soldiers, the ladies couldn't avoid battles forever.

Maybe he'd have to expose Callie's secret. She'd be madder than a hornet, but she'd be alive. It might be the only way to protect her.

A few more acorns went into his sack. Then Zach returned to the fire. "Look what I found, fellas." An acorn rolled on his open palm.

Jonesy whooped. "We'll drink coffee for breakfast."

"That we will." Spence leaped to his feet. "Where'd you find them?"

Zach pointed to the oak tree and gave his candle to Spence. Others followed while Zach laid a handful of acorns outside the hot embers to dry.

Two slumped figures approached at a snail's pace. Zach studied Callie's profile, illuminated by the firelight, as she and Louisa neared its dubious warmth, the fire not large enough for comfort against the chilly night air. How had the sisters managed to mask their womanly curves so successfully? He averted his eyes as his face warmed.

"I think I'm too tired to eat." Louisa—Lou—dropped her belongings on the ground with a groan.

"Gotta eat, Lou, to keep up your strength." Callie studied her sister thoughtfully. "We'll be marching again tomorrow." She met Zach's gaze. "Right?"

"'Fraid so." Though almost as tired as she looked, he longed to pull her into his arms and lay her head against his shoulder. She'd had several hard days—and today's march had been difficult. Tomorrow might be worse if the haze that hid the stars brought rain. "Best eat and then rest all you can. Tomorrow will be even harder."

Callie raised her eyebrows.

"You're already sore from today's walk, aren't you?"

"More than you know." She rubbed her lower back. "Do you know where our tent is? I want to set that up while I still have the energy to move."

His heart sank. "Do you remember I told you that the wagons carrying our supplies lag behind us on marches? It's doubtful you'll have a tent until we make camp again."

Color drained from Callie's face. "I'd forgotten." She exchanged a look with Louisa, who lifted one shoulder in a half-hearted shrug.

"There's one saving grace." He didn't like her sleeping in the midst of hardened soldiers any better than she did. The circumstances ate at his craw, but they were safe. No one suspected anything, but they'd wonder if the *brothers* made too much fuss over the tent. "We're camped under oak trees."

Her gaze shifted to the men scrambling to stuff their haversacks with acorns.

"I'm drying some acorns now. When they open, I'll roast them. We'll have coffee in the mornings."

Her big brown eyes softened with an inner glow. "How lovely."

Men didn't say that. His muscles tensed as he widened his eyes in warning. "I'll teach you and your brother how to make it. I gathered a few extra to share so you can start cooking your meal."

Her shoulders sagged. "Much obliged."

He nodded and strode to his belongings. He didn't have the stamina to figure out if anyone heard Callie's feminine comment.

They'd be discovered before week's end.

Callie's musket grew heavier with each step. They'd been climbing this mountain road long enough to be at the top of Lookout Mountain … only they weren't heading to Chattanooga. She peered around the broad shoulders of the stranger ahead of her. The poor man, like too many others, wore no shoes. She frowned at the mud caked on his feet. Perhaps it offered some protection. She shuddered. Snow would be another matter entirely. Southern citizens were willing to send shoes … except their lot wasn't much better than the soldiers'. She stumbled on a rock as her gaze traveled ahead. The bend revealed an incline beyond.

Stifling a groan, she refocused on her own feet, or rather, where to place them. The torn-up road became progressively more difficult to travel. Dank smelling mud plastered her gray trousers to her shins. No one talked today. Louisa, trampling beside her, had not spoken in over an hour. Even the band was silent.

Zach and Nate were way ahead of them on the march. Callie and Louisa, both unaccustomed to hard marches, had fallen out to rest four times. They had rejoined the march when able, now less of a line than when the day started because they weren't the only ones dropping out for a time.

She'd have cheered when they started down the mountain … if she'd had enough energy. The sagamite she ate for lunch seemed hours ago, but it was hard to tell the passage of time on the gray afternoon.

Soft rain fell. Callie sniffed back tears. It wasn't soldierly to cry though weakness permeated her exhausted body.

The valley will be easier, she repeated to herself over and over.

But it wasn't when she finally made it there. Muddy roads tried to snatch her shoes, so she and Louisa tramped on the side whenever feasible. As her misery increased, so did her respect for the soldiers who marched with her. Many had endured these conditions for better than three years, Zach and Nate included.

Her legs ached. She was past hunger. Soaked to the skin and too tired to think, she stared at her muddy brogans and forced her feet to take one more step.

And then another.

And then another.

CHAPTER TWELVE

Well past dark, Zach groaned and dropped his knapsack, canteen, haversack, and blanket on the wet grass. Everything he carried was soaked anyway—it couldn't get much wetter. What he wanted was a cozy fire, a warm place to sleep, and a hot cup of coffee. He sighed, breathing in the welcome smell of pine. Memories of his parents' home by the creek, nestled between evergreens, catapulted him back to his childhood. He could almost taste his mama's chicken stew.

A drop of rain struck his nose, nudging him back to the misery of the present. He stacked his musket in a growing stack with Nate's. "Have you seen our new recruits?"

"Not since lunch." Nate wiped raindrops off his face and beard. "You worried about 'em?"

"A bit." Zach peered at the men trudging past on the road, still paces away from their brigade's stop for the night. He licked his lips and tasted rain. "They're not used to marches."

"They were resting with their backs against an elm tree last time I saw 'em." Spence, breathing hard, placed his musket in the stack. "Looked plum tuckered out."

That didn't sound promising. "When was that?"

"Mid-afternoon." The tall man stretched. "Rested a couple of times myself after that. Just got here."

"Didn't they say they was farmers?" Jonesy dropped his possessions in a heap. "Marches shouldn't take a hard toll on farm boys."

Zach scratched his head, trying to remember exactly what the sisters had said about themselves. Either way, it didn't do to call attention to them. "Tough conditions out here. Rain. Mountains. Muddy trails. Toting a musket with a knapsack on your back for miles." He shook his head. "Not so easy for us veterans either."

"I reckon they'll be along." Jonesy rummaged in his knapsack and pulled out a candle. "I aim to hunt for dryer wood than this." He shivered. "You comin', Spence?"

"This ain't gonna burn." Spence kicked a leafless, downed tree limb, splattering his shoe with water droplets. "Reckon two sets of eyes are better than one."

Several others set off into the woods after them, grumbling about the rain, the cold, and the march.

And these men were accustomed to hardship. Zach crossed his arms, contemplating the soldiers trudging down the road. Where were the girls?

"Think the Shaws gave up on us and went home?" Nate stood by his side, peering at the road. "They're not the first ones to desert at the first sign of trouble. Had my bellyful of that kind of soldier."

If all the Southerners who had deserted came back tomorrow, the South would win this thing … but the girls didn't know how to get home even if they wanted to. "Those brothers are made of sturdier stuff than that." Worse luck. Zach's life had become harder with the girls in Hood's army. A grudging respect mingled with his concern over their whereabouts.

"Good to hear." Nate's shoulders relaxed. "Thinking about looking for 'em? They are just boys."

"Yep." He tugged at his collar. His mama had raised him to treat women as a gentleman should—with respect and honor. Most men in this army were happy to help a woman over the difficult trail or give up his horse or his place in a wagon for her. But they didn't know. Zach knew.

Nate slung water from his kepi then placed it back on his head. "War will make men out of them before winter sets in."

Impossible. Thankfully, his cousin was unaware of it, or he'd give the masquerade away by exchanging flirtatious looks with Louisa. Maybe the girls had been right about hiding their identity from him. "I'm going back to look for them." Zach rummaged through his belongings, extracting two candles and matches that he tucked inside his blouse. He contemplated his knapsack. Best leave it as he might be toting Callie's possessions on the way back to camp. "You with me?"

"You know I am." Nate fell into stride next to Zach, nodding to folks heading the other way. "But they could be miles back."

That's what he was afraid of. He lengthened his stride.

"Hey, where ya goin'?" A passing soldier frowned. "Isn't camp just ahead?"

Nate stopped. "You're almost there." He grinned and pointed.

The smell of mud mingled with wet pine. Clouds hid the moon, making for a dark night indeed. Were the girls marching alone? Afraid?

Zach peered at the looming shapes on the road ahead. The girls were short but not smaller than the shortest soldiers. He paid attention to anyone close to their height in the darkness, grateful that his normally talkative cousin kept his peace for several minutes. Worry for the sisters escalated with each step.

Some carried lanterns or lit candles on the path. Zach silently thanked them for the light, pushing his tired limbs to a faster pace. His arms ached from carrying his musket for hours. The longer he waited to light a candle, the better.

"Maybe they found a tree to sleep under when it got dark." Nate's long stride slapped into the loose mud, splattering Zach's trousers. "If they ain't even on the road, how are we gonna find them?"

Zach grunted. That was a possibility. They'd walked better than a mile from camp without finding them. Distance between stragglers had lengthened.

"It's getting pretty dark under these trees." Nate looked at the underbrush on his right. "Think we should light one of those candles?"

Zach gazed ahead at dark moving shapes. "I wanted to save them for the march back." When they'd likely have the road to themselves. If those girls had kept up, they'd all be sleeping by now. "Reckon we should." He lit a candle.

"I can carry it since you're too tired." Nate grinned.

Zach chuckled at his cousin's irrepressible spirits and gave him the candle. "You're a good man, Nate McClary. Thanks for helping me look for the g-boys. They're pretty raw."

"Can't be worse than we were when we started." Nate laughed. "Remember our first drill? Harry shot himself in the foot learning how to Load in Nine Times."

"Got him out of the war, as I recollect." Zach smiled. He'd felt plum sorry for Harry until he realized his old comrade slept in a warm cozy bed every night.

"Glad it didn't go that way for us." Nate's gaze darted to both sides of the road. "Been thinking about making the army my life's work along with you. Our horse farm will take years to rebuild."

"Think Louisa will like you being gone for months? Maybe a year or better?" He kept his gaze trained ahead.

"Whatever I do will be fine with her."

Nate's overly confident tone jarred Zach. Louisa didn't seem the type to remain silent if something bothered her. Then he started. Two lone figures ahead. "Is that them?"

"Might be. Right height." Nate whistled. "Them fellas are struggling. They could use a hand whoever they are."

"Yep." Sweat broke out on Zach's forehead at the pair slumped over yet trudging onward. "Let's go."

Nate cupped his hand over the candle's glow as they double-quicked to the soldiers.

"Cal? Lou?" Zach, hand on Callie's shoulder, bent down to peer into her eyes.

"Zach. You came for us." She looked at him.

"Yes. Nate's here." Though he longed to scoop her up and carry her back to camp, it wouldn't do. Not with Nate here. "Spence saw you brothers resting under a tree hours ago."

"We fell asleep." She smiled faintly. "We felt better when we woke up, but our regiment had passed us by."

Zach forced a chuckle though he doubted her ability to maintain a soldier's pace. She'd proven she couldn't handle this difficult soldiers' life.

"That explains all." Nate laughed. "We were just talking about our early days of soldiering. We made about every mistake a man can make, right, Zach?"

"I'll say." He smiled. "Want me to carry your knapsack and musket?"

Callie and Louisa exchanged a glance. "Anyone ever carry your weapon for you?" Callie tilted her head up at him.

Zach scratched his head. Not that he could remember. "Maybe not."

"We'll make it." At Louisa's bracing nod, Callie's shoulders straightened. "Just … can you keep us company? That light's a welcome sight."

"Course we can." Nate fell into step by Louisa as they picked up the pace. "Camp's just up the road. Be there before you know it."

Callie pushed her knapsack further up on her shoulders.

Despite his misgivings about their strength giving out, some of Zach's exhaustion slipped away at her determination. Her spunk was a quality he'd missed back home. His admiration for her grew daily.

These girls were made of sterner stuff than he'd imagined.

CHAPTER THIRTEEN

After four days of marching, Callie gasped at her first glimpse of the Tennessee River. In a valley near soldiers scrambling to make camp and hunt for firewood, she stood apart to survey water much too deep to wade, in awe of its majestic beauty. This river shared the name of her beloved home state. Her heart swelled.

Her gaze swept the river to the green banks on the other side. Alabama. Trees had lost most of their leaves from recent rains, giving a stark beauty to the whole scene. The river separated Hood's army from their eventual goal of marching into Tennessee.

"Pretty, ain't it?" Zach strode up and folded his arms as he stared at the river.

"I'll say." She wrinkled her nose at the fishy smell. Late afternoon sun cast beams of light through a cloudy sky to skim across the water. It almost made Callie forget her aching legs and feet. That ache now reminded her of her soldier's masquerade. She crossed her arms and widened her stance to emulate a manly posture as best she could. "How will we cross it?"

"They'll lay planks over a pontoon bridge for us to walk across. It'll be slippery." He glanced at her. "The creeks we waded before are nothing compared to this."

No fooling. Callie and Louisa had removed their shoes at crossings. Her cheeks burned to recall the few men who removed their trousers as well. She'd kept her nose pointed to her own bare feet while wading those freezing streams. It was one more test of her endurance. The main thing was to hold her musket aloft and keep the cartridges dry, which she'd accomplished.

Imagine—she'd cross the mighty Tennessee River on a pontoon bridge. "I want to sit here to watch the sunset."

"No time for that. Both of us have picket duty tonight. Corporal Morefield has given you and Loui—Lou a chance to learn a soldier's skills before ordering you to stand guard, but we all take our turn at guarding camp."

Callie might have to use her weapon tonight. She peeked over at the stacked arms for her musket and gulped. "How about my s—brother? Is he on picket?"

"Not tonight. You won't have the same duties every day." He glanced around.

Callie followed his gaze. No one paid any attention to them. Folks started campfires. Others were already cooking supper.

"Being assigned duties where you don't have to watch out for each other will help you concentrate on the task at hand," Zach spoke in hushed tones. He leaned down. "The corporal told me Lou will be on picket tomorrow with Nate and a few men she doesn't know well. My cousin hasn't stood picket much lately. He's due. The whole group is seasoned veterans. Lou will be fine."

She sucked in her breath. Louisa hadn't been alone with Nate yet. "How about tonight? Lou will be alone while we stand picket."

Zach raised his eyebrows. "In this crowd? There's better than two thousand men in plain sight."

Callie glared up at him. "You know what I'm asking."

"I do." He sighed, glancing to his left where they'd left their possessions. "Nate and a few officers are eating with a local family tonight. Someone's aunt or cousin—he wasn't certain of the family relationship. He'll likely return late."

Callie lifted her chin, forgetting her admiration of her future brother-in-law's military skills. He'd better not come back and brag of flirtations with a local woman. Nothing could more deeply test Louisa's fiery temper.

Callie's, too, if the truth be known. She wasn't about to look the other way if Nate proved himself unfaithful.

At dusk, Callie dipped her hand in the cold waters of the Tennessee River and watched it stream through her fingers.

"Spence told me that Nate is eating supper tonight with Sarge's sister." Louisa rubbed wet fingers over lye soap then reached for a cup she used at supper. "A home-cooked meal. Wonder what she's cooking. Can't you just taste it, Cal? A stew ... or maybe chicken and dumplings like Ma used to make." She rinsed the cup, peered inside, and then scrubbed again. "Sarge could have invited me. Don't understand why Nate is favored over the rest of us."

Callie didn't understand that either though there was no need to fuel the fires of jealousy. "Search me." She sighed and reached for a dirty spoon. "Maybe Nate did him a favor or something. Or maybe Sarge will invite Zach or Spence or Sam to go next time."

"You're probably right." Louisa scowled. "There'd better not be any pretty ladies present."

Footsteps approached. Callie widened her eyes at Louisa before looking around. Jonesy squatted beside her, tin cup in hand. "You fellas talking about Nate's supper?"

Callie exchanged a warning glance with Louisa. "Yes, Spence mentioned that he's having supper with Sergeant Ogle's sister."

"And you're worried Nate's going to meet the pretty girls before you do." Jonesy grinned at Louisa. "He will. Rest easy on that one. He always does."

Sparks lit in Louisa's eyes.

"No need to get mad about it." Dipping his cup several times, he frowned. His gaze remained on Lou as he pointed, "Can I borrow that soap?"

Hardly daring to breathe, Callie gave it to him and laid a bracing hand on her sister's arm. They must remain calm, no matter what.

"Much obliged. Only thing left of my soap after yesterday's rain was bubbles." Jonesy shot Lou another glance. "Yep, sometimes the officers invite Nate to supper with them. Heard it was because he ain't bashful with the ladies. That fella can charm birds right out of the trees."

"Zach said Nate's betrothed. That he's got a girl waiting back home." At least Louisa kept her voice gruff.

"Yep. Nate told me about her." After rinsing his cup, Jonesy filled his cup with river water.

"What did he say?" Louisa straightened her shoulders as she stared at Jonesy.

He stopped swirling water in his cup and looked at her directly. "To hear him tell it, she's the prettiest girl this side of the Mississippi River. He does like a pretty face."

Louisa's face glowed.

"But Nate's in no hurry to wed." Jonesy gulped down his water. "Reckon he's still got a wild streak in him. Me, I don't understand it. I can't wait to get back home to marry my Benita. I write to her every chance I get."

"You're a fortunate man." Callie's throat tightened at the pain in her sister's eyes. Still, all that Jonesy really accused him of was looking at pretty girls. Perhaps he was guilty of nothing more.

"Don't I know it." He clapped Lou on the back and walked off.

Another group walked to the river a few paces from them before Callie could speak. They gathered their dishes and walked back to their fire. "Don't do anything rash," she whispered. "Control your temper. Remember where we are. Remember *who* we are."

"Oh, I remember." Louisa's eyes glittered. "I never forget anything."

Callie's heart skipped a beat. "Promise not to confront him in front of the others. We don't know he's doing something he ought not do. Even if he is, you must talk to him alone."

Louisa's eyes flashed before she strode ahead.

Callie's heart sank. They'd been in the army scarcely more than a week. What if Louisa destroyed the only haven—albeit a dangerous one—left to Callie?

Zach's stomach rumbled as he stared out over the dark waters of the Tennessee River. No way for corn fritters to fill a grown man's stomach, but fritters were a sight more filling than dried corn.

He stole a glance at Callie, who stood five paces to his right. Picket duty was an obligation of every rank and file soldier, so she had to take a turn. Her hands had shaken when she'd picked up her musket to follow the corporal.

"Watch for Yankee boats on the river tonight." Corporal Morefield had pointed to the water. "Don't shoot unless they head to shore. You might see a ship or a rowboat. Never can tell. Report what you see. Shaw, this is your first picket duty. Your job is simple—guard our camp. Communicate with Zach if you see anything suspicious. He'll know whether to report it, open fire on the enemy, shout an alarm, or ignore it. Understood?"

Callie turned her head to the river. Shuffling her feet, she nodded.

"There's a Federal garrison on this side of the river. At Decatur. That's not far from us. Don't know if we'll attack the garrison or not. Of course, if you see anything, don't keep it to yourself."

Callie's eyes had looked too large for her pale face.

Zach's heart beat faster at the news. There might be some action tonight after all.

"Stay back from the bank near the bushes and trees so you won't be seen. We might lose that cloud cover. I don't expect trouble, but I don't have to tell you veterans how fast things can happen." His gaze dwelt on Callie. "Stand picket next to Zach. Ask him if you have questions. Whisper. Sound carries across water."

Clutching her musket, she gave a shaky nod.

Zach remembered how his stomach churned on his first picket. Her thoughts probably whipped her to a fever pitch over the possibility of meeting up with Yankees. She glanced back at camp as if wanting nothing more than to crawl into her bedroll and stay there.

She had squared her shoulders and braced her feet.

That's the spirit, Callie. No other woman—or man—could be more determined to learn everything required to serve in the army at record speed. Though everyone was tired from four days of marching, she hadn't complained about losing sleep tonight. Pride welled in his chest for his courageous girl.

Well, no. Not his girl. His spirits plummeted.

After the corporal left, he'd shown her where to stand—or sit, if nothing obstructed her view. They'd been silent for the past hour.

He'd familiarized himself with the trees, bushes, and logs before settling in. They were close enough to smell the fishy scent of the river. What a treat it would be to plop a fishing line in and wait for a bite. Callie could fry up the catch and make it delicious even without seasonings. He shook his head. Best not think about what he couldn't have.

The moon ducked out from behind some clouds and illuminated the river. No movement. No large shapes floating past.

He hadn't heard any orders about marching again tomorrow. The Yankee garrison nearby had him wondering about the next day's activities. Then again, General Hood might decide to cross the Tennessee here. Or choose another spot. Surveying the wide river with a practiced eye, Zach frowned. It might take days to erect a pontoon bridge across it.

Not his worry. The engineers would build the bridge wherever Hood decided.

Even in the darkness, Callie's presence distracted him. He tried to keep his gaze on the river but glanced at her anyway.

Cradling her musket against her chest, she met his gaze.

"Did you see something?" he whispered.

"No."

Her panicked whisper smote Zach. He didn't mean to scare her.

"Zach?" On Callie's right, Sam Watkins swiveled toward him.

"What is it?"

"Nothing," Zach whispered. His inability to keep his mind off Callie was about to raise an alarm. He'd have to do better than this. "Didn't see any movement on the river."

"Anywhere else? You're awful jumpy." Sam slunk over to him.

You would be too, if your girl stood on picket with you. "No, it was nothing. Just sleepy, I reckon." It was the one argument the others understood. No one in the whole army ever got enough rest.

"Want me to get someone else to stand in for you?" Sam peered at him in the darkness. "There's better than three hours to go."

"No." Heat rose up Zach's face. He never shirked his duty—at least not since his pa passed. This was getting out of hand … and in front of Callie, no less. "I'm fine now."

Sam returned to his spot.

She stared at him before turning to face the river.

Gazing directly ahead, Zach crouched over his musket. The misunderstanding was a lesson to keep his mind on the business at hand.

Easier said than done. Callie was far too distracting for his peace of mind—another good reason for women to stay out of the army.

CHAPTER FOURTEEN

The bugler's blast awakened Callie the next morning. She could hardly call that blaring noise a tune when it came before sunrise. She sat up and looked around. With no tent, she and Louisa arranged their belongings on either side to provide a few feet of space between them and the men surrounding them. Zach always managed to stay on one side and placed his knapsack and haversack between them. His protective presence at night comforted her as she gradually grew accustomed to being in the company of men who believed her to be a man.

She yawned, exhausted from the long hours of picket duty the previous night, and rose in the blackness of night, ever grateful for the soldiers' custom to sleep fully clothed.

More than the morning's chill made her shiver. Guarding camp had been scary. Her heart had beat double-quick when it seemed Zach saw something. That Yankee garrison being close by had unnerved her. Zach seemed restless, too. Trusting him, his distraction nearly sent her running headlong back to camp. But it had turned out to be nothing, thank the Lord.

Louisa rummaged through the haversack they shared.

Zach added wood to a fire too far away from her bedroll to warm the early morning air. Nate stumbled over to the fire, rubbing his eyes.

While pouring cornmeal into a tin cup, Louisa stared at him with hard eyes before turning her attention to preparing batter.

Once the fire blazed, the cousins left.

Callie nudged Louisa's arm, but her sister waved her away.

There had been no opportunity to talk with her privately since Jonesy sprung his gossip on them. Well, not gossip really. Callie knew he told the truth. She respected her sister's need for privacy and would keep her peace—for now.

No one talked much until breakfast. They joined a few comrades cooking their meal. Corn cakes again. Not very exciting, but they filled the stomach. She'd been hungry for too long not to appreciate even small meals. She filled her tin cup with water from a canteen and plopped a roasted acorn inside. No coffeepot but that didn't bother her much. One less thing to tote on her back. She rested the tin on glowing embers at the fire's edge. With only a handful of acorns left, she and Louisa drank one cup of coffee daily to stretch the treat for as many days as possible.

Nate and Zach joined the group already around the fire.

"Use my skillet." Looking at the cousins, Spence gestured the small skillet resting on the embers. "It's good and hot."

"Much obliged." Zach put a handful of coarse meal into a tin cup and then added water. "Cold morning."

"That it is." Jonesy spread his hand toward the fire's glow. "Hope it don't rain again."

"How was supper last evening, Nate?" Spence's eyes narrowed as he looked at Nate.

Louisa lifted her chin.

"Good. Nice family." Nate stared at the fire.

"What did you eat?"

Callie stirred at Spence's question, her eyes on Louisa's tense face. This was certainly a sore subject with everyone hungry. Why rub salt in their wounds?

"Chicken and dumplings." Nate squirmed. "With fried apple pie."

Callie's mouth watered. It was a shame that all of them couldn't have gone to supper with Sarge.

"Any pretty girls?" Jonesy asked.

"Yep." Nate grinned. "The schoolteacher ate with us. I walked her home afterward. That woman is very devoted to the Southern cause."

Scarlet infused Louisa's face as she glared at Nate.

"Ain't no need to get jealous." Nate quirked an eyebrow at Lou. "Your turn will come soon enough. You're still a mite young."

Zach shoved a corn cake into his cousin's mouth. "Eat while it's hot."

"Ow. That liked to burn me up." Nate glared at him. "What's the hurry?"

"I'm on forage detail." Zach's glance darted from Louisa to Callie before resting on Nate.

"I'll be there, too." Jonesy stood and stretched. "Reckon I'd best clean up." He picked up two cups and a spoon and traipsed toward the river.

"I'm shoveling sinks." Spence pulled a long face. "Necessary job."

"I'll be hauling water." Though toting water to camp in buckets was an unenviable and strenuous job, Callie shuddered for Spence to be digging latrines. Of course, she and Louisa always visited the woods for calls of nature. A few others who also chose the privacy afforded by the trees made it tricky for the sisters, but they had managed. Perhaps it was an unwritten code to respect a man's privacy.

"I've got picket duty starting at noon." Nate rubbed his eyes. "On two hours and off two hours. Last shift starts at midnight. Gonna be a long day."

"Me too." Louisa's chin lifted. "I'll be cleaning my musket before then."

Her sister wasn't really mad enough to threaten Nate with a musket, was she? One glance at her sister's scarlet face and glaring eyes—maybe she was. She needed a few hours away from Nate to calm herself, or he'd get an earful—along with half the camp. "Don't you think you'd better get going?" She looked up at a watchful Zach. Her eyes pleaded silently.

His gaze bounced from her to Louisa. "Yep. Sarge said after breakfast."

"I reckon I'll write to Louisa this morning. Can't figure why she ain't written to me. She usually sends two letters to my one." Nate yawned again. "Hope it's quiet on the picket line today."

Louisa stood. "I'm looking forward to it."

Callie pressed her lips together.

Nate stood, tin cup in hand. "Must be your first time guarding camp." He half-turned away. "I'll wash our dishes, Zach. You go on."

Another soldier known as Billy stood and stretched. "Cal, I'm hauling water with you today."

There was no time to speak with Louisa. A pulse throbbed in her sister's temple. That wasn't good. "I'll wash our dishes and be right there, Billy."

He nodded and strode away.

The few still sitting around the fire scattered. Except Zach.

Louisa, eyes on Nate's retreating figure, put her hands on her hips. Finding her sister's stance a bit too feminine, Callie nudged her. Louisa set to cleaning up without a word.

Callie met Zach's troubled gaze with a slight nod. He had good reason to be concerned.

Louisa's temper was riled.

Callie fretted all morning over her sister's temper. Louisa would stand picket duty with Nate—among others—all day and into the night sharing the same breaks. It was too much to hope for her sister to keep her peace.

Callie's one break came at noon. She hurried to her campsite with aching legs and shoulders. Louisa was already gone. Nate was nowhere in sight.

Her heart sank. Undoubtedly Corporal Morefield, who

brought in new soldiers to relieve those already on picket duty, had escorted them to the picket line. *Behave yourself, Louisa. Remember what awaits me should the army send us home. I can't go back.*

Sighing for what she couldn't control, Callie withdrew a hard cracker from her haversack. Her comrades called it hardtack. With the consistency of a brick, anyone biting into it risked chipping a tooth. She took her lead from the others and soaked it in water before frying it in her small skillet. A piece of ham or bacon would taste good about now.

But no meat had been issued for rations.

Others from her regiment who shared the same fire wandered up. After spending the morning with Billy, she appreciated his irrepressibly happy spirit though her heart was too weighed by worry to share it.

She'd also seen more of the camp than usual that morning—not all of it good. She had toted a bucket of water past an officer's tent whose slave cooked breakfast for him. The hair had stiffened on the back of her neck. Lincoln had freed the slaves, though she guessed the president of another country had little authority here.

Still, the sight had bothered her. The thought of one man owning another didn't sit well with her.

Too dispirited to join in the camaraderie of complaints about new aches caused by the morning's work, she gazed to the tree line on her left. Somewhere in those woods, her sister guarded the camp. With Nate.

She ate the first bite of fried bread. It had lost its hardness in the water and then lost a bit of its soggy quality in the frying, yet it was still hard to stomach. She crammed in another bite. It was better than starving.

Her stomach grumbled. She'd eat another one—maybe two—to stave off hunger pains until supper. She reached for her haversack.

If only Zach didn't have forage detail, maybe he could have done something to keep Nate away from Louisa. But what? He couldn't interfere with another soldier's orders. No, the only thing

Zach might have done was comfort Callie. Even after his rejection, she still longed for his nearness. Even that might be taken from her if Louisa lost her temper.

Callie paused with her hand on the hard tack. What would this day bring?

The cares of the war, worries over Louisa's reaction to Nate, and his fears over repercussions from Callie's discovery lingered as Zach spent the day fishing in the river. Sarge knew the local fishing holes and had divided his men into four groups to catch as many fish as possible in a few hours. He warned them to take cover if federal gunboats were spotted. These boats had been in the vicinity, so the Federals knew their location. Sarge didn't want an engagement when he had only a score of men.

This sobering reminder of war escalated Zach's determination to keep a watchful eye on the river. He didn't fault others for their lighthearted banter—days when he found pleasure in work details were few and far between. Fishing reminded him of summer days when he and Nate hurried through chores to while away long hours at the stream on a Saturday afternoon, before the weight of the war descended on their boyish shoulders.

Zach's catch of smallmouth bass, black crappie, and lake trout soon filled his bucket. His regiment would eat well this evening … if they returned in time.

A young boy watched the group a hundred yards down the bank. Within fifteen minutes, the boy had rowed three of Zach's comrades onto the river. They whooped and hollered when catching a striped bass longer than a man's leg.

A four-foot blue catfish snapped a fishing pole in two, but the hungry soldiers managed to grab the half with the line attached.

"Hold on!" A comrade on the shore cried out.

"Don't fall out of the boat!" Another stood while minding his own pole.

"Get him!" Jonesy waved a fist in the air.

Zach, whistling at the fish's size, marveled that everyone managed to stay on board. The catfish's tenacious fight didn't compare to the hunger of the soldiers intent on eating it.

He chuckled at the embellished tale of that catch when they all gathered together later that afternoon—the best fish story of the day. That fish alone could feed better than a dozen hungry men, maybe twice that. Zach's own catch included eleven fish. The meaty part of half of them was no larger than his hand though the rest were longer than his feet. Two exceeded thirty inches.

Their combined catches nearly filled two wagon beds. Buckets of river water sloshed with every turn of the wheel. A fishy smell wafted back to Zach, who trailed behind the creaking wagons as the sun slipped behind the trees.

"Mm." Jonesy breathed deeply at Zach's side. "Don't that smell like good eatin'?"

"Reckon so. Some of 'em are still flopping." Zach grinned. "I prefer my fish fried in a skillet."

"Man, I'm so hungry I could eat it raw." Jonesy's stomach rumbled louder than the creaky wheels.

Zach laughed. "Good thing we're almost back, just in time to make supper."

It wasn't often a day's work filled him with satisfaction anymore. The war had stolen that joy. But today was different. Filling empty bellies … that was a joy. Thoughts of Callie's smile when she saw such abundance lightened a bit of the burden of Louisa's anger toward Nate. That confrontation wasn't going to be pleasant for his cousin. Worries overtook him again. His steps faltered until he lagged behind the rest of the forage party. After bragging about the schoolteacher's expression of gratitude, Nate deserved it.

Only he didn't know Lou was really Louisa—not until his fiery-tempered fiancée chose to reveal it.

Groaning, Zach grabbed his head. He could have prevented

this situation by being straight with his cousin. He should have told him Louisa's identity.

But that would have hurt Callie. Betrayed her trust.

He leaned a hand against the rough bark of a mighty oak. He'd never willingly hurt Callie, though this time it came at a high price for his cousin.

He loved how she turned to him with her questions, how her brown eyes glowed at his praise. And she had earned it with her hard work, her determination. If only he could do things for her, lighten her workload, but he couldn't. He'd caught himself staring at her twice at breakfast, mourning the loss of her long auburn locks. While she pretended to be male, he'd best remember to treat her as one.

With this sobering thought, he set off to camp, arriving as Sarge directed the wagons to the quartermaster to be divided for the men. Zach's empty stomach rebelled at the order. Such an abundant catch might require hours to divvy up. He was hungry now.

Then he remembered the officers. They'd receive the best portions. Zach should have stuffed a carp down his jacket. He pulled the loose garment away from his body in disgust. It would have fallen out. He'd lost weight this year. Little wonder when he never had enough to eat.

He trudged to his campsite where Callie, her beautiful hair catching the fire's glow, bent over a skillet. He peered over her shoulder. The firelight fell on Spence, Sam, Billy, and a few others gathered to eat. Even Jonesy had beaten him to supper.

Where was Nate? And Louisa?

A cold knot gathered in his belly. It was well after six—their last two-hour shift ended at the top of that hour. He squinted in the darkness toward the woods. Where were they? Had Louisa waited for the setting sun to confront his cousin?

If so, Zach hoped she'd chosen an appropriate, private location, that she kept her voice down, and that she controlled her temper.

Little chance of that fiery blonde keeping her jealousy under control. He figured the wrong sister inherited their mother's red hair. His gaze rested on Callie's curls. Now that she was here, he loved knowing what she was doing each day—but only for marches and camps. Battles were another story. She had to be out of here before the next big engagement.

No doubt her leaving was for the best. Just not forced into it by her sister's volatile temper. Not shamed into it. If Louisa threw caution to the wind, they'd be discovered, sparking ridicule by most soldiers who marched with them. Possibly heralded as a heroine in newspapers. Louisa basked in the type of admiring attention Callie shunned.

Worst of all, Callie and Louisa risked their virtuous reputations. Soldiers and citizens alike questioned the morals of women who'd camped with overwhelming numbers of men—a cloud of suspicion that might follow them the rest of their lives, their integrity always doubted by some.

Even wives of Confederate soldiers who served as laundresses weren't really welcomed in army camps. The sisters certainly weren't like camp followers—women who demoralized the men, spread diseases, and acted as spies. Even masquerading as men, Callie and Louisa's presence here damaged their reputations if caught.

Discovery wasn't what he wanted for her. Not unless *Callie* chose it. But she must leave. Her safety and his sanity hinged on it.

Though her shooting skills rivaled his, he knew she'd never aim a loaded musket at another person and pull the trigger. Blood ran as ice in his veins. He had to do everything in his power to save her—including giving up his life—but his sacrifice might come for naught with bullets flying in all directions.

Callie didn't comprehend the danger he knew all too well.

His gaze shifted to the river. Federal gunboats were nearby. Hood's army marched toward battle. The only question was when they'd fight.

He broke into a cold sweat. She had to go.

CHAPTER FIFTEEN

Every muscle in Callie's body ached as she sank to the ground in the shadows of the dying fire. The starry sky didn't illuminate the camp where everyone finished up last minute tasks before bedtime.

Roll had already been called. Callie answered that Lou was on picket, but where had she been the rest of the evening? She'd missed supper … so had Nate.

Callie listened half-heartedly to yarns of a four-foot catfish and a three-foot striped bass from Zach and Jonesy. Who ever heard of such of thing? But the others didn't question the claims, so fish must grow bigger in the wide Tennessee River.

All she knew was the quartermaster didn't distribute fresh fish for supper. Her disappointment was no easier to stomach because it was mirrored on the faces around her.

She had offered to fry corn fritters for everyone tonight. The fellows gladly turned over their portions, eager to be waited on for a change. Having one person do the cooking made the most sense to Callie—otherwise, they all vied for the best place to set their skillet on the burning embers.

She had fried enough for Louisa and Nate and then sat to eat. It seemed the men in her company never ran out of stories. To hear each one tell it, no one else worked as hard as he did. She didn't doubt their exhaustion. Their mere presence in the Confederate army proved their perseverance.

She stared at the tree line hiding Louisa from view. She was back on picket, not to return until after taps. There was no talking after that. Candles nestled in upended bayonets were doused. Folks settled for the night. She'd have to wait until morning to find out if Louisa confronted Nate.

She clenched and unclenched her fists. He'd better not hurt Louisa, who loved that charmer to the stars and back.

A mournful tune played nearby. She looked for the source. It was Johnny—Martha Rose's Johnny—playing the bugle tonight. Their bugler must be on picket or some such duty. She smiled as he continued. If only Martha Rose could hear him play. The privilege of being part of this army—something bigger than herself—soared through Callie as she listened. How many women wore a soldier's garb tonight? How many women lay to sleep in the open after taps?

Only two that she knew of … and one of those guarded the camp.

The last notes died away. Zach strode down the road separating the rows of lounging men. He rebuilt the fire.

Callie snuggled into her blanket as he knelt a dozen feet away.

Folks spread their bedrolls. The camp quieted. An owl hooted as Zach sank onto his blanket on the other side of Callie's gear. His presence soothed her for a moment.

A whippoorwill called out, and its mate answered.

Peaceful sounds. Not peaceful times.

Callie's aching muscles protested when she shifted to her left side. She stifled a whimper and stared at the empty space beside her. No Louisa. Her last shift ended at two in the morning. Was her sister behaving?

Despite exhaustion, worry stole her sleep. Snores almost drowned the sound of approaching footsteps. One set stopped near Zach and crumpled onto the ground with a groan. The other stopped by her bedroll.

Callie sat up. "Where have you been?" She whispered as Louisa knelt beside her.

"Picket duty. And I have to go back in two hours." Louisa,

speaking in a whisper, rummaged through the haversack. "Is there anything to eat?"

"Corn fritters." Callie unwrapped a linen cloth where her sister's meal lay hidden. "We need to talk."

"Later." Louisa bit into the fritter then wrapped herself in her blanket. "Sleepy."

Callie laid back, her worries eased. Maybe her sister was too tired to hold onto her anger.

Callie jumped at a bugler's lively tune. The sun hadn't risen though the sky lightened to the east. Dawn was over the horizon.

"That bugler ought to be in the guardhouse," a male voice grumbled.

"Turn out, folks," another chimed in.

"Reckon it's that time."

Darkness hid those speaking. Callie rubbed her eyes, shivering in the chill. Dew covered her blanket. The men complained about everything—why didn't they complain about wet bedrolls?

Louisa didn't stir.

Callie nudged her shoulder. "Wake up, Lou. We've only minutes before Johnny plays assembly."

"Go away."

Callie straightened and looked around as slow-moving figures lit candles, struggled to their feet, or shuffled toward the back of camp. One man rubbed soap on his hands while another poured water over them from his canteen. No one seemed to have noticed that Louisa spoke in a female voice. Leaning over, Callie put her lips to Louisa's ear. "You're a man, remember? Talk like one."

She dragged her blanket over her head.

Brief conversations began. Callie sighed, expecting normal morning movements to awaken her sister. If not, the next bugle's blast ought to do the job.

Callie drove the sharp point of her bayonet into the ground then placed a candle on the other end. She lit it with matches from her knapsack, thrilled that soldiers had found a far better use of the bayonet than to spear their fellow man.

Lights from other candles dimly lit the camp. Zach spread his blanket over a bush to dry. Nate pushed himself to his feet and stretched. He gazed at Louisa's sleeping form. His eyes met Callie's.

Recognition.

He knows. Her breath caught in her throat as she searched his face, missing all traces of the charming Southern soldier. In that moment he seemed vulnerable, uncertain … emotions Callie had never seen in him.

She raised her eyebrows in a silent question. *Will you keep our secret?*

He turned away.

Zach looked at Callie and then Nate. "Good morning. Late night on the picket line."

"Yep." Nate stared at Louisa still lying on the ground. "Lively time. Filled with surprises."

Callie's heartbeat accelerated. Her gaze flew to Zach. *Don't let him give us away.*

Other heads turned at Nate's announcement. "Yeah?" Spence stepped forward, buttoning his coat. "You see any Yanks?"

His gaze slid to the ground. "Might have. Thought there was a boat on the river."

"How big?" Others stepped closer.

"I ain't sure. Clouds covered the moon just then." He yawned. "I heard what sounded like oars on the river. Lou heard it, too. We reported it to the corporal."

A bugle blasted. The sky had lightened enough to show Johnny's silhouette as he proudly blew "Assembly."

"Time to get up, Lou." Spence raised his voice. "Roll call."

"I'll get him." Callie stepped over her knapsack toward Louisa.

"He's grumpy when awoken. You fellas go on."

"I'm grumpy myself when I hear that bugler." Spence grinned. "If we didn't need that horn for battle orders, I might be tempted to stuff it with mud."

The men chuckled and loped away.

Nate shook his head at Callie. Zach put his hand on his cousin's shoulder. "Let's talk later."

Shaking Zach's hand off, Nate glared at him before following the others.

Watching him walk away, Zach's brow furrowed. His concerned gaze met Callie's. "Best get Lou up now. Probably not marching today, but you never know. Be ready for anything."

Was that a warning to watch out for Nate? Callie gave a quick nod before turning her attention to her sister. Filled with trepidation, her breath came in shallow, shaky gasps. What had happened last night?

CHAPTER SIXTEEN

Marching again. Word was that General Hood searched for a place to cross the impressive Tennessee River. Zach whistled as he stared at the wide river. When was Hood going to get on with it? He and Nate were likely to be gray-haired by the time they made it to the other side.

Zach stole a glance at his cousin two rows back. Nate marched alongside Louisa—Lou—today. Their shoulders touched as they marched.

Zach clenched his jaw. The pair acted too chummy for his liking. The couple had somehow mended their fences while picketing four days ago. Nate must have done some fancy talking to calm the storm in Louisa's eyes. The betrothed couple was finally together after an absence of months—dangerous while she pretended to be a soldier.

His gaze shifted to Louisa's right side. Callie's downturned face didn't hide her frown. She had confided to Zach that Louisa refused to answer any questions. Callie's concerns centered on the couple's marked attentions to each other.

He agreed. Other soldiers were bound to notice the pair gazing at one another like lovelorn newlyweds.

Nate had rejected Zach's attempts to apologize for keeping the sisters' secret.

Commotion ahead snagged his attention. A smiling group of women and young ladies held overflowing baskets and bowls. Soldiers held tin cups toward a gray-haired woman dipping liquid from a large black pot nestled at her feet.

"Gentlemen." A woman, whose faded floral dress might have been new when the war began, flashed a smile that caused many heads to turn. "My family and neighbors have prepared a few dishes for you, our brave soldiers. We have sweet potato biscuits and spoon bread. If you have a tin cup handy, we have rice pudding, vegetable soup, or rye coffee ready to serve."

Weeks had passed since Zach had consumed anything like this feast. His mouth watered. He was four rows back from the women. If everyone took one helping of one item, he'd get something. Sweet potato biscuits were his favorite.

Zach shifted his knapsack over his shoulder and untied his tin cup hanging on the outside. He joined the single line that had formed almost as soon as the lady opened her mouth. A glance behind showed four men stood between him and Callie, Louisa, and Nate.

Smiling, Callie lifted her empty tin cup.

Zach raised his own tin cup in silent salute to the unexpected blessing. He stepped aside to allow those between them to pass. "You're in for a treat."

"I know." Her eyes sparkled.

Her excitement made her careless. She spoke in a normal, feminine voice. He frowned.

She blanched. "I mean," her tone deepened, "parched corn gets old quickly."

"That it does." He gave her a slow smile. "Will you ask for soup or coffee?"

"Neither. I want rice pudding. That satisfies my hunger."

"That's what I want." Louisa rubbed her hand over her cup. "Hope it tastes the way Ma used to make it."

"Won't matter." Nate took a step forward, his eyes on the bowls and baskets of food. "Anything's welcome when we're starved."

Zach stepped in front of the ladies with arms draped around huge wooden bowls.

"Soldier, do you want a biscuit or spoon bread?"

Both bowls were half-filled with another at their feet. "A biscuit, please."

"Thank you for fighting for us." The smiling woman gave him a biscuit almost the size of her palm. "Tell my mother," she pointed to a white-haired woman sitting in front of a cauldron of coffee, "if you want pudding, soup, or coffee."

Zach fingered the gift. "Much obliged." "Thanks" seemed inadequate for what it meant to receive the bounty.

"My pleasure." She smiled and turned to Callie. "Biscuit or spoon bread?"

Callie gestured to the bowl of biscuits as Zach moved down the line.

"Pudding, soup, or coffee?" The woman glanced at the long row of men waiting behind him.

"I'll have the soup, ma'am." Corn had been the only vegetable he'd eaten for weeks. He extended his cup for a watery ladle of soup. "Much obliged."

"It's our pleasure." A lady younger than Louisa giggled.

Zach smiled and stepped away. He sipped the warm soup. Bits of onion floated on top. The other vegetables were all smaller than his fingernail. No matter. He could drink the soup as he walked.

Callie joined him, smiling. "That was so good of them."

He peeked into her half-filled cup of pudding. "Generous portion."

"I'll say. That soup looks delicious." She dipped a spoonful of pudding into her mouth.

"It is." His smile deepened at the pleasure on her face. "I guess the rice tastes good."

"Delicious." She ate another bite. "My stomach is so happy."

Zach laughed.

"I made the right choice." Louisa joined them. "I haven't eaten spoon bread since early summer."

Zach glanced back at Nate, who seemed to be holding up the line.

"Thank you kindly for the soup." Nate smiled at a blushing lady with black curls. "If soldiers got to see pretty faces like yours more often, we'd be inspired to win this war double-quick."

Eyes glowing, she threw her arms around his neck and kissed him full on the mouth.

Soup sloshed out of Nate's cup.

Louisa gasped.

Zach raised his gaze heavenward. Why did his cousin flirt with every pretty woman—especially with his betrothed standing six feet away?

"Oh, I'm sorry about your soup." The rosy-cheeked woman tilted her head upward at Nate. "Here, let me refill that."

"Much obliged." Nate gave her his cup with a side glance at Louisa.

One hand on her hip, she glared at him.

Though most men celebrated the unexpected treat with boisterous cheers and loud conversion, those closest watched Lou with wrinkled brows. Zach nudged her arm and lifted his cup in salute. "This soup's mighty tasty." Sweat broke out on his brow as he spoke to his staring comrades.

"Spoon bread was delicious." Crumbs slid down Spence's beard as he exchanged a glance with Jonesy.

"That biscuit reminded me of my ma's cooking." Jonesy turned his back on Zach. "What do you have there, Harve?"

Zach swiped his brow when their attention shifted back to the food. Most men were aware of Nate's reputation with the ladies, but Louisa had best control her temper, or the sisters' careers in the army ended today. Callie nudged her arm and Louisa's hand fell to her side. He raised his eyebrows at Louisa, but she didn't meet his gaze. Callie's stormy eyes met his. Oh, boy.

Nate joined them as soon as his cup was full.

Zach looked down at his own half-filled cup. Flirting provided some benefits. But not enough. He turned his body to shield the sisters from view. "Easy," he whispered.

Standing beside Louisa, Callie's eyes turned icy. The tilt of her chin mirrored her sister's.

Nate shrugged. "That wasn't my fault. She kissed *me*."

The sisters looked at each other then back at Nate. They turned their back on him and set a quick pace to follow those marching.

Spence watched them stalk away and then looked at Nate.

"They gave Nate a larger portion than the rest of us." Zach's head reeled from the girls' feminine reaction. Callie had learned soldiering tasks better than most recruits, but she had to somehow control Louisa's hot temper—and her own.

Callie shivered. Standing on picket duty in the chilly November rain was slightly more enjoyable than listening to her sister complain about Nate, which she did every time the sisters were alone. In fact, Callie hadn't enjoyed anything since that unexpected meal several days ago. They were camped near Tuscumbia. Still in Alabama. Still on the wrong side of the Tennessee River.

An impressive pontoon bridge had been completed. Her spirits had risen when General Steven D. Lee's corps had crossed the river by the second day of November. Speculation had been that her corps, or rather General Benjamin F. Cheatham's corps, would cross the next day.

Not to be. For some reason the rest of the army lingered on this side, pontoon bridge going to waste on a swelling river. Maybe the rains were the reason. Wind drove the rain into icy needles that struck her face. Callie tugged Pa's old soggy hat further down on her ears.

Being warm was only a memory, like when she had rested in Ma's old rocking chair in front of a blazing fire. Home sounded like heaven right now, even if there wasn't enough food to feed the whole family.

She sighed. Food was in short supply in the army, too. Her

most recent rations had been parched corn.

That didn't stretch far enough.

Her stomach rumbled. Best think of something else.

Her attention wandered to those standing guard with her, mostly strangers. Sam Watkins, another soldier from her regiment, huddled under a nearby tree, gaze trained ahead. What did he see? She peered into the darkening gloom. Nothing stirred except when raindrops pelted the few dead leaves still clinging to branches, but the Yankees were out there somewhere. Their boats had been spotted on the river. Was it safe to remain camped near Tuscumbia? Or safer to move on?

Callie swiped rain from her face with wet fingers, tensing when she recalled the strain on soldiers' faces. On Zach's face. She'd come a long way since mustering in. She'd learned enough to be a good soldier. She could do everything except … She clasped her musket to her chest. Her comrades expected her to fire the weapon upon the enemy. Her heart beat painfully at the thought. She couldn't do that. The best she'd do was aim over their heads at a tree branch. She wasn't here to kill folks who used to be her countrymen.

The mere thought caused her breath to come in gasps. Time to think of those she loved … like her sister.

Louisa's emotions weighed on Callie. Nate's talk and actions had proven that he took liberties with his promise to be faithful to his betrothed. Louisa's unhappiness stole her high spirits. She seldom met Nate's gaze yet watched him when he wasn't looking.

Louisa still loved him. She'd forgive him in a few days or weeks. Callie had no doubt about Nate becoming her future brother-in-law, so it was past time he curbed his tendencies to flirt with every pretty girl and acted like a man on the road to matrimony.

At least Louisa was going to marry the man she loved. Callie was doomed to be mere friends with Zach for the rest of her life.

Rain, puddled on her hat, bent the rim to pour a steady stream down her neck. She snatched the hat from her head, more miserable than she ever remembered. Huddled over her musket, she shook with cold.

"Cal."

A warm hand touched her shoulder. She looked up and met Zach's concerned green eyes. *Why don't you love me, Zach? I'd be home waiting for you … if you loved me.* "I'm freezing."

"I know." He took the hat from her hands, shook it, and plopped it over her dripping curls. "Wish I had an overcoat—I'd give it to you. At least you'll sleep in a tent tonight. Go on back. Your shift is over."

"Really?" Her body sagged. "Why didn't Corporal Morefield come to get me?"

"He sent me instead." Zach smiled. "Get on out of this rain. It's almost time for roll call. Then you can go to bed."

She smiled. "That sounds so good." She turned toward camp. "You coming?"

"I'll be along in a bit." He lifted his hand toward her face and then his hand dropped. "Go dry off. I'll see you in the morning."

Squelching through the mud, she was almost back to camp before she realized that the other fellows who went on picket with her were still at their posts.

Zach had taken the rest of her duty. She probably had another two hours to go. Zach sat on guard in the rain. For her.

Out of friendship.

Their friendship could blossom into love—it already had for her, long before the war started. Her feelings for him went far deeper than those of a mere friend.

He sat in the rain because he cared for her. What could she do to spark love in those green eyes? Perhaps become a better soldier? She squared her shoulders. If that's what it took, she'd be the best soldier this camp had ever seen.

CHAPTER SEVENTEEN

"We ever gonna cross that river?" Zach held his hands closer to the fire.

"Yep." Nate plopped onto the muddy ground next to Zach. "Just got our orders. Our engineers finished fixing the damage caused by debris on the flooded river. Lost a few pontoons, from what I hear."

Zach leaned forward. "Reckon the Yankees had a hand in the damage?"

Kneeling in front the fire, Callie's eyes widened.

"Don't know." Nate shrugged. "Wouldn't surprise me. All I know is the bridge has been repaired. Time to break down these tents."

"It was a relief to have shelter during all those days of rain." Jonesy bit into fried hardtack.

Sitting with his wrists on his raised knees, Spence ground a heel into the ground. "Still pretty muddy for having three days of sun."

"I feel like I'll never be clean again." Callie flipped a piece of hardtack over in the sizzling skillet.

Zach sucked in his breath at the feminine complaint.

Nate stiffened.

Laughter broke the silence.

"Boy, you gotta toughen up." Laughing, Jonesy slapped Cal on the back, nearly sending her sprawling into the fire. "A little dirt never hurt nobody."

"So, we're finally going to cross the Tennessee River." Zach steered the conversation away from scarlet-faced Callie. Jonesy slapping her on the back had helped cover for her lapse, but why had he done it? Could he suspect? No. He'd have said something. Any of them would if they knew.

"Pack up after breakfast." Nate glanced at Louisa's stony expression. "Hope the rain stays away. Might be a while before the supply trains catch up with us."

Callie and Louisa exchanged a long look.

"I'm ready to leave Alabama." Spence peered northward in the early dawn light. "We'll be in Tennessee soon. Might be a chance to steal away home to see Charlotte. She'd be a sight for sore eyes."

Spence's longing to see his wife silenced the group. Glancing around, Zach guessed each man—and woman—had used their imaginations to travel back home.

As he took down the tent he shared with his cousin, Zach dreamed about going into winter quarters but knew that November thirteenth was far too early. If they avoided big battles, Callie and Louisa would be safe when they settled in one place for the winter. They'd certainly be ready to go home in the spring—and, unless he missed his guess, Porter Jennings would be mighty happy to welcome them back.

Cageville. He missed his uncle's farm. He missed evenings he and Nate spent at Callie's home. Everyone thought he'd attended those evenings to chaperone his cousin and Louisa. No one had guessed his interest lay in the one who cooked the meals.

The same woman who now wore Confederate gray.

She could be warm and free of mud at home—if not for her pa's agreement with Ezra Culpepper. Zach pounded his fist into the canvas tent he'd just folded. Porter Jennings had driven his daughter from the safety of his home, plain and simple.

"Zach?" Nate set his half of the canvas on the ground. "You all right?"

The girls were inside their tent. Everyone else busied themselves packing knapsacks, checking rations, and filling canteens.

Zach leaned closer. "Worried about the girls. We're going to meet up with Yankees. How can we protect them?"

"Don't know as I'd worry about any Yank who threatens Louisa." Nate grinned. "She'll give 'em what-for with her musket."

"Agreed, but Callie's not so bold. She'd rather take a bullet than shoot one."

"You think?" Nate's voice rose an octave.

"Keep it down." Zach's glance darted from left to right. "And I fear for her in battle. She couldn't even hit an empty Yankee uniform."

"Bad aim?"

"That ain't it. She's a better shot than her pa—when she's hunting for her supper."

"These women will be the death of us, won't they?" Nate's gaze darted to the girls' tent. "Louisa still won't talk to me. Never knew her jealous streak was this bad."

"Can't flirt with other women when you're betrothed. If you see any pretty women near our next camp—or even plain ones—you'd best ignore them."

"Ain't no harm in smiling back." Nate tied his tin cup to his knapsack. "Louisa will have to learn to trust me."

"Act as a trustworthy man," Zach stacked his canvas half on top of Nate's "and she will."

Nate rubbed his bearded chin. "My canteen's empty. Want me to refill yours while I'm at it?"

"Wait for the g—Shaws to come out," Zach caught himself as two soldiers strode behind them, "and we'll fill theirs at the same time. They still need to take down that tent."

"Are you wearing every stitch of clothing from your knapsack?" Callie whispered from the shelter of their tent.

"Yes—all underclothes, blouses, and both my trousers." Louisa rummaged in her sack. "We've both lost weight from insufficient rations—"

"And long marches."

"Everything fits." Louisa grimaced. "But you're too skinny."

"Thanks." Callie rolled her eyes along with her bedroll. She'd never been the beauty of the family so best not fret over it. "It's warmer wearing all these clothes."

"Best part is we now have room to carry our tent." Louisa grinned. "Better to carry it than wait for supply trains to catch up. Sleeping in the rain—or snow—isn't my idea of adventure."

Callie shuddered. Weather worsened with the coming of winter. "Let's get this tent down. We aren't as quick as the others."

"They've had years to practice."

With the grim reminder of the war's duration, Callie carried her bedroll and haversack outside. The sun peeking over the tree line lifted her spirits. No rain today.

Zach stepped over. "Are you about ready?"

More than ready to implement her plan to capture a certain soldier's heart.

Callie stood between Zach and Louisa some fifty paces from the floating bridge. A band of soldiers playing "Dixie" on horns and drums led the way.

Other brigades had followed their bands, four men in each row, across the long bridge. From Callie's vantage point, they appeared to walk on water, just like Jesus did. She hummed to the music, bouncing from one foot to the other. The bulky tent canvas, tied to her knapsack, flopped against her back with each step.

Zach smiled down at her. "Excited to walk across the mighty Tennessee River?"

Her heart skipped a beat at his glowing green eyes. "For a g— boy who never went much of anywhere, it's like a grand adventure."

Nate leaned across Louisa. "One to tell your children someday."

Callie's elation ebbed. Not unless she won Zach's love.

Soldiers ahead began moving. Did folks ever fall off when crossing? She wiped clammy hands on her trousers and then almost laughed aloud. She was becoming more like the men she tried to emulate every day.

She matched her steps with Zach's, which was easier at the slow pace. She stepped onto the planks covering the makeshift bridge, which vibrated under with the weight of hundreds of men—and two women. She stared at her feet. It was like floating on the water with the river stretching far into the distance on either side.

She was the size of an ant compared to this mighty river.

The band played "The Bonnie Blue Flag." Callie lifted her chin. Even if she didn't belong with the brave men marching alongside her, she loved them one and all for their sacrifice. They'd given up so much to fight for their families, their country. It was a privilege to be part of Cheatham's Corps in the Army of Tennessee. General Hood must be proud of his soldiers. Being a small part of that … it meant something.

High bluffs rose beyond the river. Yankees were nearby, maybe shielded behind those bluffs. When their armies met, there'd be a battle. She'd never be ready, and yet she must be. Zach admired courage, bravery. She'd not let him down.

Were they watching her brigade? Did they hear Southern tunes played by the band?

She shivered.

"Are you cold?" Zach inched closer.

She wasn't but didn't want to admit her trepidation. "A little."

Zach peered ahead. "I reckon we're about halfway. These bridges are pretty safe … for foot traffic anyway."

"Yep." Nate looked behind him. "Hope we don't lose any horses or mules."

Water lapped over the boards. Callie stepped over a puddle. She hadn't considered the danger to the animals. The swaying bridge and lapping water might spook them.

Zach splashed into the puddle without changing his gait. "Best not think about it now."

Though Zach didn't say it, the water was so close that soldiers must sometimes fall in. This river was deep and she couldn't swim.

"Cal? Something wrong?" Louisa nudged her. "You're not scared, are you?"

She was trying to be brave here. She didn't need anyone pointing out her fear, especially within Zach's hearing. "Nope." Louisa knew how to rile her.

"I didn't think so." The corners of Louisa's mouth turned up.

The band, still playing "The Bonnie Blue Flag," reached dry ground. They continued marching past the river bank.

The music livened Callie's step. They'd camped for days waiting to cross this mighty river. This thrill had been worth the wait.

She heaved a sigh to step off the bridge onto a muddy bank. Charred remains of a few houses stood near the river.

"This is Florence." Zach gestured toward the untouched homes in the town.

"Were the Yankees here?" Many homes hadn't been harmed, but the charred shells of others gave mute witness to some tragedy.

"Most likely." Zach's face turned grim.

Orders came to halt in Florence. They'd make camp.

Louisa turned to Callie. "That wasn't so long to carry our tent, was it?"

"No."

"If our supply trains don't cross until late tonight, at least we'll have a tent for shelter." Louisa clapped her on the shoulder. "Whoever thought of toting it on our backs had a good idea."

Callie laughed, pleased that her sister had followed the soldierly custom of smacking her on the shoulder. Small successes, but they were making them. "I believe that was your idea, brother." Her eyes glowed. "A mighty fine one, too."

CHAPTER EIGHTEEN

"Is that General Hood?" Callie nodded toward a tall man with a full beard. She wiped raindrops from her cheeks. It was worth standing in the chilly rain to see her commander. Maybe he'd speak to them.

"Yep," Zach said. "His left arm troubles him—thanks to a wound at Gettysburg. From what I hear, his left hand is mostly numb."

The general's arm hung loose at his side. Callie rubbed the wet sleeve covering her left arm. "Why does he walk with a crutch?"

"You didn't hear?" Shaking her head, she darted a glance all around. Men huddled in groups of varying size in the stormy chill.

"Lost his right leg at Chickamauga," Zach whispered.

"But I see his leg ... and his boot has spurs."

"That's an artificial leg."

And he remained in the army? His sacrifice put a new perspective on standing in the pouring rain, renewing her commitment to serve as the best soldier she could be. "He must be a brave man."

"Agreed." Zach folded his arms across his chest, his gaze returning to his commander. "Injuries don't stop him. Gotta admire that in a man. Seen fellas go home for good for a lot less."

Though the general's auburn hair was paler than hers, it gave them something in common. Compassion welled up in Callie. His refusal to quit inspired her. She'd think twice before complaining.

"Where's Lou?" Zach's gaze darted around the gathering crowd of soldiers.

"He's resting in the tent. Went there straight from supper."

Callie turned around. A crowd of soldiers blocked the view of their camp. "Says he's wore out from moving camp."

"It's gonna get a lot worse. Winter's coming on."

Her face heated at the implied criticism. "A body has a right to feel tired now and then." She crossed her arms and stared at him without smiling.

"No need to get on your high horse." He waved an open palm at her. "I just thought he'd want to see General Hood."

"Never mind about Lou. Where's Nate?" She'd heard about the kisses the women in town had given the first soldiers who arrived. That was overly patriotic to her way of thinking.

His gaze dropped to his brogans. "A few officers were invited to a local home for supper. Nate tagged along."

She stared at him until he looked at her. "Don't tell Lou about this. Sh—he's almost over …" Her glance darted at men within earshot. Everyone's attention focused on General Hood, but it'd be foolish to forget herself and betray Louisa. "I'll talk to Nate myself."

"I already talked to him. Didn't do any good."

"I'll talk to him."

"Worth a try." His gaze shifted beyond her. He whistled. "There's General Forrest. Glad to see his cavalry back with us."

Callie followed his gaze to a dashing officer striding toward Hood. The man's piercing eyes spoke of confident authority. She'd heard of him, of course. This general led divisions of cavalry forces. She needed a dose of his self-assurance for this soldiering job.

"No wonder everyone is gathering." He glanced at her. "Doubt that Lou wants to miss this."

"You're right." Callie reached for her skirts to run back to camp, realizing a second too late that she wore trousers. She brushed at mud clinging to the fabric to mask her blunder. "I'll fetch him."

She ran back to camp against the flow of men walking toward the generals. She berated herself for faltering in front of her comrades. In the gloom, it took her a few minutes to find their tent among the additional tents standing tonight.

She halted at her tent. Bending over, she stepped inside. Louisa, wrapped in a blanket, lay unmoving. "Lou?" Callie shook her sister's shoulder. "Feel any better?"

"I'm sleepy." She grunted. "Go away."

"I will if you want me to. Just thought you'd like to see General Hood and General Forrest." Callie sat next to her. "Seems like most of our comrades are gathered there."

Louisa sat up. "General Nathan Forrest? The cavalry officer?"

"The very one." Callie smiled at Louisa's bright-eyed look. "He's as dashing as they say."

She peered outside with a sigh. "It's still raining."

"Who knows when the chance to see Forrest and Hood together will come again?" She refused to allow the storm to keep her away. "Want to go with me?"

She pushed the blanket off. "I'll come. Where's Nate?"

Glancing away, Callie stood. "He's somewhere around. Let's hurry."

The strains of hundreds of male voices singing "Dixie" filled the air.

"That's a beautiful sound." Louisa's face glowed. "Let's take our female voices and join in."

She laughed and led the way.

Though they hurried through the darkened camp, the song died away.

"What's happening?" Callie peered ahead. The back of the crowd had expanded.

"I don't know," Louisa hurried past, "but I'm not missing it."

Callie ran to keep up with her.

They reached the outskirts. Everyone stood silent, some with arms crossed, others at attention. "Zach's over this way."

"Shut up." A stranger in gray glared at Callie. "General Hood is speaking."

She blinked, sorrier to miss the general's speech than regretful to disturb a cranky soldier. She maneuvered through the crowd until she glimpsed General Hood in the distance. He stood respectfully silent now as General Forrest spoke.

Standing too far from the speaker to catch more than an occasional word, she cheered when those in front cheered. She and Louisa joined the singing afterward.

When the crowd dispersed, Louisa looked around in the darkness. "Do you see Nate?"

"No." Her spirited sister wasn't herself—thanks to him. Callie's blood simmered at the unhappy droop of Louisa's mouth and hoped to calm down a bit before she talked with him. "I don't see Zach either."

"Crowd's too large, I reckon." Louisa sighed. "Let's get back to camp. I'm ready for bed."

"All right." Callie frowned. Today had been one of their easier days. Maybe the rain had drained her sister's energy.

Rain fell that night and continued the next day. The sisters stayed in the shelter of their tent when not performing duties. The canvas kept the worst of the moisture away. The persistent thud of raindrops lulled a subdued Louisa to sleep. Callie stared at her wan, tired face. She much preferred her sister's anger over the listless, tired woman who only wanted to sleep in her free time. Might just be the weather. Goodness knows they'd had enough rain to float the ark in the past two weeks ... but Callie didn't believe the storms caused her sister's downhearted spirits.

Nate.

But was it all his fault when Louisa's prickly behavior kept him away? Someone had to say something. Callie shifted to the front of their tent. She hadn't seen Nate since breakfast, and it was about time to make supper.

Rain prevented cooking over a fire tonight. They'd have to

make do with soaked hardtack. She grimaced at the coming meal, then shoved the thought away. At least they'd have something to eat. They'd eaten several meals of fish before crossing. A steer had fallen from the pontoon bridge, providing fresh beef for last night's supper and breakfast, so she had no cause to complain.

She peered into the rain. Men stood in line to get their haircut outside a tent across the way. Most soldiers had pitched tents yesterday. Nate and Zach's shelter was on her right.

A bearded man of medium height sauntered into view. Finally. She stepped into the rain. "Nate." Her voice came out too feminine. She'd correct that.

He turned swiftly. "Oh, it's you, Cal. I'm in a hurry. Can we talk later?"

"No." Her tone sharpened. "This won't take long and now is a very good time."

He raised his eyebrows. "Let's walk this way."

He led the way to woods at the edge of camp. Adjusting her hat, Callie fell into step beside him. She liked him well enough, though he seemed to think highly of his own charms. It was his flirting that had to stop. Time to give her future brother-in-law a piece of her mind.

He stopped under the dubious shelter of a maple tree. "What's eating you, Cal?"

"Well, that's a mighty good way of putting it." She folded her arms over her chest. "I'll get right to it. My sister loves you, and you're not treating her right."

His face blanched. "Wh … what are you talking about?"

Maybe he was remorseful. She liked seeing him upset about hurting her sister. "Kissing that girl on the side of the road for starters."

"Oh, that didn't mean nothing." Color returned to his face. He leaned against the tree's sturdy trunk. "Some of the younger ladies are mighty devoted to the Southern cause. Grateful to us soldiers. That's all."

"You don't go around kissing other girls when you're betrothed." Callie stiffened. How dare he make light of his behavior? "And that girl kissed you because you flirted with her. It has to stop."

"Wait just one stinking minute." He glared at her. "Who do you think you are, telling me what to do? I ain't going to wed you."

"Thank the Lord for that mercy." She rolled her eyes. "I speak on my sister's behalf. She's been too mad to talk to you, and now she's …"

He straightened. "She's what?"

"She's not herself, that's what. And you're to blame for it."

Rain slid down his face as he peered toward camp. "I gotta go."

"Where are you off to?"

"The corporal got an invitation to supper at one of the homes. They said he could bring a buddy. He asked me."

No soggy hardtack for him. "You could have refused."

"Turn down home cooking?" He grunted. "You know any soldier who'd reject an offer to eat in comfort, sit around the fire after supper?"

Good question. They were all too hungry to walk away from a home-cooked meal, no matter how humble.

"See? Use your noggin." He strode toward camp. "I won't talk about the meal at breakfast."

"Nate?" She stopped.

He turned back.

"No flirting."

"When did you get so bossy?"

"When my sister got so unhappy."

They glared at each other.

"Don't hurt my sister."

His face flushed. He turned on his heel and left.

She watched him enter the row of tents at a run. He'd better mend his ways.

Zach awoke to a bugler's blast before dawn. Rain pelted the tent. Wonderful. Another wet day. He sighed. It wasn't like he wasn't used to it. And the weather was bound to get worse, as he'd warned Callie.

President Jefferson Davis had proclaimed a Day of Prayer for Wednesday, November sixteenth—today. Hood had ordered them to observe it all day and attend a place of worship.

The South could use the prayers. Several pontoons sank—the very day they'd crossed the Tennessee River—costing the army some steers and a couple of mules. Though he hated this loss, they'd had beef for supper that night. Callie had fried their steaks in the skillets. Even with only salt as a seasoning, the meal satisfied him. A full belly had become a rare treat. They'd even had enough for breakfast. His mouth watered for another meal just like it.

Because of the broken pontoon bridge, part of the army hadn't crossed yet. And to top it off, the blasted rain meant the river continued to rise.

Not to mention the next battle with the Yankees. It was coming. He'd just as soon get it over with if not for Callie and Louisa. The girls would be part of the fighting unless Zach figured out something in the meantime.

The mere thought of them in battle sent him into a cold sweat. Comrades had fallen dead at his side more times than he could count. Those memories, and so many more, never left him. Even if the girls managed to escape without a scratch, they'd see sights they'd never be able to un-see.

He didn't want that for either of them.

Louisa had kept to herself more and more. He was used to her high-spirited dashes into the next adventure. Army camps and war provided plenty of new experiences to go around. Yet, she acted listless. She'd been so happy to be reconciled with Nate that their relationship had threatened to give away the sisters' secret. Until that woman with the biscuits had kissed him. Was she really so jealous of a stranger's kiss?

He rubbed his chin. Maybe so. If Zach saw some man kiss Callie, he'd see red. His feelings for her had grown since she'd mustered in. Working beside her day after day. Watching her give the army all she had. Sleeping within reach of her every night. He flopped over onto his stomach.

He couldn't allow his feelings to grow. The army was his future. He wasn't going to be the quitter his father had accused him of being. He had to prove that boy had become a responsible adult, even if it meant not pursuing a romantic relationship with Callie.

He grabbed his canteen, scooted out of the tent, and strode to the river. A long walk should calm him. Maybe a little talk with the Lord.

Callie's main concerns were soldiering and her sister. With the scrapes the high-spirited Louisa dragged her into, she had a full plate.

Louisa had to learn to cope with Nate's behavior or break their engagement. If she decided not to marry Nate, his cousin would be devastated. He always said he loved Louisa best.

On the other hand, Louisa might desire to get as far away from Nate as possible. She could leave, find feminine garb, and dress as a woman again with none the wiser. Taking Callie with her.

He rubbed the sore spot over his heart. At least they'd be alive. They'd get out before the next battle. Might be for the best.

So why did the pain in his chest increase?

Yep, couldn't hurt to spend the day asking for help from the Almighty.

CHAPTER NINETEEN

Five days later, frigid winds bit through Callie's frame while standing for morning roll call. How she longed for a warm winter overcoat. She'd never been this cold.

"Men, we're going on the march." Sergeant Ogle paced back and forth in front of their regiment. "This will be a hard campaign. We're heading back home to Tennessee where we'll find them Yanks and fight 'em on our own land."

A battle. This was what Zach had warned her about for weeks. She clutched her arms to her chest.

Zach and Nate cheered with others. Louisa, whose energy had been revived by several days of rest, stood rigid at Callie's side. Neither cheered.

"Our base of supplies will be behind us." Sarge continued to pace. "We'll persevere through disciplined marching and fighting."

Callie's heartbeat thrashed against her ears.

"Soldiers, we will no longer fight on our enemy's terms."

Another cheer.

"We will be assured of adequate strength before battle." Crossing his arms, Sergeant Ogle faced the line of soldiers. "The choice of ground will be ours. As such, risk of defeat in our homeland of Tennessee is small."

Men shouted encouragement. Zach's fist pumped into the air. Then he met Callie's gaze. Triumph faded from his face as his hand fell to his side.

Callie rocked on her heels.

"Men, hardships lie ahead. You know all about those." Sarge's glance passed over each face in the front line. "With determined patriotism to our dear country, a cheerful, manly spirit will win the day."

She gazed at the frozen mud beneath her feet as men cheered. Not much to be glad about to her way of thinking—hard marching, low rations, frigid temperatures.

And a battlefield looming ahead.

"Let's reclaim our state!" Sarge raised his musket high.

Dizziness threatened. She steadied herself against Louisa's arm as she and her silent sister followed the boisterous crowd back to camp. Why were they happy about a battle? Probably because it was one battle closer to the end of the war.

Snowflakes fell on Callie's eyelashes. She dreamed about the warm winter cloak she'd left at home as the cold penetrated to her bones. She wore every scrap of clothing from her knapsack not only to keep warm but also to make room for the tent canvas.

"It has to snow while we're marching." Louisa shifted the weight of the other canvas half on her back. "Glad we'll have a tent as shelter tonight."

"That canvas gets heavy after a while." Zach fell into step beside Callie. "But you'll be happy to have it while the rest of us will envy you."

Brushing snowflakes from her eyelashes, Callie glanced up. "You had the opportunity to carry your tent."

"Yep. Got tired of toting so much on my back, and that's a fact." He peered over the troops marching in front of them. "Looks like muddy roads will continue."

Callie sighed, her gaze returning to half-frozen mud. Her feet were as cold as the rest of her. "Why didn't the whole army come this way?"

"We often break by divisions to cover more ground. Do you

remember what division we're in?"

"Cheatham's Corps is all I know." She had enough to remember with masquerading as a man and a soldier.

"You're in Brown's Division and Carter's Brigade." He clucked his tongue. "That's something you have to know. It's important—especially in battle."

Then it didn't matter because she didn't intend to fight. No need to give away her plan to simply watch the action.

"We'll be in Tennessee soon," he said.

"It will be a pleasure to return to our home state."

He tapped her shoulder with his knuckles and pointed to a few soldiers resting on a log. "Did you notice their shoes?"

She fought the urge to hold her nose against the stench of rotting meat. "What are they made from?"

"Beef hides. General Cheatham ordered his soldiers without shoes to stitch up new ones using beef hides. We're cold without a coat. Can you imagine how you'd feel with no shoes?"

She shivered. Her shoes didn't have holes, but long marches on rough terrain could change that. "Where's Nate?"

"He's talking to some of the fellas from another Tennessee regiment." He glanced at Louisa. "He'll find us when we make camp."

Callie's talk with Nate didn't appear to have borne any fruit. Louisa trudged on beside her, silent and stoic through the cold. There was nothing Callie could do about it now. And with the battle looming … maybe it wouldn't matter.

Zach peered at the long line of men before him. No sign of his commander's horse, who traveled near them today. The trees were barren of leaves. Last year that sight had sparked a loneliness in his soul. Why didn't it this year?

Callie.

He adjusted his collar against the biting wind. He worried about her, shivering at his side on this second day of marching. She shouldn't have to endure such wintry conditions. She should be warm and dry in front of her father's fireplace. Blast this war that drove caring fathers to desperation.

He rubbed his hands together as they avoided the deep mud on the roads by walking through fields and woods. They had marched hard yesterday and stopped at dark, camping at Rawhide near the Alabama and Tennessee border. Today they headed toward Waynesboro. Were the Yankees there?

Zach had an ominous feeling. It had robbed him of precious sleep last night. He had no idea where or when, but something bad was going to happen. Nate must have felt it too. They both stayed near the girls today.

He glanced at Callie trudging through the woods at his side. Did his trepidation stem from worry for her safety?

"See that sign ahead?"

Zach followed Louisa's pointing finger. "Where?"

"On the right. It says, 'Tennessee, a grave or a free home.'" She shivered. "How morbid."

Callie's hands shook, whether from cold or the ominous message, Zach could only guess. He decided to focus on the positive. "Well, folks, looks like we made it to Tennessee."

Callie smiled amidst whoops and shouts. "Good to be home again."

"That it is. Say, who is that fellow with General Hood?" A man, balding on top with tufts of hair bulging out on the sides, stood with their commander.

"Why that's Governor Harris," Spence spoke from the row behind. "Well, reckon I'd best say exiled governor since the Yankees took over the state."

A warm glow lit Zach's heart. "Reckon he's welcoming us troops back home?"

"Looks like it." Spence's tone deepened. "Good to see, ain't it?"

"Yep." This welcome meant more than a hot fire—and that was saying something.

Callie rubbed her arms to stimulate some feeling from the numbing cold. Stomach pangs reminded her it must be about suppertime on this second day of marching. Would she ever be warm again?

Shots rang out ahead of them. The cold forgotten, she clutched Zach's arm. "What's happening?"

Eyes wide, he shook his head.

Maybe soldiers didn't grab each other's arm. She pried her hand away. "Is that a battle?"

More shots and they came closer together, almost a constant popping.

"Too soon to tell." Zach gripped the musket in his arms. "Someone's exchanging fire."

"What do we do?" Her voice sounded shrill to her own ears. She sought her sister's frightened glance.

"We follow our training." He spoke calmly, authoritatively. "We await orders."

"Are they shooting at us?" Louisa's gaze darted in every direction.

"Not directly at *us*. At least … not yet." He stared up ahead. "I see our corporal. He's motioning for us to keep marching. But keep your wits about you."

"Is it the Yanks?" Callie asked.

He shot her an exasperated look. "Who'd you think?"

"Then who are they shooting at?" She didn't even care if Zach thought her questions were stupid—this was the first time anyone had shot at them since she'd arrived. Her face tightened at the surge of emotions that mixed with her fear.

"Our cavalry rides ahead of us. They're fighting and require assistance from leading regiments."

"Us?" She gulped.

"Always a possibility." His green eyes looked steadily into hers. "Watch me. Remember what I said—keep your wits about you. Be ready to shoot your musket to protect your life, your si—brother's life, and your comrades' lives."

Knowing the other soldiers nearby didn't understand her hesitancy, she tried to suppress a shudder.

They advanced. Her heart raced faster than the rapid fire. Musket shots came from further away. Heeding Zach's advice, she watched the woods ahead. She listened as shots slowed. Then the shooting stopped.

Not long after, orders came to bivouac for the night. As they strode into camp, her heart pumping, Zach turned to her. "I'm glad this wasn't worse. But mark my words, if you stay in the army, it will be."

A chill climbed up Callie's back. She didn't doubt the truth behind his warning.

Her military haven wasn't a shelter anymore.

CHAPTER TWENTY

Late the next afternoon, Callie caught her first glimpse of Waynesboro. She'd heard of the town from girlhood. It was nothing like she expected.

War had visited Waynesboro and changed it forever. Houses had been torn down. Charred remains of homes. Destroyed gardens. A hide-tanning yard had been gutted, probably for its timber. The place was deserted.

Callie met Louisa's alarmed glance. "This is what war looks like."

"Yes." Louisa tilted her head. "You wouldn't have fired your musket if Yankees had shot at you yesterday."

She met the accusing stare of a Tennessee soldier, a stranger to her. He stood close enough to hear the question. She pushed Louisa ahead of her to a deacon seat near a charred home and sat down. "Don't speak so loud."

"Answer me." Glaring at her, Louisa remained standing. "You'd not shoot to save your own life."

"I told you before we left that I can't shoot anyone," she whispered. "Why bring this up now?"

"And I told you that I'd shoot to protect my loved ones." She clutched her musket. "Can you?"

Her glance fell on the musket resting against her shoulder, always there while marching. "I ... I—"

"That's what I figured." Louisa's eyes flashed. "You're in the army now. Yankees are going to shoot at you ... at me. Decide now what you will do."

"But I might kill somebody. How do I live with myself then?"

"Things are different in wartime." Louisa straightened her shoulders. "I'd shoot someone who aimed at you. Can I count on you in times of great need?"

"Always." Was it true? She shifted under the piercing stare. Louisa had always been the spirited one, the courageous one. It was time for Callie to prove herself—just not by killing someone.

The fire left Louisa's eyes. "I need to talk to you."

"Of course." Callie's gaze darted to soldiers ambling through the town's wreckage. With hundreds of men exploring the remains of a once-vibrant town, there'd be little privacy to discuss her sister's relationship with Nate. She'd waited weeks for this conversation. "As soon as we're alone."

She raised miserable blue eyes. "That will be best."

"Lou?" She'd never seen such fearful sadness in her eyes. "Is this about …"

Louisa's shoulders sagged. "You'll know soon enough."

Her lips tightened. She only knew one person with the ability to steal her sister's exuberant, feisty spirits. What had Nate done?

News that the corps' wagon train broke down some four miles to the rear hit Callie hard that evening. No new rations. Though her back ached from the weight of the canvas, she was comforted that she and Louisa would sleep under shelter.

They silently pitched their tent amidst talk of the damage to Waynesboro and grumbling—the food they each carried in their haversacks must now stretch longer. Callie had hard bread and not much else. She'd make do with one of these for each meal. She mourned her long-gone supply of roasted acorns. A hot cup of coffee might warm the day's cold from her bones.

Maybe. Bright sunshine hadn't warmed the air. The gap on either end of the tent insured the temperature was nearly the same inside as outside.

"Cal, Lou, do you need water in your canteens?" Zach stood near the tent opening. "A few of us are walking to the stream. I can take yours and refill them."

"Thanks." Stepping outside, Callie lifted the strap over her head and handed it to him.

"Mine's empty." Louisa exited the tent and gave him her canteen. She rubbed her lower back. "Much obliged."

He slung both containers over his shoulder. Nate, Jonesy, Spence, and several others joined the group.

"Might have to break some ice." Nate pushed up his collar.

Zach grunted. "We've been through worse."

A chorus of "Ain't that the truth," "Truer words were never spoken," and "Quit your belly-achin'," followed.

Callie hid a smile. It was as difficult to not complain of the rough conditions as it was to listen to others complain. She watched them walk away, her admiration of her brave soldiers growing with each passing day.

"Let's go for a walk." Louisa didn't look up. "We might find some acorns or walnuts. Anything."

"Anything will help." Now she'd find out what troubled her sister.

They set off at dusk in the opposite direction from the one taken by Zach's comrades. They soon reached a clearing. "This is a good place to talk." Louisa led the way to a downed tree near the edge of the open meadow. "We'll see anyone who comes along."

Callie sat beside her, reaching to arrange her skirts.

"Not there, are they?" The corners of Louisa's mouth drooped. "We haven't lived as women for weeks." A sigh came from deep within. "It's Wednesday, November twenty-third."

"I didn't know you kept a watch on the days."

"Oh, I've counted the days of late." Louisa wrung her hands. "My menstruation didn't come this month."

"That's probably due to the long, hard marches with little

food." She waved away her sister's worry. "My last one barely lasted a day. We are malnourished. It stands to reason our cycles will be affected."

Louisa stared down at her hands. "That … may account for yours. I looked for mine to start while we waited to cross the Tennessee River."

"What are you saying?" Louisa didn't meet her gaze. A niggling worry became a rock in her stomach. "What else could it be?"

Louisa turned her face away.

"Louisa?" She rose. "What are you not telling me?"

"I'm afraid I'm with child."

"What?" Callie's head spun. Her sister, who wore Confederate gray, pregnant? "But … I don't understand. When …"

"It happened that night Nate found out who I was." Her cheeks blotched with patches of scarlet. "Remember we had a long day of picket duty together?"

Words wouldn't squeeze from her throat. All she could do was nod.

"Nate was so happy to see me. He said he has a hard time waiting for me … that soldiers die in battle all the time." She wrapped her arms around her stomach. "I didn't want him to die not knowing me … that way. So I agreed."

"What a scoundrel!" Callie ground her teeth in the gathering darkness. That—that scalawag had worked on her sister's natural fears for her future husband's life. "Oh, I'd like to wring his neck. How dare he?"

"I'm not innocent, Callie." She bent over. "Ma always taught us to wait for the wedding. That men don't respect you if you allow them liberties with your person. And it's true. He's ignored me the better part of a month."

Callie turned away, unable to take in the terrible truth. Her dear sister … pregnant. She'd anticipated becoming an aunt since Louisa announced her betrothal. But not like this. Not without the bonds of matrimony.

Louisa would be scorned, ridiculed, when babe grew large enough for her stomach to expand. Soldiers around them weren't dull-witted—they'd notice. Not only would her femininity be discovered, but they'd look at Callie closer. They'd both be branded as the frauds they were. They'd sneer at Callie's character as well. Men would question her virtue, perhaps leading them to vile acts against her if they caught her alone.

And wasn't she to blame—at least partially? She'd ignored the signs and brought Louisa to Nate. If Callie hadn't made the journey to muster into the army, Louisa would have stayed home. She'd be safe … and Callie would be married to a whiskey-loving irregular older than her father.

But she'd have saved her sister.

She hadn't seen this coming. She'd failed her sister, whom she'd have died to save.

Almost as bad was the looming loss of her temporary shelter. Louisa's actions had robbed her of her sanctuary. Three, four, maybe even five months was all the time left before … what? Where could Callie go if Louisa didn't marry Nate and invite her into their home?

Senses reeling in a kaleidoscope of anger, fear, disappointment, loss, and a deep, aching sadness, she sank to the ground. Louisa's dream had been every girl's dream—to marry the man she loved and raise a family. Her reputation was ruined. Good men cared about their women, protected their reputations. Nate's selfishness proved he didn't deserve her.

Yet their paths were irrevocably yoked now, and Louisa loved him. Tears clogged Callie's throat in grief for the pain this hasty decision brought.

"Callie?" Louisa touched her shoulder. "Won't you say something?"

She swiped at her wet cheeks.

Hands covering her face, Louisa sank to her knees, weeping.

Filled with compassion, Callie put an arm around her shoulders.

"He played on your fear for his safety. He ought not to have done that."

Louisa's body stiffened. "I've been so ashamed, wondering what you'd think of me."

"I love you. Nothing you can do will change that." She smiled at the hope rising in her sister's face. "Quit trying to test me."

Louisa gave a shaky laugh. "You're not ashamed of me?"

"No. Disappointed, I guess, but never ashamed." Callie closed her mind to the dark days ahead and those who'd scorn her sister. "Have you told Nate?"

A tear trickled down her cheek. "No. The way he's treated me, I'm not certain he'll care."

"Oh, he'll care, all right. He's going to marry you at the first church we find. Your son or daughter will bear their daddy's name."

"What if he refuses?"

Just let him try to refuse. "You're betrothed, aren't you? We'll simply move up the wedding date."

"But we're masquerading as men because we can't go home. We have no place to go."

"You do."

"Not anymore." Louisa pointed to her flat stomach.

The first thing Pa would do was grab his musket and challenge Nate for dishonoring his daughter. "Maybe you're right. We have to stay in the army a while longer. We'll find a preacher and a church—"

"I don't have a dress. We buried our clothes back in Alabama."

Soldier's garb made the situation awkward. Callie's heart squeezed until it seemed to be shrinking. Not the wedding she wanted for her sister. "We'll tell the preacher the truth. The baby will persuade him to help us."

Louisa's eyes sparked with an inner glow. "How can we manage to slip away and marry?"

"Nate can figure that out. You have to tell him he's going to be a father."

"But what if I'm just late, like you said?"

"Do you feel like you're with child?"

"I know I am."

"Then you must talk to Nate." Callie pressed her wet face against Louisa's. "And if he gives you any trouble, send him to me."

CHAPTER TWENTY-ONE

Zach tried to ignore his gurgling stomach. What he wouldn't give for a decent meal.

A band played "Lorena" while some folks whistled along.

He couldn't relax and join in because something was up with the girls. He didn't know what, but it wasn't good. Louisa cast furtive glances at her beau who stared stoically at the blaze. Callie took turns between glaring at Nate and the fire. The orange flames hadn't done her any harm, so her anger must be against his cousin.

Zach wasn't the most intuitive man who ever lived, but even he could smell trouble in the wind. Perhaps Louisa was ready to forgive her betrothed for his flirtatious ways. That didn't account for Callie's scowls though, and they were starting to draw unwanted attention. Something had to change.

Time to stir the waters.

He stood and stretched. "It's a mite nippy just sitting here. Think I'll take a little walk. Nate, you up for that?"

He leaped to his feet. "Might warm my toes."

Zach looked at Callie and Louisa. "Didn't you two take a walk today?"

Callie nodded warily.

"How 'bout showing us where you went?" He blew on his hands for warmth as the girls rose. "As long as it's within the picket lines."

"That's fine." Louisa darted a glance at Nate. "It's cold, even around the campfire."

"Clear nights are colder, but the stars are awful pretty." Spence leaned back against a stone. "We'd come with you except Jonesy and me are standing picket tonight."

Thank heaven for that mercy. Zach wanted to give the couple an opportunity to talk—privately. He nodded to Spence and then set a quick pace in case someone else decided to join them.

They passed several fires lining the path, Nate's troubled expression revealed in the dim light. He stared at the muddy trail as if on his way to the gallows.

"It's this way." Callie pointed to the right.

They followed the skinny path until the campfires were behind them. As soon as they were out of earshot, Zach halted the group with an outstretched hand. "What's going on between you two? Unless I miss my guess, Louisa is ready to talk to you, Nate. It's time for you to listen."

Louisa blanched. "It's private."

"We'll wait here." Zach dusted frosty crystals from a log. "Don't be long. Roll call is in a few minutes."

Shadows swallowed the couple. Their footsteps faded.

"Thank you for wresting us away from the campfire." Callie peered in the direction they took. "They have important matters to discuss."

Low voices spoke too far away to discern the words—only the beat of the conversation.

"Beyond his penchant for flirtation?" Her dogged concentration in what the couple was saying piqued his curiosity.

A quick nod without glancing in his direction.

"Are you concerned?"

That earned him a scoffing look. "Your cousin needs to grow up ... face responsibility like a man."

What did that mean? "Agreed." There was more stirring the pot than he'd realized. "Want to let me in on the secret?"

"What secret?"

"Never mind." He folded his arms across his chest. "I'll ask Nate."

"You do that," she sputtered.

"Are you mad at Nate or at me?"

She darted a glance his way and then lowered her head. "Sorry. It's Nate who's got my dander up."

Nate's voice carried back to them, quickly shushed. The hum of the low conversation continued.

"My cousin has a way of doing that." Zach sighed. "Try to remember he means well."

"He doesn't *always* mean well." Her words were clipped. "He has a chance to redeem himself."

Her words made no sense. Unless— "What blame are you laying at his door?"

"Naught but his own guilt."

Did she mean ... no, she couldn't. There hadn't been time. No, wait. Nate and Louisa had been missing for hours the first night they stood picket together. About four weeks ago.

Long enough for a woman to suspect herself to be with child.

He groaned aloud.

"Shh." She glanced at him. "I see you've reached the proper conclusion."

What could he say? Sweat beaded on Zach's forehead. His chest tightened.

"He'll have to marry her." She tilted her chin. "They're already betrothed so presumably he wants to marry her."

Nate loved her, sure enough, but needed to grow up first. This was a fine kettle of fish. His cousin had behaved abominably.

Little wonder that Callie had glared at Nate all evening.

Footsteps approached.

Callie's muscles tensed. She'd soon discover the measure of the man Louisa loved. Would he stand beside her and her babe?

"Zach? Cal? Where are you?" Nate's voice shook.

"Over here." Zach's lips flattened.

They stepped into view, Louisa's hand tucked in the crook of Nate's arm.

"Well?" Callie searched her sister's glowing face.

"Zach," Nate shook his head as if dazed, "I'm going to be a father."

"What are you going to do about it?"

She'd never heard Zach use that belligerent tone with his cousin.

"There's going to be a wedding," Nate said a bit sheepishly.

"That's wonderful." Zach clapped Nate's shoulder. "That'll keep me from punching you in the eye."

A scarlet flush crept up his neck. "I know I done wrong. I'll make it right."

Louisa gave him a radiant smile. "We'll get married at the first church we pass—"

"That has a preacher inside." Nate patted her hand. "Can't go traipsing around the countryside hunting for a minister to marry us with a war on. And we've agreed not to ask the chaplain."

Callie thought about the clergymen serving as chaplains. "Why not?"

"To protect you," Nate said. "The only ones who know the true identity of the Shaw brothers are standing right here. Anyone else knowing—even the chaplain—makes discovery more likely."

Louisa shuddered. "Don't want Pa to find out about the baby by the army discharging us, sending us home in disgrace, or gossip ruining our reputations."

Pa.

Louisa's actions had robbed him of the joy of giving his daughter away. Callie's heart ached for her pa, though it was for the best that he wasn't here to confront his future son-in-law under the circumstances. She blinked away tears that the wedding would be held, not in their own church with Pastor Brown beaming at the happy couple as he recited their vows, but in a strange church with a stranger presiding over the ceremony. And this they had to be grateful for.

"Agreed." Zach glanced at Callie. "The girls have to remain in the army … for now. The best way to protect them is to keep silent."

Callie dropped her gaze. She'd share the shame if Louisa's condition was discovered.

"We'll be on the march tomorrow," Zach said. "Do you have a dress?"

Louisa wilted in the silence that followed.

There'd be no fancy dress. No orange blossoms pinned on Louisa's beautiful hair. Callie shot him a scornful glance. Why did he have to bring up such a sore subject? "We have to find a church off the main road or march as close to the end of the line as we can." Her mind raced. "Remember that day Louisa and I fell asleep while on march? Our friends know about that. We can pretend to do that again."

"This march will lead to a battle." Zach rubbed his jaw. "I feel it in my bones. Soon, too, unless I miss my guess. You'll need to wed before that in case—"

Nate kicked Zach's shin.

"In case we get stuck fighting for days in one location." Zach kept his eyes on his cousin.

Did Zach fear one of them would die in battle? Callie flinched. Of course, he did. They all should.

"We'll have to keep our wits about us." Nate patted Louisa's hand. "But we'll be man and wife before the week's out."

Louisa smiled up at him.

"You're still in the army," Zach spoke frankly. "She's masquerading as a man. You can't live as man and wife."

Nate agreed hastily.

"The girls will still share a tent. You'll sleep under the stars unless the supply train catches up with us."

"Which ain't likely, as quickly as we're moving." Nate frowned.

"That will give you time to make plans for your future." He

glanced at Callie. "Don't neglect your bride's sister. She has no place to live."

Plain speaking, indeed. Callie's face flamed. If she imagined Zach might propose a double wedding, he'd dashed those hopes. She was in everyone's way. No man loved her. Zach knew her best, and he didn't love her, despite her best attempts to earn his love by being the best soldier she could be. Well, minus having to shoot anyone.

"Of course, Callie will always have a place to stay with us. Right, darling?" Louisa's smile bespoke confidence.

"Uh, right."

No need to search anyone's face for hidden meanings. Callie's future was still uncertain. Nate's noncommittal tone told her she'd not be welcome for long. She pushed that worry aside—it was a problem for another day. It was Louisa and her child that should be the focus right now.

"Let's keep our attention on the matter at hand." She worked to instill a confident tone. "Find a church and a minister who will marry these two at the earliest opportunity."

"Agreed." Zach smiled at them. "I look forward to kissing the bride."

"Me, too." Nate grinned at his blushing soon-to-be bride. "Me, too."

CHAPTER TWENTY-TWO

Three days later, the army was still on the march. Zach wiped cold raindrops from his face. It was safer for the girls' sake since the three corps had converged again on the Mount Pleasant and Columbia pike. Grateful the rain didn't muddy the hard surface of the road, Zach kept his eyes open for Yankees and a church. Too bad the one they'd found yesterday had been empty. He'd like to get this business done quickly, but a minister to marry the couple was as important as the church.

"We'll find a better church," Callie had comforted her crestfallen sister.

Though Nate could be slow to accept responsibilities, he was not one to allow grass to grow under his feet once he'd decided on an action. He had patted Louisa's shoulder, echoing her sister's assurance.

Zach had no doubt they'd pass a church—finding a minister nearby to perform the ceremony was another problem altogether.

A battle brewed—of that he was certain. His pulse raced at the mere thought. The only way he could ensure the girls' safety was to keep them off the battlefield. Other than tasking them with fetching water for their canteens right before the fight, he had no idea how to protect them.

If only there were some safe place for them to go after the wedding, they'd be gone in a heartbeat. He'd take them there himself. But where? Not Cageville where their pa would find them and force Callie into marriage.

Callie nudged him. "Look at the pretty church over there."

A quaint Gothic chapel nestled among tall magnolia trees. The grove of trees offered privacy from soldiers marching past. "Let's stop by those bushes ahead. I'm parched."

"I need a rest myself." She gave a quick nod to Louisa and Nate.

When he was near the bushes, Zach left the march. The other three followed.

"I'm thirsty." Eyes on the church to their side, Nate took a long swallow from his canteen.

"Need a minute's rest," Zach spoke loudly enough for the soldiers passing by to hear.

"There's a church over there." Louisa pointed toward the ivy-covered tower. "I'd like to go inside and say a prayer."

Perfect. Anyone within earshot understood a soldier's desire to pray before battle. "Sounds good to me." Zach gave her a satisfied smile.

They crossed between trees on lush green grass—so different from the impoverished land in Alabama—toward the building.

"I told you we'd find a better church," Callie said.

"It's perfect." Louisa sighed with pleasure. "Such a romantic setting for a wedding."

"Hope the preacher's inside," Nate said. "Then it will be perfect."

Callie halted. "Who's that officer among the gravestones?"

Callie stared at the man in gray, his frock coat and shiny gold buttons showing his high rank.

"That's General Pat Cleburne. He's the best general in the Army of Tennessee." Zach whistled low. "If he asks why we're here, tell him we've come to pray. We'll stick with that story."

"But who is General Cleburne?" Callie recalled the name but couldn't remember how she knew of him.

Sandra Merville Hart

"He commands one of the divisions in Cheatham's Corps—our corps." His brow wrinkled as he gazed at the general. "We're in General Brown's Division, remember?"

Having memorized what seemed to be vital information, Callie nodded. "And we're part of Carter's Brigade."

"Right." Zach's glance didn't shift from the officer who paused at each headstone. "Cleburne's Division is one of the best in our army. His men would follow him into h—" He cleared his throat. "Anywhere."

"I heard tales of his bravery even back in Cageville." Louisa's gaze darted from the officer to the church. "He's very dashing."

"You're spoken for," Nate grumbled in a low voice.

"Soldiers." General Cleburne called across the yard. "What is your business at this church?"

They snapped to attention.

"We feel a need to pray for the upcoming battle … and our safety." Zach spoke with respect.

"Then carry on. And if you can spare a prayer for me and my men, I'd be obliged." The general's piercing gaze swept the group.

"We'd be honored to pray for you, General Cleburne." Zach stood taller.

The general inclined his head, resuming his perusal of inscriptions on the graves.

"Let's get inside," Nate ushered them toward the door, "before we attract more attention."

Callie had been so enamored with meeting the famous general that she momentarily forgot their purpose. Her stomach twisted. A commanding general was the worst person possible to stumble upon her sister's wedding. *Please stay in the cemetery until we're done, General Cleburne. Then you can have the church to yourself.*

A musty smell greeted them as they entered the church. The pews were arranged in one large center row and two small rows of pews on each side.

A man stood from the front pew. He wore dark pantaloons, not

Confederate gray. His coat almost hid his blue vest. Callie sighed deeply. It had been weeks since she'd seen a man wear anything except military garb. "Welcome, soldiers."

He stared at their muskets. Zach propped his musket in the back corner. She placed her weapon next to his. The others followed suit.

"I'm Pastor Neftzer." He ambled toward them down the left side aisle. "When I saw our army passing by, I came to the church in case a soldier wanted to talk or pray with me." He beamed at them. "And here I find four of our brave men. How may I help you gentlemen?"

Callie flushed. Being called a brave man—especially by a man of the cloth—rubbed against her conscience, reminding her how far from God she'd fallen.

Louisa took a step backward.

Nate halted her with a hand on her arm. "We have a special request … perhaps an odd one."

The man of God inclined his head. "No request is too great after all you've sacrificed to serve our country. What may I do for you?"

Nate looked at Louisa and then squared his shoulders. "We are not what we seem."

"Oh?" The pastor's glance swept the group before settling on Nate with a frown. "You are not soldiers?"

"No, we *are* soldiers." Nate took a deep breath. "We are not all men."

"Forgive me." Pastor Neftzer rubbed his brow. "I don't believe I quite heard—"

"My sister and I joined the army," Callie pointed to Louisa. "We'd fallen on hard times. We masquerade as brothers."

"The army is a dangerous shelter indeed. But I don't quite understand …" The pastor leaned against the back of the pew. "You … are all women soldiers?"

"No." Nate said. "Just Callie and Louisa," he put an arm around her shoulders, "my betrothed."

The poor man opened his mouth and closed it.

Callie looked at Nate, willing him to be the man and take responsibility.

"I must make a confession, Pastor Neftzer." Nate paused and waited.

He simply stared back at Nate. Had he lost the power of speech?

"I'm afraid that Louisa and I ... anticipated our vows." His face was as scarlet as Louisa's. "She is with child."

His stare moved to her gray trousers. "I begin to comprehend why you are telling me all this. You want me to perform a wedding."

"Yes. Are you willing? I have no money to pay you—only my sincere gratitude."

Pushing himself upright, the pastor gave a slight shake of his head. "Does anyone else know these soldiers are actually sisters?"

"No." Nate glanced at Zach. "Me and my cousin are the only ones who know."

"That's amazing." The pastor stared at the sisters. "I see it clearly ... such beautiful women. How were all those men fooled?"

"You expect women to wear dresses. Cook. Sew." Nate shrugged. "Not wear soldiers' gray and carry a musket."

Pastor Neftzer studied them a moment. "I fear you have the right of it. I don't have to tell you this is the most unusual request I've received."

Callie held her breath. *Please. You must help them.*

"I'll do it for the sake of the babe." He clasped his hands in a prayerful pose. "I assume you folks are in a hurry?"

Nate smiled at his bride. "We are in a mite of a hurry. Don't want anyone coming in during the ceremony."

Louisa slid her knapsack, canvas, blanket, haversack, and canteen from her shoulders. The others shed their heavy belongings onto the pew beside hers. Callie clasped her sister's hand with a shaky laugh. She hadn't known how she feared he'd refuse until this moment.

The pastor walked to the front of the church. Two long windows situated on either side of the lectern came together at a point on top. He peered out first one and then the other before picking up a pair of spectacles from the lectern. "There is one young man, an officer, in the cemetery. He's been there a while. Someone waits for him a respectable distance away. Those two are the only ones I see."

"That's General Cleburne. We don't want him to witness the ceremony. I didn't notice anyone else, but his aide is probably with him." Zach's urgent tones drew Callie's gaze. "No disrespect, but can we do this as quickly as possible? We have to be back on the march."

Callie's scowl burned hot enough to scorch Zach's skin.

He brushed her irritation aside—he had more pressing matters. "Do you mind if they said their vows from back here, away from the windows?"

"Well, I … This is highly irregular." The pastor's gaze fell on Louisa's anxious face. "I suppose I could make an exception for our brave soldiers."

The same ones the pastor had promised to serve when they first walked inside the church. Zach pushed the wry observation away. "Much obliged."

Nate shot Zach a quick glance. "Yes, thank you. Now I suppose you'll need our Christian names."

"Of course, my good man." The pastor opened a leather-covered register and picked up a pencil. "Your name first."

Now that the nuptials were taking place, Zach stopped listening to the conversation and tuned his ears, sharpened by the war, to the noises outside.

Rain pattered on the roof. No footsteps. No creaking of the door.

And no one else here except a highly-disciplined, much-loved general roaming the cemetery. Zach's mouth went dry. If General Cleburne chose that moment to step inside the church, the wedding revealed the girls' secret—and he'd probably discover the deeper secret of Louisa's child.

Having added their names, the pastor finally closed the register. He opened a small black book. "Dearly Beloved, we are gathered here …"

Could the man speak any slower? The muscles of Zach's neck strained as he peered over the pastor's shoulder to the window. He could only see a yard outside the window. That meant a person must stand beside the window and peer inside to see their little group.

He was sweating worse than Nate now.

"Is there a ring to mark the exchange of these vows?"

A ring announcing to everyone that Lou suddenly got hitched while on the march? Was the man daft? Zach met Nate's wild gaze and then looked at the pastor. "No, we will see to that later."

"What therefore God hath joined together, let not man put asunder."

Zach had never seen Louisa look more radiantly beautiful. His cousin was a fortunate man, after all, to be loved like that … far more than his previous behavior deserved.

He looked at Callie, the true beauty of the family. In his eyes, anyway. A myriad of emotions crossed her face as she stared at the happy couple. Relief, certainly, and joy. But did that sheen of tears betray a sense of sadness?

Her unshed tears wrenched at his heart. She always acted so strong. She performed every task demanded of her as a soldier and a sister. Callie deserved happiness, too. If only Zach weren't committed to the army, hadn't aimed to make a career of soldiering, then maybe he'd try his hand at winning her heart.

As matters stood, she was better off without him. Danger lurked in every battle. He might live to old age. He might die in the next fight. That hard life was too much to demand of a wife.

"I now pronounce you husband and wife."

Nate waited. Glanced at the pastor, who closed his book with a snap. "Preacher, you didn't say, 'You may kiss your bride,' but I'm going to take the words as if you'd said them." He smiled at Louisa, swept her into his arms, and kissed her thoroughly.

Zach rolled his eyes. "Not now, Nate. We have to get back on the march before someone comes in."

The door creaked.

Nate dropped his arms and stepped back.

A man in gray stepped inside. A stranger. "Preacher? If you're not too busy, I'm in need of prayer."

"Certainly, my boy. No request is too great after all you've sacrificed to serve our country. Gentlemen, I believe we are finished here."

"Yes, sir." Nate shook his hand. "Much obliged."

They gathered their gear.

"My prayers go with you." He smiled at them and turned to the man who'd sat in the last pew. "What's your name, soldier?"

Zach opened the door.

"It's Porter, sir."

At the threshold, Louisa gasped and grabbed Callie's sleeve. Then they smiled at one another as they stepped outside.

A soldier with their pa's name. Zach's heart lightened. Seemed like Providence had given them a sign. Porter Jennings would have approved.

CHAPTER TWENTY-THREE

Three days later at sunrise, Callie waited her turn to cross the swollen Duck River outside Columbia. Standing between Zach and Louisa near the riverbank, Callie's shivers had nothing to do with the morning's clear skies and warm temperature—a welcome relief from cold rain. Yesterday, the distant popping of guns had kept her on edge as General Forrest and his cavalry troops pushed the Federals further from the Confederate army.

Yankees were near her division's position at the river.

Light banter surrounded her. Were her comrades really as unconcerned about meeting the Federal army again as they pretended?

"Keep a watchful eye today, Cal." Zach leaned close to her ear. "Them Billy Yanks aren't far from us now. You might see action today."

Callie tried to breathe normally. "What do I do?"

"Follow orders. Our officers will shout orders, but it's hard to hear them over the din of battle." Shots fired in the distance. His gaze shifted toward the sound. "Listen for direction from the buglers and drummers."

Her mind flew back to that first day of training. "I can't remember what any of the tunes mean." She smoothed back her hair with trembling fingers. What had she gotten herself into?

He groaned. "Can't do anything about that now. Watch me and Nate. We know them."

The newly wedded couple stood beside them. They'd both stood picket last night and returned long after the others who picketed with them. Right now, they were exchanging a secretive smile. She poked Louisa sharply in the ribs. "Careful, *Lou.*" She whispered. "Keep your mind on soldiering."

"Ouch." Louisa glared at her. "That hurt. And I *am* paying attention. What's all the fuss? We've crossed bigger rivers than this one."

"It's not the river we're crossing." Her voice raised an octave. She lowered both the tone and the volume. "It's the Yankees up ahead."

"I know about them. Isn't it exciting?"

"Have you lost your mind?" Had wedded bliss addled Louisa's brain? "This isn't an adventure. I shouldn't need to remind you to pay attention." Her eyes dropped briefly to her sister's flat stomach.

"No, you don't, brother." Her tone sharpened. "And I'll remind you of your promise. Remember to shoot."

Heat flooded Callie's cheeks.

Soldiers closest to them stopped talking. Shifted from one foot to another.

"I'm unlikely to forget." Her sister was too happy as Nate's wife to contemplate much else, but she didn't have to raise doubts about Callie's abilities. She clamped her mouth shut and looked at Zach.

"Lou's right." His green gaze pierced to her soul. "Don't forget to shoot."

That was one promise Callie couldn't make as their column approached the river.

Zach could only be grateful their regiment had crossed the pontoon bridge on Duck River before their artillery began a sustained barrage that shook the ground. Color drained from Callie's face as the fighting continued for a couple of hours. Fearing she'd faint, he whispered encouragement when their buglers didn't order an advance.

She remained pale as a bed sheet even after the shooting became sporadic. Her body tensed at every blast of artillery.

He shifted his musket at a horn's blaring. "We're marching again."

"Is that good news?" Her brown eyes were huge as she stared at him.

Her fear moved him. He caught himself before he could pull her into his embrace. "Means things aren't as hot in Columbia anymore." He stood and watched the movement of those in front. "Headed north again."

They'd been promised a hard campaign—so far that'd been right. Marching for days had exhausted him. How much harder must it be for Callie?

Zach figured that was just about the time they'd be ordered to fight.

As they followed comrades through woods, the sounds of battle grew louder. Darting a glance at Callie's pinched face, his breathing accelerated. The situation was too active to avoid a fight altogether, but he was perplexed by musketry ahead that was intense at times, sporadic at others.

"What do you think is happening?" Callie stepped over a downed tree limb.

"Don't know. Sounds like it's not a big engagement. Cleburne's Division is likely in the thick of things up ahead."

Her eyes darkened.

"Bates's Division is next in line." He shared her anxiety this afternoon—he'd protect her from the whole war if he could. "Probably be over before we get there. Sounds like just a skirmish."

"What's the difference between a battle and a skirmish?"

"Limited number of men in the fight. Skirmishes are short. But soldiers die in skirmishes, too."

Her trembling hand tucked a stray auburn curl under her slouch hat.

He could kick himself for his fool mouth. No need to remind her of the havoc that shot and shell wreaked on a person. Best change the course of the conversation. "Have you seen Nate and Lou since lunch?"

"No, they lingered over their meal. Said they'd be along." Her face bloomed as red as it had been pale moments ago.

His wayward cousin would do well to keep his mind on the task at hand with a battle brewing. Nate's bride preoccupied him a mite too much for safety's sake. He kept his thoughts to himself—Callie was embarrassed enough already. "Creek ahead. Folks are removing their shoes and socks to cross."

She peered ahead and then behind her.

He looked around. No sign of the married couple.

Resting her musket against a tree, she sat beside him on a rock and removed a shoe.

Conversations heated up ahead, drawing Zach's gaze. "Jonesy? Did you hear something?"

"Yep." Jonesy tucked his socks into his shoes. "We've been ordered forward. We'll join the battle on Cleburne's right."

Callie's worst nightmare. She'd be engaged in her first battle with her sister nowhere in sight. She had no way to protect Louisa.

That was Nate's job now.

With his despicable treatment of Louisa leading up to the marriage, he had yet to prove himself to Callie. She reckoned the marriage changed him, but until she saw evidence of him protecting his wife as a husband should, she'd keep a watchful eye on her sister as she had done for years. Or would, if she knew where they were.

Racing across an icy creek soaked her trousers, causing them to stick to her legs. Despite the milder temperatures, she shivered. She swiped leaves across her bare feet to remove mud from the bank before putting her socks and shoes on.

She followed Zach and others deeper into the woods. Smoke from an earlier skirmish lingered in the air. The smell of gunpowder pressed home the reality of the impending fight as her regiment moved into position next to Cleburne's Division on the rolling, wooded area. Callie's heartbeat quickened as she lay on winter-dormant grass next to Zach in the gathering twilight.

She was grateful beyond words for his comforting presence. More than her soldierly mentor and a representation of home, he was the man she loved. Her admiration of him had grown as she saw his soldierly training respond to danger. His comrades looked up to him. He'd demonstrated his leadership qualities since that first day when he'd drilled them so hard.

To save their lives. He excelled at serving in the army. Her heart sank to realize he'd made the right choice to make soldering his career.

She had no place in his life. Her attempt to win his love by hard work was futile. Why did that truth have to hit her now with the coming battle before her when she needed her head clear and her heart unbroken? Was anything in her life ever fair? No. It wasn't. And she needed to wake up and smell the gunpowder. This was war. This was what she signed up for. Not romance. Not love. Not … Zach.

The orders to take Spring Hill rustled down the line, breaking through her sadness. She'd no time to think about her future. If she had one at all once this battle ended. Something moved on the small hill before them. Soldiers in blue.

Yankees.

Dizziness threatened to overcome her. What was she doing here? She didn't know the first thing about fighting.

Her gaze darted in every direction, looking for someone to save her from this fight. There was a wooded knoll to her east. Was that more movement? Gathering darkness masked details.

A group of men from their division ran into the field. She clutched her loaded musket.

"Be ready." Zach's voice was calm. Serious. "Stay near me. You'll be all right."

Then their men halted not far from their Confederate line. They remained there.

She cast a frantic look at Zach.

His attention stayed focused on the front.

Minutes passed. Her heart beat loudly enough to alert the Yankees if they had half an ear. Her hands shook until she feared shooting the musket wasn't the issue, holding onto it was. Why was nothing happening?

No gunshots. No fighting. What did this mean?

Darkness had fallen by the time Callie followed the rest of her division a short walk from Spring Hill where they set up camp, or *bivouacked*, as the other soldiers called it. She was learning.

Believing the fight was done for the day, the pounding of her heart slowed to a normal rhythm. She unfolded her half of the tent and peered toward the road. Where were Louisa and Nate? She still hadn't seen them.

Soldiers built small fires to cook their supper and heat their coffee, if they had any. Callie only had hardtack left in her haversack. She'd fry that and leave the skillet out for Louisa.

Zach had dropped his belongings near her bedroll and then disappeared. Spence and Jonesy started a fire.

Wishing to be alone with her thoughts, Callie kept her distance from everyone until they were done cooking. Then she fried a piece of soaked bread.

Not much talking tonight. The now familiar faces around the fire were lined with worry and fatigue. Jonesy, leaning close to the firelight, wrote in his journal.

They seemed to share her pensive mood. Her feet and legs hurt from days of marching. Her back ached from toting a piece of canvas that grew heavier with each half mile. All that faded before the anxiety that gnawed her stomach—tomorrow.

Should she take part in a battle? All she needed to do to get out of it was tell Sarge who she really was. The temptation to do that made it hard to sit still.

"Cal, where's Lou?" Spence covered his shoulders with a blanket. "Ain't seen hide nor hair of him since pert near breakfast."

Jonesy looked around the group. "Zach and Nate are missing, too."

"Probably lookin' for Lou." Sam frowned. "He's probably back in the woods above Columbia, fast asleep."

"Yep, noticed him looking mighty peaked back in Florence." Spence stared into the flames.

"We're not accustomed to living like this." Callie defended her sister, who had been fighting unusually strong fatigue. She had a good reason for her exhaustion—one that these men couldn't understand.

"That earlier icy sleet and wind cuts right through a body." Spence rubbed his hands together. "Glad for this milder spell."

Three dark shapes approached the fire.

"Hey, Cal." Louisa dropped her possessions. "Got any supper left?"

"I can fry a piece of bread. Or two." Her sister looked all done in. She needed nourishment, and their rations had to be replenished soon.

Zach picked up Louisa's things. "Your brother's bedroll is over here." He toted them over to rest by Callie's knapsack.

Callie fetched bread from her haversack. She met Zach's eyes in the dim light.

"They're fine." He whispered. "They found us after we left Spring Hill. Lou's exhausted."

"Yes." It was too risky to say more with others so close. She carried the hard crackers back to the fire and plopped one of them into her cup of water.

"What do you think will happen tomorrow, Nate?" Jonesy placed his journal by his side. He looped his hands over his upturned knees. "You hear anything from the officers we don't know?"

"Nah." Nate flopped to the ground beside Lou. "Reckon we'll have another run in with the Yankees soon."

Spence grunted. "Probably tomorrow. Don't know what happened this evening."

"I'll take furlough as soon as I can." Sam's face turned to the south. "Shame not to see my family and the girl I left behind me while I'm this close to Columbia."

"Some of the fellas got to visit home." Jonesy picked up his journal again.

"I know." Sam stood. "Reckon I'm done for the day, boys. Have a bad feeling that tomorrow will be a long one."

Callie placed a piece of soaked bread on a skillet still resting on burning embers. "Supper will be ready shortly, Lou." She put another piece of hardtack into the water.

"You coddle your little brother too much, Cal." Jonesy looked at her over the top of his book. "He needs to make his own way iffn he's gonna make a good soldier."

"We're family." Callie's gaze slid to Louisa, whose eyes were almost closed. She had to shift the focus off her sister. "We watch out for one another. You and Spence watch out for each other."

"That's a fact." He looked over at the man beside him. "I mean to marry his wife's friend when this thing is over."

Callie shook her sister awake and gave her the hot bread. The other piece soon sizzled.

"I wed Charlotte after we fired on Sumpter." Spence grinned. "Knew I'd be part of the fight."

Jonesy's eyes took on a faraway look. "And I proposed to Benita at your wedding."

Callie offered the next serving to Nate, who downed it in three bites.

"Lou, are you ready to put our tent together?"

"Yep. I'm ready to turn in." She stood and stretched her arms over her head.

The others murmured their excuses and walked away.

"I think I'll write a letter to Benita tonight." Jonesy sat alone at the fire.

A few minutes later, Callie lay in her tent, ignoring the activity going on in other sections of camp. If something was wrong, there were plenty of soldiers who'd find out and let her know. She was too tired—too disheartened—to care.

She burrowed into her blanket.

Jonesy's pencil scratching blended with total exhaustion to lull her to sleep.

CHAPTER TWENTY-FOUR

Zach looped rope around his bedroll onto his knapsack after his group had finished their breakfast. He frowned at the commotion in camp a short distance away. Officers rushing this way and that boded ill for soldiers. He tugged at the rope to tie it.

Callie stowed her possessions in a knapsack nearby.

"Fall in." Corporal Morefield rushed by. "Fall in."

Zach met Callie's wild-eyed gaze. "Grab your musket. Got your cartridge box?"

Trembling fingers touched the box on her belt. She turned to her sister. "Lou. We have to go."

"Oh." Louisa clutched her stomach. "I'm ailing this morning."

"Quick, men." The corporal rushed back through the narrow path between men scurrying to follow orders. "Make haste."

"Get your canteens and haversacks," Zach spoke to the girls, but his gaze darted at men grabbing muskets from stacked arms all around, their faces set in grim determination. "Leave that tent where it is. It's too heavy to tote." His heartbeat drummed against his chest. An attack must be imminent. Everything was happening so fast he didn't know how to protect Callie. Yet. He'd keep his eyes open.

"Quick," Ben shouted orders. "Fall in. Quick time."

Callie tossed the straps of Louisa's canteen and haversack over her head. Nate handed them each a musket.

Men dashed around in pandemonium that lasted only a moment before they began to form a line.

"March. Quick time." The corporal continued to bark orders

echoed by other officers. Soldiers in other regiments also joined the march.

The bugler played marching orders.

"Stay close to me." Zach raised his voice to be heard over the shouts. "Looks like there will be an attack. Soon."

Callie stared at the shoulders of the soldier in front of her. That she was prepared to go through with fighting didn't reassure him at all. He should have exposed her. He should have forced her to remain behind. Where it was safe. If it was safe anywhere.

They made it to the turnpike near Spring Hill and stopped. Broken wagons, guns, and knapsacks were strewn about the lane. His stomach hardened. Left behind by the Federal army? But they had been ahead of the Yankees. What happened?

Scanning the hillside and the fields, he gripped his musket. No Yankees.

"Where are they?" A voice ahead drifted back.

"They're gone." Then many voices fought to be heard. "What! The whole Yankee army gone?"

"No, that can't be."

"How'd they get by us?"

"They passed while we slept."

"I could have slept through a stampede last night."

Zach turned to Callie. "I don't understand. I thought we were ahead of the Yankees. I saw them on the hill last night."

"I did, too—before it got too dark." She looked dazed. "We aren't going to fight?"

"Oh, we're going to fight. Depend upon it. Today, unless I miss my guess. Wait for our orders."

He rubbed his jaw as he stared at her worried face. This situation turned uglier by the minute. How could he protect her?

Last night had scared Callie—whether they'd been called on to shoot or not. The time she'd dreaded was here. She'd seen her first Yankee with a loaded rifle ready to aim in her direction if ordered.

Zach had warned her they might do battle today and then he'd fallen silent, unlike others around them who discussed everything from rubbish along the road to the fight they'd have when catching up with the Yanks.

Her head spun. Her musket seemed to weigh a hundred pounds, so heavy did it lay against her shoulder on the march along the Columbia pike. She didn't want to use it. Didn't want to point the barrel at another human being as Louisa said she must. She shuddered at the thought.

She glanced at the woods on one side of the road. Nothing would be easier than for her and Louisa to hunt for a stream to refill their canteens and then linger on the bank. Make a bed on crunchy dead leaves and fall asleep—allow Louisa to steal the rest she required for her babe to grow strong. Her sister might agree to the plan.

Yet Callie had taken on the role of the soldier. Slept beneath the sheltering arm of the Confederate army. Shirking her duties wasn't fair to the officers who relied on her, to her comrades who'd fight with her.

She rubbed the ache at her temples. What should she do?

The Federal army awaited north … the direction they headed. Yankees had abandoned several wagons in what appeared to be a headlong rush toward Franklin. She stepped over knapsacks, canteens, blankets, and other debris in the road. A soldier, laughing at a companion's joke, reached down for a bedroll and tossed it over his shoulder.

Soldiers all around her talked in a boisterous manner.

"We're gonna find them Yanks wherever they hide."

"They won't know what hit 'em."

"The pride of the South!"

Men cheered.

A band played "Dixie." Voices singing along almost drowned

out the instruments.

Zach leaned close to her ear. "Are you all right?"

Her shoulders curled inward, pulling into herself like a turtle. If only she could escape that easily. A shallow ditch along the road seemed a good place for her and her sister to hide until the fighting ended. "I don't know what to think." She looked at the faces around her—some stoic, some laughing, some singing. "I've never been more scared in all my life."

"Battles are fearsome, that's for certain." He rubbed his bearded jaw. "Been thinking ... about how you and Lou can avoid the whole thing."

With the lively singing, she struggled to hear his whispered words. His gaze bored into hers. If he meant to suggest that they confess to being women ... "No. We need shelter a while longer." Her married sister hadn't mentioned her future living arrangements yet. Callie had hoped to hear of Nate's plans to send Louisa and her back to his parents' home in Cageville. As far as she knew, they'd not discussed this possibility. That placed her in a tough position today.

They passed a wagon beside the road. The mules, still in their harnesses, had been shot. She shrank from the gruesome sight.

"You'll see worse if you don't find Lou and drop out to rest. You can rest a long time and then pretend to *lose* your way until after the fighting's done."

Exactly what she'd considered doing, yet somehow the spoken suggestion made it sound more dishonorable than it had in her thoughts. A silent soldier ahead of them walked with slumped shoulders. Did he wish to hide from the coming conflict as much as she? Could she live with herself if she shirked her duty? Her legs slowed as heaviness descended over her.

"Lou's feeling a mite better now." She stepped to the side to search for her. Zach followed. Louisa's face hadn't been as pale when she last saw her a few minutes ago, but she couldn't maintain the quick pace of the march. "S—he fell back a few rows with Nate.

I don't see them."

"Let's rest a minute. Let them catch up." They stood on the side of the country lane. "Pretty through here."

How could he think of the land's beauty at a time such as this? She barely raised her eyes to the green countryside before focusing her attention on passing soldiers. Where was her sister?

She stared into the faces of men passing by. She peered deeper, to the expressions masked by layers of grime from the fields on which they slept. Some men laughed and thumped their companions on the back as if their day held nothing more than hunting game. Some sang, loud and off-key, to the band's accompaniment of "The Girl I Left Behind Me." Others walked silently, clutching their muskets and staring at the trees ahead with trembling chins.

Their fright didn't relieve her fears, yet knowing many veteran soldiers feared the battle ahead while continuing to push on inspired her. Their courage strengthened her resolve. She wasn't the only one afraid to face what lay ahead. If they could march, resolute, toward their fate, then so could she.

"There they are." Zach pointed a few rows back.

Callie spotted Nate's tall form before she saw her sister, who walked slowly but with head held high. Good. Louisa's queasiness must have passed. They stepped off the lane and joined Callie and Zach, who waited underneath the barren branches of a maple tree.

"You're looking much better," Callie said to Louisa.

"I am. I feel better with each passing hour—ready to face what awaits."

"You don't have to. You can pretend to feel worse." Zach looked at Callie. "Cal can take you to the surgeons."

Callie pressed her lips together. Was anyone going to ask her opinion?

"That's not a bad idea," Nate said. "Plenty of folks noticed you feeling poorly the past few days."

Louisa stared up at her husband. "The unsettled feeling has passed." She turned to Callie. "I need to answer nature's call."

Callie nodded. The sisters needed a private conversation. "That copse of trees behind this field will give us privacy."

"We need it." She tilted her chin. "Will you men wait?"

The men exchanged a look. "We'll be here." Nate leaned against the tree and slid his back down the sturdy trunk.

Zach plopped on the ground beside him. "We'll talk when you get back."

"Yes, we will." Callie gave him a sideways glance before turning away.

Louisa set off for the trees. "We've hardly had a chance to talk since the wed—" She glanced at the crowded, noisy lane behind them. "Since that day at the church."

"A lot has happened in four days. I know you want to be with your husband every minute—"

"You'll understand some day."

Callie'd never know her sister's happiness—Zach hadn't fallen in love with her, despite her best efforts. "We only have a few minutes." She shoved her unhappiness away. "I don't want to accompany you to see the surgeons, but I think you should go without me."

"Not a chance, Sister. Where you go, I go. We're in this together."

Tears sprang to Callie's eyes. "I don't know how you feel, but I've thought about the battle ahead. Whether it happens today, tomorrow, or next week, I choose not to shirk my duty."

Louisa stared at her.

"The army sheltered us when we had nowhere to go. They've given us rations—"

"Such as they are." Louisa sighed.

"Exactly. Our brave soldiers fight for us on empty stomachs. Are we better than them?" Her resolve grew with every word. "How can we live with ourselves if we accept what the army has given us, and turn our backs when they need us the most?"

"I'm proud of you, Callie." A sheen of tears glistened in her eyes. "You've grown. You were always strong, but you're stronger now."

Warmth spread through Callie as they reached the shelter of the trees. "You were always the strong one."

"Not me." Louisa touched her stomach. "No, I'm the sister who chases adventure and fun. You're the one who follows your convictions. I admire you."

"Thank you." She thought of the fear that gripped her on the battlefield that previous evening. Even without firing on the enemy, she felt stronger for facing that hurdle. Her first battle—no, Zach had called it a skirmish. Either way, folks died. "I can't pretend to be sick or lost to avoid the battle. What if everyone did that?" Callie still didn't intend to shoot anyone, but no one needed to know. The smell of gunpowder reminded her that her musket was still loaded from being called into battle formation the previous evening. She hated the musket ball being inside the weapon, hated all it represented. Even so, her presence in the fight might encourage her comrades. She had to offer them that, at least.

"What stories we will tell our children and grandchildren. We can say that when enemies invaded our country, we fought for our land."

"Or squashed a tomato with our fingers when invading soldiers refused to pay what it was worth." Callie shook her head. "You scared me then, but, oh, I was proud of you."

"We didn't back down when things got tough for the South." Louisa grasped her hand. "Telling our children will make them strong, too."

"I've never been prouder of you." Callie hugged her. "My fiery, impulsive sister."

A tear slid down Louisa's cheek. "Even though a babe grew inside me before my wedding vows?"

"Nothing will ever change the way I love you." Callie met her sister's blue gaze squarely. "God blessed me with the best sister in the world."

"No, that's my blessing." Louisa hugged her again. "You're the best. Never forget it."

As they returned to the men. Callie's heart was full. It was good that they'd had this talk, that they'd cleared the air between them. If the worst happened in the battle to come … at least they'd made peace.

CHAPTER TWENTY-FIVE

Zach blew out a frustrated breath as he marched along the road to Franklin. Long strides had taken him far ahead of Nate and the sisters who insisted it was their duty to fight.

Duty.

It had been their duty to stay home where their father, no matter how drunk, would have fought to protect them.

He wiped sweat from his brow. Those girls had no idea what was coming. The chaos. Shouted orders. Bugles blaring. Cannons bursting shot and shell. Comrades you called friends dropping like swatted flies, to rise no more.

And today was a particularly bad day. He'd heard mutterings from passing soldiers while the girls talked—Hood was fit to be tied that the Federal army had fled north while the Southerners slept.

He couldn't figure it out either. How had those standing picket last night missed that much activity on the road? Wagon wheels squeaked. Horses neighed. Mules got stubborn and had to be coaxed to obey. How had the Northerners escaped detection? He figured that's what the officers wanted to know, Hood in particular. Now if only their leader's frustration and anger didn't lead to foolhardy decisions.

"Push on, boys." A group of civilians smiled at soldiers marching past from the side of the lane. "Them Yankees passed at a dead run not more than two hours ago."

That sounded promising. Discarded knapsacks and canteens on the road started to make sense. Recalling his manners, Zach tipped his hat at the ladies present.

"Don't worry, son." A stooped, gray-haired man patted his shoulder. "You'll capture them Yankees soon."

Soldiers within earshot cheered.

Zach nodded but couldn't manage a smile. The man meant to be encouraging.

"I'll wager there were more than a score of Yankee wagons abandoned on the roadside today." One soldier laughed.

"I counted four and thirty." Another said, joining the laughter.

"They're on the run."

"Run all the way to the Ohio River." One man punched his neighbor in the arm. That led to good-natured shoving.

Confederate soldiers filled the road as far as Zach could see. He scanned the horizon. Two hours. Yankees couldn't be too far ahead.

Cheatham's Corps trailed behind Stewart's Corps today, so it surprised Zach to reach the outskirts of Franklin in the lead. Stewart had taken a side route. Zach was well behind the first troops when he emerged into the open from a wooded lane.

"There were Yanks on those hills."

Zach stopped to listen to fellas from another regiment. His gaze followed the man's finger pointed at a pretty hillside lined with cedar trees. No sign of the Northerners now.

"We went into battle formation to whip up on the skirmishers and they left." Disappointment dripped from his tone.

"Without making a fight." A third man shook his head.

"Off to Franklin." The first swept his arm to the side.

Across a rolling, treeless river valley stood the town of Franklin on a hill. There were two lines of earthworks in advance of houses with blue-coated men scurrying around.

A well-fortified position.

Zach's heart dropped at the two-mile expanse of open fields

between his army and Franklin. If Hood ordered a frontal assault, they'd make easy targets for enemies behind the earthworks. Zach prayed his commander decided on a flank attack—right or left, he didn't care. Any way he looked at it, this was going to be a tough fight.

Once he explained to Callie what they were up against, he was certain she'd change her mind about fighting.

She must change her mind.

Callie hadn't enjoyed Nate's company this much since they'd mustered into the army. Nate must have set out to charm both her and Louisa, though he didn't have to labor to win Louisa's regard. He told tales of his early training, well before he was sent to meet with any Northerners on the battlefield.

"We were practicing Load in Nine Times one day." Nate grinned as he glanced at his audience, which by now included a couple of rows ahead of men who stopped talking and turned their heads toward him. "It was early days. No one was much good at hitting our practice targets. But not old Joe Sullivan—Sully, we called him. Well, Sully had just finished loading. He started to pick up his musket when it went off. Squirrel fell out of the tree over his head."

Callie almost choked on her laughter, which sounded far too feminine for her liking. Thankfully, the guffaws and shouts around her drowned her female giggles.

"The poor critter fell on the shoulder of the fella next to him."
More laughter.

"Sully got a new name. We called him Squirrely after that."
That set off another round of laughter.

Her uncontrollable giggles cleansed her of her heartache over Louisa losing out on Pa giving her away at her wedding, her worry that Nate didn't welcome her to live with them, and her sadness

A Musket in My Hands

that Zach didn't love her.

She hadn't laughed this hard since … since the Yankees invaded Tennessee. Part of her knew it wasn't Nate's story. It was the upcoming battle and the need to occupy her mind with something else. Anything else. The need to feel alive and normal, whatever that was anymore.

Zach appeared beside her, and her laughter died away. He'd huffed away two hours ago after failing to convince her to abandon the fight. It was now mid-afternoon. She'd hoped that his anger had cooled. His steely gaze suggested otherwise.

"Just got a glimpse of Franklin. This ain't gonna be pretty."

All her joy vanished. "Sorry to hear that." She ran a finger along her musket. Walking away wasn't fair to the others. He knew that. Why was he making this difficult for her?

Talking died down as they marched ahead on the hilly path.

"Change your mind yet?" He pushed his shoulders back. "This will be a hard fight for veteran soldiers."

"Which I'm not." He needn't throw her inadequacies in her face.

"No." His whispered tone was ruthless. "You're not. This is foolishness, plain and simple. You have the power to put a stop to it."

He was right. If she went to Sergeant Ogle and confessed that she and Louisa were sisters—not brothers as they'd claimed— he'd not allow them to participate in the battle. They'd be safe from Yankee bullets. On the other hand, they might be arrested or sent home. Either way, Callie lost her sanctuary. Her shelter. Her temporary home. "I can't do that," she whispered, "and lower your voice."

"Oh, don't think I'm not tempted to—"

She elbowed him as men fell silent. Did they guess her secret?

As she emerged from the wooded lane to a beautiful stretch of valley ahead, she understood all too well why the men stopped talking.

It wasn't to listen to her and Zach argue.

Beyond the valley lay a town on a hill. Fortified with military earthworks. The kind that soldiers hid behind during attacks.

Blue-coated soldiers stared at them from across the valley.

Blood rushed to her ears. As inexperienced as she was, she knew she'd rather be hiding behind the barricades than dashing across an open pasture with no fences in sight.

Zach was right. This wasn't going to be pretty.

Especially for a girl whose weapon must remain silent.

CHAPTER TWENTY-SIX

Callie cringed as color drained from Zach's face. She'd never seen him so shaken. They'd just been told that Cheatham's Corps—her corps—would lead a charge to the center. Their regiment was detailed as skirmishers.

His uneasiness was mirrored on nearly every face in her vicinity. She peered across a beautiful meadow to blue-clad soldiers guarding the town of Franklin. She covered her mouth with icy fingers.

One soldier strode over to a chaplain who stood beneath a tree a few feet from Callie. "Chaplain Davis, I'd be obliged if you'd hold onto my pocket watch while I'm in battle." He turned the man of God's hand palm up and placed a watch and chain on it. "If I don't return, send that to my wife for my little boy. It was my pa's …" he drew a shaky breath, "and I want my son to carry it when I'm gone."

Tears rose in Callie's eyes at the emotion in the soldier's voice. She didn't know the man, yet a terrible premonition washed over her that he'd never see his family again.

Others nearby rooted through knapsacks or scribbled on pages while Chaplain Davis prayed for him. Then, head bent low, the soldier walked away.

Another man gave up his Bible. Soon the chaplain's bag held two pocket watches, a ring, three journals, and two New Testaments. Chaplain Davis, eyes filled with grief, promised to send the precious items along, if necessary and prayed for each man.

What could she leave behind for Pa? He didn't know that his daughters mustered into the army. He'd probably searched every foot of territory within fifty miles of their home. *I'm back in Tennessee, Pa. You don't even know we left. It was wrong not to let you know sooner where we went, but I couldn't do as you asked.*

She longed to see him, hug him, ask his forgiveness for causing him to worry.

They might die today without Pa knowing what happened to them. That was wrong. What he did, he did out of love for his daughters, even though he should have asked, not demanded her compliance. He'd reacted to circumstances beyond his control.

She realized that she'd forgiven him somewhere along her journey. None of her anger remained—only compassion and the love of a daughter for her father.

Pa deserved to know the truth.

Jonesy sat nearby, leaning against a leafless tree, writing in his journal. "Jonesy, can you spare a piece of paper? I want to write my pa."

"A mighty fine idea." He smiled a little sadly as he ripped out a page. "Haven't seen you write to anyone. Wasn't certain you knew how."

"Perhaps I forgot for a little while." She accepted the torn page. "Mighty grateful for this."

He nodded. "You can borrow my pencil if you hurry. I'm writing to Benita. She's not far from here. I'm going to visit her when all this is over. Me and Spence plan to speak to Sarge about a furlough. Can't figure why he'd refuse."

"I can't either. Tell Benita I'd be pleased to make her acquaintance when this war is over."

"She'd like that. Now write your pa so's I can finish my letter."

She turned away and met Zach's gaze.

"Yes, that's a good idea, Cal. He'll be pleased to hear from you."

Callie glowed at the first genuine smile she'd received from Zach since their argument. He wouldn't ever be hers, but for this moment, she could almost let herself hope.

Zach's chest tightened as if a band of steel tried to cut off his air. If he'd gone to Sarge and exposed Callie's secret, she'd be safe. He'd have risked infuriating her if exposing her hadn't also left her homeless and without supplies. Until Nate made arrangements for both women to go back to Cageville, they needed this dangerous haven.

The best he could do now was try to keep her close.

"Stay beside me, even at this distance." They waited in a single line about ten paces apart, making them less easy targets. They were ready to cross a two-mile valley on the left side of Columbia pike as skirmishers to screen the major forces behind them. Yankees waited on the other side of the valley, protected by strong earthworks and barricades. This was madness. "Unless I tell you otherwise."

"I promise." Her brown eyes were huge in her pale, yet determined, face.

"Fire as you advance. Don't matter if you hit nothing." How he wished to save her from this day. "You'll probably get off two or three shots before the main line catches up."

Ashen faced, she looked toward the town on the hill.

"I'll try to watch over you." How did anyone believe she was a man with those beautiful eyes? He shook that thought away, shedding all weakness. "It takes courage to cross this field." He lowered his voice. "You won't be the only one to fall back."

"I won't be falling back." Her lips set in a mutinous line.

His sigh came from deep within. "Remember to shoot and reload as you go. We won't be alone out here too long."

She tucked a thick strand of auburn hair behind her ears. "I'll try to take comfort in that."

Zach looked over her head at Nate.

His cousin gave a tiny shrug of one shoulder. No sign of his earlier funny stories now. He met Zach's eyes squarely. When the signal came, they'd fix bayonets. They'd run across the field. Death might separate the cousins today.

Nate's serious gaze dropped to Louisa at his side and returned swiftly to him.

Zach nodded. If something happened to Nate, Zach would take care of his bride. He dropped his gaze just as swiftly to Callie and back. Nate gave a quick nod.

Good. That was settled. They turned to face the enemy, awaiting the signal.

Callie fixed her bayonet, which glinted in the late afternoon sunlight. The red sun dipped toward western hills, spreading a chill over her back. The quick approach of night must surely end the fighting, mustn't it?

A band behind her played "The Bonnie Blue Flag," sparking a patriotic flare in her soul. She couldn't have foreseen a year ago that she'd march into battle for her beloved South. Awe warred with trepidation in her spirit. If she died today, it was in service to her country. Zach needn't suffer any guilt over refusing to marry her. Pa's worry over feeding her disappeared. Nate's possible resentment of sheltering his wife's sister until she found work need never become a bone of contention between the couple.

If she didn't survive the battle.

But her sister must live for the wee babe growing inside her. For her husband.

Louisa gave her a curt nod. "We can do this. Remember all we've learned."

Zach gazed at Callie steadily. "Remember to pull the trigger. The Federals will remind you since they'll be shooting at you."

Her heart raced. Before she knew it, she was running with the rest, bayonets in the air.

No shots came from the hillside. Must be out of range.

Running toward them demanded all her courage.

Movement ahead. Rabbits scampered across the meadow.

Thousands of quail circled overhead, landed, and then took flight again.

A burst of artillery showered the soldiers from the hillside. Several yards away, men fell to the ground.

Breathing hard in a mixture of terror and dread, Callie paused when her comrades did.

"Forward, men!"

Callie joined her sister and the brave men running headlong into danger.

They were getting closer to where the Yankee army waited. Flashes came from the first line of earthworks in sheets of fire. Men near Callie fell, groaning and writhing in pain.

She stopped.

Zach grabbed her arm. "Drop or move. Standing still makes you a target."

She ran.

The main line caught up with them. It seemed to Callie that she'd been swallowed up by shouting soldiers behind her. Zach, Louisa, and Nate shifted until the four Cageville residents crossed the valley, quick time. They were together again.

Confederate bands played "Dixie" as Northerners in the first line of earthworks dashed for safety behind them. Southerners in the lead ran up the slope and crossed the main line with a loud, prolonged cheer. Bayonets flashed as men fought hand to hand.

Brave men stormed the earthworks and climbed out again as Northerners fled from the back. The sisters lost Zach and Nate in the melee. Callie's heart lodged in her throat.

Glinting bayonets. Flashes of gunfire.

"They're shooting at us. I see Zach." Callie grabbed her sister's hand. "Let's catch up with them." They lowered their heads and ran toward their men. She was glad when those before her fell back several steps.

Zach fired and reloaded as he pushed forward.

Bullets struck the ground beside them.

Muskets flashed all around her. Artillery behind her and in front of her raised a terrifying din.

Men screamed in agony. Others called for help. Bugles blared. Officers looked back, mouths moving as they shouted orders she couldn't hear. Nothing she'd learned in training had prepared her for this pandemonium.

"We're charging." Zach's face was a mask. Only his green eyes betrayed his turmoil.

Her voice failed her.

They followed those rushing toward the Yankee line. They stormed an earthwork. Callie was able to take a deep breath only when she found no Yankees still occupying the ditch.

Mayhem reigned. Cannons thundered. Amidst bullets whizzing past her ears, she searched for her sister, then ran to her side.

Louisa paused to aim, then a flash as she squeezed the trigger. Callie kept pace with her as Louisa slowed to reload.

Rapid fire pushed them back.

From several paces ahead, Zach turned back to her. "Some of our men are back in the earthworks we stormed over." He jerked his head toward the left. "Follow me."

She grabbed Louisa's hand. "This way. Nate!"

Nate looked toward them. Then he fired off one more shot before following.

A bullet struck the ground beside Callie's shoe as they ran to the ditch. She toppled inside, then stood with her back against the muddy wall. "What now?"

A bugle blast rose above the din.

"We stay here until we get new orders." A bullet struck the ground. Zach lowered his head. "Charging again is suicide. So is retreat."

She shivered.

"I'm sorry, Callie."

Her real name slipped out, but she doubted anyone heard over the boom of cannons, shells falling, and muskets firing.

"It's not your fault."

"I shouldn't have let you come. I knew it'd be a hard battle. Not like this. I've never seen such frenzied combat."

They'd meet God together today. Callie touched his arm, glad that her letter to Pa was safe in the chaplain's keeping. She didn't see any of them surviving this fight, this hell on earth.

Soldiers all around raised up to aim and fire then drop down to reload. Louisa didn't reload as quickly, yet she bravely stood to fire off another round.

Two men dropped to the ground, hands slackened on their muskets.

Callie gasped. The men had been her comrades.

Another stood. Shots took him down before he aimed.

"Louisa!" Callie tugged on her sister's coat. "Get down here. You'll be killed."

"Maybe." She shot. Then down on her knees again, she extracted a cartridge from the cartridge box on her belt. "My life isn't worth more than anyone else's. Our corps needs every soldier we can get."

Callie's cheeks burned. Her gaze fell to the unused weapon in her hand. "Think of your babe."

Gunpowder trickled down the barrel of Louisa's musket. Her hands trembled. "You're right. I'd risk my life. I won't risk my baby's." A groan. Another soldier fell. "But I must do something."

"Let's reload while Zach and Nate shoot. They can shoot twice as fast and they're better shots than us."

"Good idea."

Flashes of gunfire. Bullets struck the ditch.

Callie fought rising panic. This shelter wasn't much of sanctuary. Those flashes came from the right.

Reaching into his cartridge box, Zach squatted.

"Here, take mine." Callie exchanged her loaded weapon for his.

"Good idea. Reload mine, will you?" He squeezed her shoulder.

His touch revived her, released the hold of fear. "We'll be a team."

His troubled eyes sought hers. "Always." He stood and fired.

Callie tore cartridge paper with her teeth, gunpowder dusting her tongue with its acrid taste. She'd found a way to be useful.

A man fell with a thud down the line. He didn't move.

Bugles blared a frantic tune. What did it mean?

Shooting such as she'd never heard rained down bullets on her comrades. Would this nightmare never end?

If ever a situation warranted prayer, it was this one. She'd fallen out of the habit of praying. She hoped God didn't mind hearing from her after a dry spell. "God, please hear me. Save us. Protect Zach. Louisa. Nate. Me. Please, God. We need you."

The sky darkened as she rammed the next cartridge in place. Zach exchanged weapons with her, half-cocked his musket, then retrieved a percussion cap from his pouch.

They did this over and over as the battle raged.

Smoke settled over the ground, burning in her lungs. Bullets flew at them from the front, the right, and the left. How could anyone survive?

"Load faster." Zach raised his head to peek over the wall.

CHAPTER TWENTY-SEVEN

Callie replaced the ramrod in her weapon as Zach's musket flashed again. He thrust the gun toward her and grabbed her loaded one.

"Several blue coats coming this way." He bent down, shouting. Men's heads jerked toward him. "Hard to tell how many with the smoke. Everyone fire. Don't let them have our earthworks."

She poured gunpowder down the barrel and rammed the cartridge as everyone except her stood to fire. Folks fell back on the ground. Some before they'd taken their shot. Southerners fired then grabbed loaded weapons from dead companions.

Callie stood. Yankees shot into the ditch from several yards away. They couldn't miss at this range.

One took aim at Louisa.

Callie raised her musket and squeezed the trigger. The Yankee grabbed his arm and fell to the ground. She stared, unmoving, as the man rose and stumbled back to his line.

Louisa dragged her close to the wall. "I can't believe it. You saved my life."

Callie shook as if her bones would come apart.

"I'm proud of you." Louisa pulled her close. "One day I'll tell your nieces and nephews what a brave aunt they have."

Callie closed her eyes and saw again a blue kepi over a bearded face.

"Good job, Callie." Nate bent down. "Keep loading."

His command jolted her back to the shot and shell flying overhead. Gun smoke hovered over them in a thick haze. A bullet

A Musket in My Hands

struck a confederate soldier in a butternut uniform yards down the ditch. He slumped over his fallen comrades.

She wanted to run, to retreat back across that field she'd crossed, but she'd be cut down before taking three steps. She wanted to hide but there was no place to go. She wanted to scream, but terror blocked her throat.

Zach grabbed her by the shoulders and pressed his face close to hers. "Callie?"

She raised her head. Tried to focus.

"I've never been prouder of anyone. I'll keep shooting if you keep loading. Can you do that?"

Zach needed her. Her strength flooded back. She nodded.

"That's my girl." He brushed back her hair with a gentle hand.

"Your girl?" Her heart pounded. Leave it to Zach to wait to declare his feelings for a time like this.

"I—" He looked away.

A moaning soldier slumped against him.

Zach eased him to the ground.

Callie trembled as the stranger's eyes glazed.

His moaning ceased.

Her gaze flew to Zach's. "When will the killing stop?"

He shook his head and gave her his musket. "We must fight until a retreat is ordered. Or we die." He picked up the dead man's musket and tore a cartridge open with his teeth. "Pray that Hood comes to his senses before then."

Dozens of men lay wounded or dead in the darkening ditch, bodies piled on each other where they fell.

She mustn't look at that. This wasn't a fight against the enemy anymore. It was a fight for survival. She must focus on reloading.

She extracted a cartridge from her belt. Tasted the gritty gunpowder as she tore it open. She poured it inside the barrel and rammed it.

"Nate!"

She jerked around at Louisa's agonized scream. Nate lay on the ground, a red stain spreading across his shoulder. Louisa dropped to her knees, tears smearing the dirt on her face.

Callie rested her loaded musket against the wall as Zach rushed to his cousin's side. She crawled to her sister.

"Nate, old boy." Zach knelt beside him. "Look at me."

He opened pain-filled eyes. "What'd you hit me with?"

"It was them Yanks." Zach pushed back the tear in his cousin's coat. Brow creasing, he inspected the wound. His grin seemed forced. "I've seen worse. You'll be all right. There has to be a hospital set up behind the lines. We'll take you there."

"Can't." Nate panted. "Don't want Yanks making … target practice of us. We'll go when the shooting stops."

Zach studied Louisa's stricken expression. "He's right." His face turned grim as he met Callie's eyes. "It's too risky. Do what you can to bind the wound." He returned to the wall.

"Nate, my love." Louisa clasped his hand. "Don't leave me."

Callie met the wide-eyed stare of a soldier, his grimy face unrecognizable, reloading a few feet from her. His gaze dropped to Louisa holding Nate's hand. "Please don't give my sister away."

"Lady, I got bigger problems right now." He stood and fired off a shot.

Requesting Louisa restrain herself was out of the question. She'd care for her husband, no matter what.

Rust stains spread on Nate's coat. Callie had little experience in the sick room—and none with bullet wounds. How was she supposed to stanch the bleeding?

There was no fabric in her knapsack, which she'd left behind anyway. That was no help. If only she had her petticoat on. What was available? She touched her gray coat that was part of her Confederate uniform. She wore two blouses underneath for warmth. One could be torn into strips for bandages, but that meant removing it in front of all these men—immodest behavior even with another blouse and multiple layers underneath.

She glanced around. Everyone concentrated on shooting or

reloading. No one looked at her. Facing the wall, she removed her coat then pulled one blouse over her head while Louisa continued to sob.

Shivering, Callie donned her coat before ripping the white fabric into long strips. Then she leaned over Nate. "I'll be as gentle as I can, Nate. It's time we get that wound wrapped."

Men shouted. Bugles blared more orders. What did they mean?

"Do what you must." He didn't open his eyes.

She folded one long strip.

"Don't leave me. I'm nothing without you." Louisa put her cheek on his chest. "I hear your heartbeat. Please, God, let it keep beating. Heal my husband so he can live to be an old man."

A few heads whipped around at her odd behavior and then returned to their desperate reloading. They heard her sister appeal to their Maker on her husband's behalf. Their secret was revealed. Callie couldn't worry about that now. Placing the folded pad directly on the gaping wound, she quickly wound strips around it. She covered that with two additional strips, sending up a prayer that it stopped the bleeding.

Zach's weapon jammed. He tried to remove the percussion cap. It was wedged on tightly. Muttering, he laid it on the ground and picked up a dead man's musket.

Buglers blared out a rapid tune.

Nothing in Callie's life had prepared her for this terrible day. She returned her attention to her brother-in-law. No red stains on the strips. She didn't know what to do for him beyond bandaging the wound. Was it fatal? Had her sister married him only to watch him die?

Her heart ached for them. For Zach. Dusk had passed, making it difficult to see more than a few feet away. Where was Zach?

She crawled to where he had last stood. Men lay unmoving all around. *Please, God, don't let Zach be one of them.*

Zach could need help. He might have been shot while she tended his cousin. Steeling herself, she knelt beside an unmoving soldier.

Grasped his shoulder. Turned him. A mere schoolboy, not yet old enough to shave. His face was a peaceful mask. She prayed for his soul and then searched the surroundings.

No Zach. Most of the men who'd been shooting over the wall were gone. Where?

Louisa lifted Nate on his uninjured side. She raised a canteen to his lips.

Callie hunkered down and made her way back to them. "Nate, I can't find Zach." She touched his uninjured arm. "Where is he?"

He opened his eyes. "Don't look for him. I hear … bayonets." He closed his eyes. "Hand … to hand combat. Stay here. Can't do … anything … for him now."

Horror poured over her and the sounds she'd ignored broke through her panic. Blades slammed against blades not far from their position. Rifles flashed like a thousand fireflies and lit the darkness.

She grabbed her ears to drown out the noise.

No use. Her hands only muffled it.

Angry shouts. Bugles blared. Drummers beat out orders. Shot and shell screeched through the air.

Earth and heaven met in a mighty uproar.

Zach and others had left their only sanctuary in the midst of this firestorm.

God, save him. The cry came from her soul.

Satan must be laughing with delight for hell had come to earth.

CHAPTER TWENTY-EIGHT

Men dashed toward them from behind. Callie was glad to see soldiers in gray and butternut pour into her earthworks from the rear.

"Forward, men!"

They grimly followed their officer's orders, and Callie was relieved to see it. Zach and the others from her brigade needed reinforcements. She and her sister knelt over Nate in the onslaught to protect him from stampeding feet.

Passing soldiers bumped into her, stepped on her legs, her feet. Wincing, she drew her legs up and tucked her feet close. The men went over the side.

A fallen man groaned down the line. "Water."

Callie, keeping her head down, crossed the pit toward the stranger. Red blotches stained his coat at the waist. "Can I help you, soldier?"

"Name's Johnny." He licked dry lips. "I have a powerful thirst."

"My name is Cal. I have some water left." She lifted her canteen to his mouth.

He downed half her reserved water before she lifted the mouthpiece. "Much obliged. Think you can do something to stop my wound from bleeding?"

She tried not to frown. She had a few long strips left but had planned to save them in case Za—one of her loved ones needed it. This man needed help now. He was all alone. "I have a small roll of bandages. No medicine for the pain."

"Please. Bind my wound." Brown eyes pleaded with her from

a grimy face.

"Let me see it." She pushed aside his coat and red underclothes to peer at a ragged wound. She swallowed her queasiness. "I will." She extracted the bandages from her sleeve where she had stored it.

He groaned as she shifted him to wrap the bandages around his body. Binding the wound required all the fabric.

"Much obliged, Cal." He gestured to a dead soldier on his right. "Harve here has a canteen around his neck. Can you get it for me?"

Rob a dead man? Johnny demanded too much.

Or did he? These were desperate times. Water only had value for the living.

She forced herself to crawl to Harve, recognizing the man who had yelled at her for walking too slowly on her first march. He didn't deserve this end. Her hands shook as she lifted his head to disengage the strap. She laid the canteen on Johnny's chest and ran back to Louisa before he requested something else that cost too much.

Other wounded cried out in pain.

She prayed for them. For Zach, who returned before she ended her prayer.

He dropped into the ditch and then squatted low as he walked toward them. "Situation's hot out there. Ain't never seen nothing like it. No one's seen Sarge, Corporal Morefield, or any of our officers."

Nate opened his eyes. "For how long?"

"Too long." Zach spat the words out. "I don't like the looks of this battle. It's cost us too many good men."

Callie's heart went cold. Corporal Morefield, Sergeant Ogle … dead? Her head whirled.

Comrades poured into the earthworks.

"Forward, men!"

A Rebel yell reverberated the earthworks as soldiers, bayonets fixed, passed through.

Zach gave a slight shake of his head and grabbed his rifle.

His tormented gaze met Callie's. Then, joining the Rebel yell, he followed the tide of gray and butternut over the wall again.

"No! Don't go." Callie stared at Zach's back as he vaulted the wall. He took a terrible chance with his life every time he left. They all did.

"Nate, don't leave me." Louisa held her husband's hand, sandwiched between her own. "We've only begun our life together. Live."

He opened his eyes. "Can't a man take a nap?" The corners of his mouth turned up.

"In this din?" She kissed his hand. "If you can sleep amidst all this noise …"

"Don't mind if I do." An irrepressible twinkle had returned to his blue eyes. "Try not to worry. I'll be fine once a surgeon sees to my wound."

She nodded.

Callie turned her gaze to the smoky ground above them. She clutched her throat at the clash of steel against steel. Nate was as comfortable as loving companions could make him under the circumstances, but Zach wasn't safe. He was out there in hand-to-hand combat. Why hadn't he come back by now?

She picked up a loaded musket. Creeping to the wall, she raised her head over the embankment. Darkness hadn't yet descended to hide the tragedy unfolding before her. Her stomach lurched at the sight of men fighting each other while their comrades—blue and gray alike—littered the field.

Mustn't think about that. Focus on Zach. Where was he?

A bullet struck the mud two feet from her face. Gasping, she ducked her head. Heart beating wildly, she raised it again. Peering through the smoke, she saw Zach as a man struck his face with the butt of his rifle.

The blow loosened Zach's grip on his musket. He fell to his knees, half-facing the trench where Callie hid. As he made to rise, the soldier in blue raised his rifle once more.

"No!" Callie lifted her musket and fired.

The Yankee soldier yelled. Dropping his musket, he clutched his elbow.

"Zach!" Callie met his gaze, smoke still rising from her weapon. "Retreat!"

Grabbing his musket, he ran to her. Dropping over the side, he leaned against solid earth. Sides heaving, he looked over at her. "Did you shoot that Yankee?"

She gave a slow nod. "He was going to smash your head with his rifle."

"I know. You saved my life." He pulled her in for an embrace.

Trembling, she touched his bruised face.

He winced. "I'll likely be sore 'til Christmas. At least I'll be alive to celebrate it now—thanks to you."

Tears filled her eyes, spilled down her cheeks. Zach had almost died in this horrid battle. What premonition had prompted her to risk her life to search for him through the haze?

Spence and Jonesy tumbled over the wall, along with a scant handful of others. Far too few.

Zach released Callie.

She moved away and swiped at her cheeks with her sleeve, suddenly hating her pretense. She wasn't a man and no longer wanted to masquerade as one.

"Never saw such a frenzy." Jonesy's eyes were wide as he sank onto the ground next to a fallen comrade.

"No more charges for me." Spence dropped as if dead on his feet near Zach. "I'd not survive another one."

"Agreed." Zach touched the bruised welt across his cheek. "This is madness."

She met Zach's gaze. "I agree."

A bugler played a frantic tune, possibly ordering another

charge. None of the men moved.

The day's warmth had turned into a bitter night. Smoke and the black of night hid Callie's companions from her. Buglers played orders she didn't understand. Officers shouted orders snatched away by shot and shell.

Zach had not left the earthworks again, for which she was grateful. He sat beside Callie around Nate to keep the patient as warm as possible.

Spence and Jonesy stayed with them. She was as relieved to have them near as if they were family. They'd explained that they'd been separated from their regiment in the original charge.

The battle still raged in front of them. Every now and then, a nearby soldier groaned in response to flashes of musketry. Another bullet somehow found its mark. Zach had warned them not to talk or move. Those aiming for them might see the movement and shoot.

Nate ran a fever, though the frosty night might be enough to lower that. Louisa, who had confessed to queasiness not due to the grisly sights around them, lay with her head against his chest on his uninjured side. They had no way to warm him, no place to move him out of the wintry night air.

Callie shivered. No blankets to warm anyone—those lay with the rest of their belongings in the rear of the army.

The Southern town was under the control of the North. Undoubtedly there were citizens hiding in Franklin homes who were willing to take in a wounded Southerner. Help was so near, yet they could not carry Nate there. There was no medicine to relieve his pain.

The married couple hadn't moved. Callie hoped Nate was asleep and not unconscious. A man groaned, reminding her of the many wounded. She couldn't help them, couldn't even offer a drink from her empty canteen.

Shooting became sporadic.

She hadn't realized that the roar of battle had masked the prayers of men until the shooting stopped. Each of their prayers, cries, and groans physically hurt her. Their entreaties haunted her.

"Help. Somebody, help me, please." The voice came from her right.

"I need water. For the love of all that's holy, someone give me a drink of water." This soldier lay in the yard.

"Ma, pray me home and I'll never stray from the straight and narrow path again." Callie's heart broke at the whimper in a boy's voice.

"I'm bleeding to death. Won't someone help me?"

"Mama, please pray for me."

"God, please deliver me from my pain. It hurts so bad. I'm ready to go now if it's my time."

These voices, and so many more, cried for deliverance from their agony. Tears coursed down Callie's cheeks as she prayed for the wounded, the dying. The walls of the cold pit closed in around her, trapped her beside her injured brother-in-law—she'd never been so miserable in all her life. "Callie? You all right?" Zach clasped her hand.

"I'm freezing." His hand was just as cold as hers. Since he wasn't made of stone, he was likely as affected by the injured men's moaning as she. "I feel like I'm living a nightmare."

"You are," he whispered. He dropped her hand. Putting an arm around her, he drew her close. "We all are. A few have decided to escape to the rear under cover of darkness. Some will make it to safety."

"Can we try?"

"No. When folks escape, it draws enemy fire. Nate can't run, and we can't run and carry him at the same time. At least, not without harming him."

They'd have to run two miles, maybe more. In their exhaustion, even if Spence and Jonesy helped, they'd never be able to run that far carrying Nate.

"Sleep if you can. It's the only deliverance until morning."

He had to be as cold as she, yet his body warmed her. She snuggled against him with her head on his chest with only a passing thought for the impropriety. They were chaperoned by no less than one hundred men and the night was so cold. "Only if you fall asleep too."

"I'll try." He held her with both arms now. "Close your eyes, my sweet, brave Callie."

That sounded nice. Did his words hold a deeper caring? His embrace felt like heaven after the day's torment. She closed her eyes, too tired to think. The fighting was done until morning. For now—and perhaps for the last time—she was safe in Zach's arms.

CHAPTER TWENTY-NINE

Thunder awakened Zach in the middle of the night. No, not thunder. Artillery. Cannons from his side of the lines blasted toward town.

Shells whizzed through the air and then shook the earth. No one had come by with orders. Had the Federals scurried away after the battle?

Zach hoped so, but best to find out. If the enemy had fled Franklin, maybe a kind Southern woman would make room for Nate in her house. His cousin needed to be out of the frigid air.

He glanced down at the woman sleeping against his chest. Despite his exhaustion, his misery over his dead comrades, and his anger at General Hood for ordering the slaughter, holding Callie while she slept had given him the most peaceful, sweetest sleep he'd ever known.

But it was time to see to Nate's wounds.

Making small shifts to the left, Zach slid away from her, holding her head while he guided it to the embankment.

He stood and peered into the field in front of them. A fire blazed in the distance. The Federals must have abandoned the town and torched some buildings.

Shadows bent over men lying on the field that had been so treacherous hours ago. Some looked for loved ones. With so many barefoot, poorly-clad soldiers, others searched for shoes, socks, pants.

He knelt beside his cousin. "Nate? You awake?"

He groaned. "How can a ... soldier sleep ... with all that

cannonading?"

The complaint heartened him. Nate wasn't too ill to respond to the fearsome noise they'd grown far too accustomed to. "How's your shoulder?"

"Burns like blazes."

"Figured."

"Hospitals must be set up in the rear by now. Can't walk that far." He panted for breath while the artillery continued. "Will you carry me?"

"You know I will." They'd been through thick and thin. There was no question of abandoning him. "But I've got another plan."

"What?" He lifted his head and peered around.

A freezing draft swept the earthworks. "Franklin homes are closer. There's movement in the yard, but most are still holed in ditches. That means that every house may not be filled yet. Or we'll find a barn." He shivered. "Any shelter that will get you and the girls out of this wind."

"Sounds best." He rested his head on the ground again. "Hurry back."

"That I will. Sleep if you can." He gave his cousin an awkward pat on the hand. A glance at Callie showed she still slept, even with the roar of cannons. His brave girl was exhausted.

They all were. He'd taken part of so many charges yesterday that he'd lost count. They'd used muskets as clubs against each other. That last frenzied fight had convinced him he'd not survive another charge. He touched his sore face. There'd have been no surviving that one if Callie hadn't shot that Yankee. The soldier she shot would live—with his shooting arm out of commission.

He'd been so worried she'd not defend herself. His steps faltered. He reckoned she hadn't shot to defend herself … just him and Louisa.

He gazed at Callie, still sleeping on the cold ground. She grew more precious to him every day. His gaze traveled to his cousin, who still needed his wound tended.

Zach hefted himself from the ditch. The distant fire gave him more a frame of reference for the shot and shell overshooting the town than light for his path. He'd take care to stay well to the side of the artillery. A better plan was to wait until the cannons stopped, but Nate needed shelter. He'd tarried long enough.

The only favor the cold wind had done the soldiers was dissipating some of the gun haze that had clung to the earth. The moon and stars dimly lit the yard.

His heart faltered at the carnage.

Both sides had lost many men in this area, so many that he had to place his feet carefully to avoid stepping on them. Far greater numbers of men wearing gray or butternut than soldiers in blue.

He had seen far too many sights not fit for humanity since he mustered into the army … but nothing compared to this tragic scene. The stench of death clung to the earth.

The cold wasn't the reason for shudders that wracked his body. If there had been anything in his stomach, he'd have lost it.

He approached a man bending over a body. "Who is it, soldier?"

"My brother." Tears glistened on his dirty face. "Died in one of the charges."

"I'm sorry." Zach squatted beside him. "How did you escape his fate?"

"I went on the first charge. I was too skeered to go back." He lowered his head. "But not Jeb. Not my big brother."

"What's your name?" Zach peered down at the dead soldier, barely more than a boy.

"Josiah."

"How old are you, Josiah?"

"Fourteen." He swiped at his nose. "Jeb was a year older than me."

Mere boys who should have had their whole lives ahead of them.

"Them Yanks retreated. The town's ours." He stared at his brother. "Jeb'd be happy to know we run them off."

"Yep. You can tell your folks at home how brave Jeb was. Any soldier who charged that dangerous field even once is a courageous man. Like you, Josiah."

The boy's head remained bowed, but he raised tormented eyes to him.

Zach had never hated this blasted war more. The Federals were likely on the road to a more fortified city ... Nashville. Josiah needed every scrap of comfort he could muster—Zach refused to steal it away. "Why don't you see about burying your brother and then go home to tell your family the news?"

He had no authority to grant a furlough. Even the suggestion was wrong ... but so was this youngster's presence in the army after today.

"Mebbe I will."

The boy's agonized grief seeped into Zach's soul. Why had he imagined he'd make a difference in this fight for Southern citizens to become a sovereign nation, for the right to govern themselves?

He had fooled himself. He'd leave, take Callie back to Cageville himself. She'd be safe ... but he'd be the quitter his dad had always accused him of. His chin sank to his chest. He couldn't bear for his father's words to be true, yet he had to ensure that Callie'd seen her last battle.

Josiah's sobs pierced his soul. The South had lost too many fine men, soldiers cut down in their prime. They'd lost this battle, and they were losing the war.

Zach stepped carefully back toward the ditch. The sky lightened, but it was not yet dawn. More folks walked among the town and the dead than had an hour ago when he'd met the grieving boy. He peered around the field. Josiah was gone.

Maybe he'd dug that grave for his brother. Zach's mouth tightened against the cruelty of war.

His mission had been successful. He'd met a young boy exploring the battle scene. Davy Ross, no more than ten years old, took him to his home. Mrs. Ross extended a warm welcome. She'd prepare a pallet on the floor for Nate and breakfast for all of them while he fetched his injured cousin.

His stomach grumbled. None of them had eaten since breakfast at Spring Hill. Though only a day had passed, that hill seemed a lifetime away.

No one could pry Louisa from Nate's side, so Zach didn't worry about her safety. Callie was another story. If yesterday's battle didn't convince her that the army wasn't a safe haven, he'd allow the walk to the Ross home to finish the job.

He untied a bedroll off the back of a dead Yankee. And then snatched up another. Good. He needed these. When the wagons would bring their supplies was anybody's guess. He'd search through more abandoned items later for what he needed.

Sobs coming from the earthworks hastened his steps. Was that Callie? Oh, no, Nate.

Zach lowered himself into the ditch where he'd spent too many hours. He placed a blanket over Nate. His relief that his cousin was still alive soon turned to shock. Nate's head was turned toward where Callie sat with Spence a few feet away. She knelt in front of a soldier.

Head propped against the earthen wall, Jonesy lay unmoving, A tear in the chest of his jacket bore mute witness to his fate—a bullet to the heart. His hands still cradled the journal he'd so loved.

"It happened in the wee hours." A tear dripped from Spence's cheek as he looked up at Zach. "Must've been one of those shots when we were all trying not to move. Maybe he reached for his journal. He was always writing in that thing."

Jonesy dead? Zach reeled. They'd marched together. Stood picket together. Eaten what seemed a lifetime of meals together. He always figured they'd made it so far that they'd end the war together. His throat tightened.

It was not to be.

"He was so good to me." Callie's sobs broke through his shock. "Always told me the truth about what to expect."

Zach placed a blanket around her shaking shoulders, forcing his hands not to linger.

"He was as good as they come," Spence said. "A true friend to me since we were schoolboys."

Zach knelt. Put his hand on Callie's arm. No way to shelter her from this sorrow.

"He planned to marry Benita when this war ended." Spence swiped at his cheeks with the back of his hand. "I'll take him to her. We'll bury him in the churchyard. Then I may come back to finish this fight." He pushed himself to his feet. "And I may not. I'm gonna have to think on it."

Nodding, Zach stood. Lots of folks might hightail it out of here after yesterday's slaughter. He wanted to quit, too. He'd have to see to Callie's well-being before making that decision "Will you help me carry Nate to the Ross home in Franklin? Mrs. Ross is preparing breakfast for us right now."

"I will." Spence stared down at his friend. "And I'll be obliged for the meal. But don't look for me after that. I'm heading home."

"I understand." Zach clasped his shoulder. "More than you know."

CHAPTER THIRTY

Sunshine lit the eastern horizon. Callie climbed out of the pit and then wished she'd stayed where she was.

Dead and dying covered the field before her. This was the area they'd been ordered to charge. Repeatedly. She was grateful she'd only obeyed the order the first time otherwise she'd be lying dead on this field with all the rest.

The horror washed over her as her gaze bounced from one prone soldier to the next. Such human devastation had to be abnormal. How did soldiers find the heart to continue fighting? And why?

"Girls, you haven't seen such sights as you are about to see." Zach's tone was hushed. "Nor will you ever see them again, if I have anything to say about it."

"This is rough on all of us." Spence's strong hand descended on Callie's shoulder. He made no comment about Zach calling them girls. "This being your first battle, it's bound to hit you hard. No one will blame you if you walk this field with your eyes closed."

"Hold on to your end of the blanket, and we'll get Nate's wound tended." Zach gave Callie a slow nod. "You can do this. For Nate."

"For Nate," Louisa whispered.

The men bore the greatest weight with Nate's head and upper body. The women each had a corner of the blanket by his feet.

"Ready?" Zach looked back at them.

No. "Yes." Callie followed her sister's lead and fixed her eyes on Nate's face.

A Musket in My Hands

The single-story brick home Zach led them to was filled with soldiers in gray and butternut. The smell of fresh cornbread greeted them, making her stomach flip. Callie hadn't eaten since this time yesterday and wondered if she could eat at all after what they'd just walked through.

Her sister was as pale as Nate.

A blond-haired woman ten years Callie's senior ushered them through the door. "How glad I am you finally made it. Oh, my gracious—his bandages need attention. This way, gentlemen."

A dozen soldiers ate, standing, in her front parlor. Two more flattened themselves against floral wallpaper in the hall while they passed.

Callie's gaze strayed to the blazing warmth of the parlor's crackling fire. After spending months in the open air, the home welcomed her like a mother's hug.

"I'm Mrs. Ross." The lady spoke over her shoulder. "I managed to save a pallet for your friend. Gracious me, if my house didn't fill as soon as I opened the door this morning—both around the table and my son's bedroom." She led them into a room on the left. There was one wounded man sleeping on the bed and two others on the floor. Mrs. Ross pointed to a blanket on the floor. "Lay him there. What did you say his name was?"

"Nate McClary," Nate spoke for himself.

Callie wondered how he got a word in edgewise. This woman loved to talk.

"Pleased to make your acquaintance, Nate." Smiling, she gave a small curtsy. "Let's just dispense with the formality for I'll never remember your name otherwise. And it's a pleasure to meet all of you brave soldiers as well, though don't bother to tell me your names." She held up her hand. "My brain can't catch up with all the names I've heard so far. Well, there's cornbread and coffee in the kitchen, though you'll have to share a cup. Come in after you get Nate settled."

"Mrs. Ross?" Callie followed her into the hallway. She raised her voice to be heard over several conversations in the parlor and surrounding rooms. "May I speak with you?"

"Of course. I always have time for the brave men who serve our country so nobly." The hospitable woman smiled though her gaze darted toward the back of the house.

She rubbed her forehead. Should she do this? How else could she ensure that Louisa got to stay here with her husband? "Mrs. Ross, I have a confession. I mustered into the army as Cal Shaw, but that's not my real name."

Mrs. Ross blinked. "Cal, that hardly concerns me—"

"My real name is Callie Jennings. I'm a woman."

Mrs. Ross's eyes dropped to Callie's soldier's garb.

Louisa stepped into the hall.

"My sister and I joined the army as brothers. Her name is Louisa McClary. She is Nate's wife." No need to mention the duration of the marriage.

"Oh, so you joined to be near your husband." She covered her mouth with her hands. "That's the most romantic story I've ever heard."

"I'd like to stay in your home to care for him if you don't mind." Louisa spoke normally for the first time in a long while. "And my sister and I will help tend the other wounded."

"Well, don't that beat all. I've heard everything now. Who'd have thought there'd be two sisters posing as soldiers—and one of them married to another soldier." Her gaze darted from one to the other. "I reckon the two of you can sleep on my bedroom floor while your husband needs care. Besides, it's far too cold for ladies to be sleeping outside."

"Yes, ma'am." It was far too cold for undernourished, exhausted men to sleep outside either. Callie kept this observation to herself. "My sister and I are much obliged to you."

"You girls are mighty thin, but I'll loan you both a dress. 'Twon't matter a bit if they are big on you."

Peace washed over Callie. The stress of pretending to be a man and a soldier were behind her. What heaven to wear a dress again. "We're beholden to you, Mrs. Ross."

"Will one of you come help me in the kitchen when you've finished breakfast?" Her gaze darted to the back of the house. "I didn't know there'd be so many."

"I'll be happy to help." Callie smiled at her hostess's fleeing back.

Zach stood at the bedroom door with Spence, hardly believing his own ears. He had prepared himself to argue with Callie about her staying in Franklin. A weight slid from his shoulders. He'd been ready to escort her to Cageville himself. The kindness of a stranger made that unnecessary. He'd hardly dared to hope she'd don a dress again.

"Want me to get you all a piece of cornbread?" Spence raised his eyebrows at Zach and then at the ladies.

"I'll go with you." Louisa and Spence hurried after Mrs. Ross.

Callie's huge brown eyes met his. "Looks like I'm done being a soldier."

"Hallelujah." Zach gave a shaky laugh. "You did the right thing."

"I know." She lowered her voice. "I didn't want to take a chance on Louisa losing the baby."

Raising his eyebrows, he blinked at her. How much did she think these poor battered soldiers within earshot could take? "Don't speak of that now," he whispered. "I'm just happy all three of you will be safe. But you'll have to hide Nate if the Yankees come back to Franklin."

She swallowed. "I will."

Spence and Louisa brought cornbread and one cup of coffee into the hall. They distributed the bread. Louisa went inside the bedroom with two pieces.

"There's more coffee." Spence drank a long swallow. "We just have to go back and refill the cup. How I wish I had my knapsack."

"Here." Callie extended her hand for the cup. "I'll refill it." She disappeared through the door at the end of the hall.

"Want to go find another knapsack?" Zach hated taking possessions from dead men though he reasoned they didn't need it any longer.

"Yep." Crumbs tumbled down Spence's bearded chin as he bit into the cornbread. "Tasty."

Zach finished his before Callie returned with a steaming cup.

"I drank mine first." She smiled up at him.

"Did you now?" He fought the urge to grab her and kiss her. "Can you share that one with me then?"

"Of course." Dimpling, she gave him the cup.

"Much obliged." He lifted it in salute.

She curtsied. "My, that feels good."

He had a hankering to see her curtsy in a dress again. "What does?" He quirked an eyebrow.

"To curtsy as a woman again."

Spence cleared his throat. "I'll wait outside for you, Zach. I hope to see you again one day, Callie Jennings."

"And I hope the same. Godspeed, Spence."

He tipped his hat. Then he strode out into the cold, shutting the front door behind him.

Callie stared at the closed door. "He didn't seem surprised."

"He didn't." How long had Spence suspected? Zach drained the cup. "I have to go. Discover what happened to our officers … our comrades." Make decisions. He sighed. "Learn of any orders."

She studied his expression. "If those are marching orders, come back before you go."

"I promise." The urge to kiss her was back, stronger than ever. He tore his gaze from hers. He'd lingered too long. Put his hand on the doorknob. "Callie?"

"Yes?"

"Can you put on that dress before I get back?"

CHAPTER THIRTY-ONE

"You knew." Zach headed to the field beside Spence.

"Yep. Jonesy figured it out first." Sunlight fell on Spence's face. "Then I saw it, plain as day. You were the one to give the secret away."

"Me?" He'd agonized over the girls betraying their femininity in the actions, and he was the one who gave it away? "How?"

"You were always looking at her. You've been protective of raw recruits until they gained experience, but this was different."

He thought he'd done a better job controlling his emotions, his worry for her safety.

"Jonesy told me before we crossed the Tennessee River."

"That long ago? And you didn't expose their secret?"

"Nope. Wasn't none of my affair. It wasn't like they didn't pull their weight. Don't know why I didn't see it right off. They're both as pretty as a painting."

The girls *had* learned faster than some recruits. "I'm obliged to you for not speaking up."

"I know you are," Spence smirked.

"What do you mean?"

"You're in love with Callie."

Zach's steps faltered. "What do you mean?"

"Well, I've never seen you hold another man."

"You saw that?"

"I heard you talking, too."

"It was so cold." He ran a finger under his high collar.

"You ain't telling me nothin' I don't know. I shook my canteen to keep ice from forming."

"This is all my fault. I've tried to protect her. Them. And didn't do a good job of it."

"Not certain she feels that way." The grin left Spence's face. "Bout time you made an honest woman of her."

Zach halted. "I beg your pardon. Callie's a lady."

"I believe you." Spence faced him. "Others might not. You know how people talk."

"What do you mean?"

"Look, man. She bivouacked surrounded by hundreds—nay thousands—of men who aren't her family. What do you expect people will think?"

"That they acted honorably as soldiers." The back of his neck heated up. "And this from a friend."

"I'm saying it *because* I'm a friend." Spence took a step back. "Look, there are so many dead and wounded that everyone will just imagine they were killed when they don't join the march."

Spence raised valid arguments, on all scores. "You're right. No one will look for the Shaw brothers to be wearing dresses and living as Franklin citizens."

"That's what I'm saying."

"I'd marry her if the army wasn't my life now."

"Do you love her?"

His mouth went dry. Did he love her? After fighting his feelings for months, he didn't know what they were.

Zach reached the battlefield and helped Spence gather what he needed. Bruised and battered men walked among the dead. Some knelt, weeping as they recognized a friend.

Spence halted. "No." He stared down at a dead soldier.

Zach steeled himself against the grief on his friend's face before looking down. "Not Ben." His own voice sounded faint. "Corporal

Ben Morefield. He was a good soldier. A good man."

"We lost sight of him after that first charge." Spence sighed deeply. "He must have fallen early in the battle. And there's Sarge."

Zach's grief intensified. He squatted beside Sergeant Ogle's unmoving body. "Chest wound. Brave man. His family needs him." He bowed his head. "His oldest child is about ten."

"He lived fifteen miles from Jonesy. I'll ride out and tell his family once we bury Jonesy." Spence shook his head. "Wish I could take them both home, but I'll be dragging my best friend along on a blanket as it is."

Zach stood and grasped Spence's forearm. "These are desperate times we live in. We all do the best we can."

"Ain't it the truth." He slung a bedroll over his shoulder. "I'm afraid to tarry. Don't want to hear any orders. If I don't know our orders, I can honestly say so when—and if—I return. Will you bury Ben and Sarge?"

"I'll see to it." A weight descended on Zach's chest. Tough times, indeed.

"I'd stay and help, but I feel a powerful hankerin' to get Jonesy home."

"I know. Do what you must."

Spence scanned the dead in the field. "'Bout had a stomach full of this accursed war. You stayin' in?"

"Trying to decide. I'm a soldier." Zach straightened his shoulders. "Hate to quit when I made a promise to stay 'til the fighting's done."

"Jonesy made the same promise."

"And he kept it." He shook Spence's hand. "Good luck to you. I'll see you again, Good Lord willing."

"There'll always be a chair on my porch for you. Keep your head down." With that, Spence headed to the ditch.

Left on his own, Zach's shoulders slumped. Their men had been ordered to take this town against all hazards. They'd sacrificed their lives. Men cut down in their prime. For what?

Anger and sadness threatened to slay him alive—he pushed the feelings aside. He had too much to do. He'd have to find comrades from his regiment, bury his officers, and find personal necessities on the field.

Folks nearby were searching the bodies. If he didn't hurry, he might not find what he needed. He tossed two Yankee bedrolls over his shoulder. Good start.

Plenty of filled cartridge boxes remained on the dead soldiers. He replenished his stock of cartridges and percussion caps. A stray knapsack contained clean clothing—shirt, drawers, candles, and two pairs of thick socks. A Bible and a packet of letters were also tucked inside. He fingered the letters. When he could, he'd return them to the sender.

He dropped to the ground and exchanged his dirty socks for both pairs he'd picked up. The added warmth on his cold feet brought little comfort amongst the carnage. He crammed the dirty pair into the knapsack for laundering. His shoes were still in decent shape, but if they did a lot of marching, he'd need another pair soon. Still, he balked at removing clothing and shoes from dead soldiers.

Many dead Yankees had been stripped of everything but shirts and drawers. Though he hated this aspect of war, he understood. Many of his comrades froze in tattered clothes. Tied rags on their bare feet to keep warm. They needed the shoes, the coats, the socks.

The wind blew up the back of his coat. It was cold already, and the worst part of winter was yet to come. Too bad he hadn't found an overcoat.

Knapsack on his back, he retrieved his musket from the ditch. He recognized some folks from his regiment wandering the field they'd crossed as skirmishers yesterday afternoon, a lifetime ago.

Dreading to tell them about Ben and Sarge, he picked his way over to them.

Sam looked at him with tormented eyes. "Did you hear? We lost General Cleburne."

"Truly?" They'd lost the best division general in Army of Tennessee? "That's a hard blow for us."

"It is." Johnny, their bugler, stared toward the town. "They put his body in the same ambulance with General Adams'."

"General Adams is dead, too?" General Stewart would miss a man like Adams.

"And General Strahl." Sam scrubbed his dirty beard with an equally dirty hand. "General Granbury."

"All dead?" At Sam's nod, Zach staggered back a step. "How about General Brown?" They needed their division leader more than ever.

"Wounded. Don't know how bad. General Gordon was captured."

The news kept getting worse. He swiped sweat from his forehead despite the cold. "How about the leader of our brigade? Is John Carter among the living?"

Sam looked at Johnny, whose job as bugler kept him in close proximity to officers.

"Last I heard. He's wounded, too. Heard it was pretty bad."

"General States Rights Gist was hit, too. Don't know if he lived." Sam said.

Johnny shook his head. "Don't think so."

The earth spun beneath Zach's feet. How could their army recover from such catastrophic losses? "I've got bad news, too."

Sam looked at him with dead eyes.

"Spence and I found Corporal Morefield and Sergeant Ogle in the field between the earthworks and the Yankee line." He drew a shaky breath. "Dead."

Sam half-turned from him. "Did you bury them yet?"

He shook his head. "We'll need to see to it." He hesitated. "Jonesy didn't make it."

Sam's shoulders stooped.

"Spence is taking him home to Benita. They'll bury him in the church where they all attended services."

Horses approached. General Hood and some of his staff rode up the pike. The general halted his horse. He gazed in every direction at the dead and dying in his army. His expression altered to melancholy sadness. Then, sitting in his saddle, the commander of the Army of Tennessee covered his face with his hand, sobs wrenching his body.

Sam and Johnny left to bury Ben and Sarge, but Zach remained on the battlefield. Hood had moved on toward town, yet the sight of his commander's grief stayed with Zach. After all, he had ordered the attack. If they'd attacked the right and left flanks instead of the center, many Confederates lying in the field would be eating breakfast this morning.

And they'd lost Cleburne. Many soldiers, including Zach, had considered him their most talented general. His men had followed him into the thick of battle yesterday. Most hadn't lived to tell about it.

"Help me."

Zach knelt beside a man missing a foot. "What's your name, soldier?"

"Joseph Miller, Sixth Texas."

"Joseph, the ambulances are collecting the wounded from the field." Zach caught a driver's eye and waved him over. "My name's Zach Pearson, First Tennessee. I'll wait with you until they arrive."

Wheels creaked toward them, stopping once. Soldiers jumped down from the wagon and moved dead men to the side.

"Much obliged, Zach." His head turned at the sound of a hoof striking a stone. "I hear them now. How bad is it?"

"You lost your foot, but you should be all right."

"It's gone? No fooling?" Bright blue eyes widened at Zach's nod. "It hurts like blazes. I worried about losing it all night … never knowing it was already gone."

Two men, each holding a corner of a gray blanket, knelt beside him. "We're here to take you to the field hospital."

"Thank you." He lay back and closed his eyes.

"His name is Joseph Miller of the Sixth Texas." Zach helped heft him onto the blanket.

"Much obliged. We'll take it from here."

Those men were as much heroes as men who carried muskets. Ambulances toted battle-scarred soldiers to the field hospitals soon after fighting began—and often while shot and shell crashed around them.

He wandered aimlessly, searching for faces of friends. Such carnage. How could he stay in after this?

Quitter.

His pa's words, spitting at a young boy in exasperation, haunted him. He couldn't make those words true.

A captain approached him on foot. "Soldier, what is your regiment?"

He straightened. "Zachariah Pearson of the First Tennessee, sir."

"Have you lost non-commissioned officers in your regiment?"

"Yes, sir. I found Corporal Morefield and Sergeant Ogle this morning … dead from bullet wounds. I've only found a handful of comrades from my regiment."

"Our losses are greater than we can bear." His mustache twitched. "Have you served our Confederacy as a soldier for a long time?"

"Yes, sir. Almost since the start."

"Ever instructed new recruits in elementary principles?"

Zach's heart rate quickened. "I have, sir."

"Just as I thought." He nodded. "You take over for your corporal now, son."

He had dreamed of getting a promotion. His gaze rested on the peaceful expression of a dead comrade nearby. But he hadn't wanted to replace his corporal like this.

"Gather your men, Corporal Pearson. We have dead to bury."

Zach peered out over the field. It wasn't the first time he'd dug graves for comrades. Yet this time his heart weighed as much as a boulder on his chest. He'd never buried so many men he admired at one time.

"You will have a new sergeant. Orders will be coming soon."

Corporal Pearson. The title had lost its luster and bound him to the army as if shackled by irons. His head still spun from battle losses. The smell of gunpowder lingered in his nose. Nate's blood stained his uniform. And now he'd have charge over a group of soldiers?

While Callie waited for him in the town across the field.

CHAPTER THIRTY-TWO

Callie hadn't been in the sick room since she and Louisa bathed and changed into dresses that morning—how heavenly to be clean again. She enjoyed the feel of petticoats under the sweep of a full skirt. Combs held back her shoulder-length hair.

She'd ripped up her soldier blouse, happy to use it for bandages. A soldier of short stature came in for a meal. Her heart lifted when Mrs. Ross suggested giving the pants and coat to the man, who wore tattered, grimy clothes. She built up the fire in the parlor, rejoicing in the soldier's heartened expression. After all, as Mrs. Ross pointed out, she had no more use for them.

The delicious blaze of the fireplace penetrated to her bones as she stirred a big pot of soup. The savory seasonings in the soup—basil, parsley, sweet marjoram—brought pure joy to her senses after doing without so long. She had prepared two pots for lunch—the first batch had been devoured within the half hour, though watered down considerably to feed the dozens of soldiers who had come to the door. They smiled and nodded their thanks as she scooped up servings to the men who'd endured far too much hardship.

Mrs. Ross preened at the soldiers' expressions of gratitude. "It's the least I can do for soldiers who fight so nobly for our country."

The men raised tin cups and cheered.

Callie's heart lightened at their smiles. After last evening's horrific battle, the kindness of a home-cooked meal went a long way to begin their healing. She began to understand why Nate always accepted supper invitations—it meant so much more than just a full stomach.

She fingered the soft fabric of her borrowed floral pink calico frock. She and her sister had even more reasons to be grateful to Mrs. Ross than the soldiers who ate around her table. She didn't have to pretend to be someone she wasn't anymore. What joy to shed those manly clothes and mannerisms. To be able to cook again, not just heat corn over a fire. She used a napkin to wipe soup from her mouth and almost laughed out loud from the sheer joy of being a woman again.

Thinking back, she hadn't done such a bad job at soldiering. Pretending to be a man in the company of thousands of men had eaten at her soul, but she'd endured it because she had to.

Shedding the pretense freed her spirit. She couldn't wait to see Zach again as her former self. No, maybe that wasn't possible, for her weeks in the army had somehow made her a stronger woman. She'd never be the same girl he'd known before.

Every time the front door opened, Callie checked to see who it was. Zach hadn't come, and the second pot of soup grew smaller. She dished him a bowl and set it in the kitchen. He'd be hungry when he arrived.

Mrs. Ross bustled from room to room with a kind word for each guest, but the busy woman had yet to visit the sick room, probably taking the siblings at their word that they'd manage. Her sister had bandaged the wounds of the four men in her care and had fed them. Now they waited for a surgeon's visit.

Louisa entered the kitchen. "Where's the doctor?"

"I don't know." Callie filled a tin cup with vegetable soup and handed it to a waiting soldier. "Is Nate worse?"

"I don't think so. Just being inside a warm house is an improvement." She peered out the window. "So many people on the streets. I wonder if the surgeon knows about the wounded in this house?"

Mrs. Ross hurried into the kitchen. "I've sent for the doctor. Again. No telling when he or any of the army surgeons will be here. How are our boys?"

"One is asleep." Louisa wrung her hands. "The rest groan in pain."

"Soldiers just carried in another wounded man. Shot in the leg. I've instructed them to carry him into the sick room, which is now full. If there are more injured men, I'll have to put them in the parlor." Their hostess clucked her tongue. "Well, there's no help for stains on my rug. Let's give those in pain a small dose of laudanum. That's the only medicine I have on hand. I wanted to consult with the doctor first, but I can't stand the thought of their suffering. I'll fetch the laudanum for you, dear. Can you see to it?"

Louisa bit her lip before straightening to her full height. "Of course. I'll remember how much medicine each man gets and then tell the doctor when he comes. He can advise us what's best after that."

"I'll fetch you some paper so you can write it down. You can write, can't you?"

"Of course."

Mrs. Ross squeezed her shoulder. "Thank you, Louisa. I never could abide the sick room. You girls are like angels straight from heaven sent to help me."

Angels. That eased Callie's fears over the siblings' intrusion into the Ross household.

"Callie, will you make another batch of soup? I've soaked some dried vegetables, and they're about ready for the pot." Mrs. Ross leaned close. "Add lots of water. I never expected so many. A bit of vegetables with the broth is better than nothing."

She nodded. So much for helping Louisa. There were too many other tasks that needed to be done. Pride welled up in her sister's sacrifice—Louisa hadn't been the best in sick rooms in the past. Her husband's injury shifted her focus off herself.

While preparing the soup, Callie's gaze often strayed to the kitchen door. Where was Zach? The corners of her mouth turned up in anticipation of the look in his eyes when he saw her in a frock once again. But that would have to wait. Zach was out in the fields searching for survivors and lost comrades. Gathering supplies. Walking among the dead in the terrible aftermath of a war that had torn her country asunder. He had more important things on his mind than what she was wearing.

She shuddered at the tragedy revealed by dawn's light when they carried Nate to shelter. No matter what the future held, she'd not don soldier's garb again. She wasn't strong enough. Her admiration for the men she'd marched with had grown a hundred-fold in the past two months.

She stoked the fire under the soup and then went to the parlor, where she spotted a man from her brigade. He nodded at her without recognition. Sipping coffee, he returned to his contemplation of the blazing fire while men around him talked. While relieved he didn't recognize her, a small part of her was a bit miffed as well. She'd done the best she could do as a soldier, even if it hadn't been enough to win Zach's love.

Zach was a hero in her eyes. Even so, she wanted to ask him to quit the war. They'd lost too many men to recover and make a fight. In fact, going into winter quarters until spring to give her men time to recover seemed the best idea to her.

Her men. Yes, in some ways she'd always belong to them, belong to the men in this parlor eating soup from tin cups … only they didn't recognize her.

Outside, the street teamed with soldiers, townsfolk. Where was Zach?

Zach located two score of survivors from the First Tennessee by noon. Some learned of the loss of Corporal Morefield and Sergeant Ogle for the first time from him. Explaining that he'd been promoted to corporal, he set them to burying their dead.

They needed more men. He found another dozen from their regiment and sent them to join the others. When he returned to the digging, a man in his thirties introduced himself as Sergeant George Crawford, his new sergeant.

"Corporal Zach Pearson." He clasped the sergeant's calloused hand. "I'm right glad to meet you." Right glad to not be in this alone.

"Understood. I've introduced myself to anyone who didn't know me." The shorter man held up a piece of paper. "I have field orders to read to our regiment. No need to form the men in a line."

Zach attracted their attention, grateful to find them obedient to his orders. Men rested their arms on their shovels and looked at Sergeant Crawford.

"Refer to me as 'Sarge' if you like. I know your hearts are as heavy as mine over recent losses." His gaze scanned the group. "I have field orders from General Hood. *The commanding general congratulates the army upon the success achieved yesterday over our enemy by their heroic and determined courage. The enemy has been sent in disorder and confusion to Nashville, and while we lament the fall of many gallant officers and brave men, we have shown to our countrymen that we can carry any position occupied by our enemy.*"

Zach snatched his mouth shut. Those orders couldn't really state that the fight had been successful, not with all the unsuccessful charges that had left so many dead and wounded.

"Even as we speak, Lee's Corps is crossing the Harpeth River to leave Franklin in pursuit of the Federals in Nashville." Sarge lifted his chin. "We will follow them, but I don't yet know when. I don't need to tell you that Cheatham's Corps—our corps—suffered great losses yesterday. The situation is very grave in some of our brigades. Some officers have no men ... some companies have no officers." He dismissed them and grimly picked up a shovel.

Zach leaned over, his hands on his knees. Catastrophic losses. Losses he had no idea how they'd ever recover from.

And his corps was ordered to pursue the fleeing enemy? They needed rest, time to recover. Food.

Recalling his new leadership role, he straightened. He had

to keep a grip on his emotions for their sake. Silently, the men returned to their tasks.

Grateful that Callie wasn't going to face another battle, Zach picked up a shovel and drove it into the cold ground.

"A neighbor boy just dropped these vegetables off to me." Mrs. Ross toted a round basket into the kitchen. "I've decided to use my large wash kettle and cook our next meal on the fireplace. That kettle holds twenty gallons. If they don't eat it all, they can come back tomorrow."

Callie laughed. "I'm certain they will. Those vegetables are a welcome sight." Sliding a dirty bowl back into the dishwater, she wiped soapy hands on her apron. "Cabbages, potatoes, turnips, and dried beans." She picked up a firm turnip, savoring its mildly sweet aroma. "It's hard to believe that I look forward to peeling vegetables. These look delicious. The crowd has left," she gestured to the room, empty of men, "but they'll be hungry again at suppertime."

"My, yes." She fanned her red face with her hands. "I'll be happy to see them return. Though there won't be as many."

She dropped the turnip with a thud. "What do you mean?"

"Why, one whole corps already crossed the Harpeth River." She picked a potato from the top of the pile. "They are on the road to Nashville."

Zach hadn't returned. He'd promised to see her if he received marching orders. He'd held her last night in the frigid temperatures. Protected. Sheltered. Safe. She'd slumbered like a babe, even through the artillery blasts she'd learned of later. He must care for her a little. Hadn't it meant more? Enough that he'd come back?

Callie dug her nails into a cabbage she'd plucked from the basket. He'd promised to return. Even a promise to a friend should be kept. "Which one?"

"Didn't ask. Does it matter?"

The first time she'd worn a dress in weeks. Today could be the last time she'd see him if there was another battle like yesterday's.

Oh, yes. It mattered more than anything else in the world.

CHAPTER THIRTY-THREE

Zach trudged to the Ross home after sunset. He hadn't been this exhausted since … maybe ever. Curling up in his bedroll near a fire appealed more to him than a hot meal. Seeing Callie once more meant more than anything.

A lantern hung by the doorframe welcomed him to the brick home. Its flickering light brought a pang to his chest. Little things meant a lot.

He knocked and waited. Conversations reached him through the closed door. Mrs. Ross probably couldn't hear him over all that, so he pushed it open. The aroma of cabbage soup changed his mind about the bed over the meal. He'd never been overly fond of the smell, but a summer rose couldn't smell prettier right now. He hoped they'd offer him a cup.

Warm air struck his cold face. How he longed to sleep one whole night with a full belly before a cozy fireplace. At least Callie, Nate, and Louisa would sleep warm tonight.

Five men were eating in the parlor. Four more stood in front of the fire, almost hiding the enormous kettle resting on the embers. He greeted them and headed to the sick room. Maybe Callie was with his cousin.

He stepped inside the crowded bedroom. No Callie. "Nate. How's that shoulder?" He grinned despite his cousin's wan face and Louisa's downtrodden expression.

"Hurts a mite." Nate's tight face moved into the semblance of a grin. "'Bout time for more laudanum while I wait for the doctor to show."

Zach's gaze swept the room. He greeted four other injured men. One soldier was bound to lose an arm. Another had bandages wrapped around his head. None of the wounds he saw had to be fatal—if treated. "Ambulances were still bringing fellas to hospitals this afternoon. Lots of wounded. Someone should be by soon."

"Hope so." Louisa's brow wrinkled. "All Callie and I know to do is clean the wounds and put on bandages. Mrs. Ross isn't good in the sick room, so she's grateful for the help."

Something was different about Louisa … it was her dress. And her blond hair was swept back with brown combs. So, the girls found time to bathe. He'd washed up in the icy Harpeth River, using soap he'd found in a knapsack. He'd cleaned his dirty clothes as best he could while he had the chance.

He knelt beside Nate. "I'm not much help either, I'm afraid. That's dried blood on your bandages. Probably means the wound stopped bleeding." He looked at Louisa. "Did you feel for the bullet in his shoulder?"

"I tried." Her gaze fastened on the bandage. "Something hard near the skin. I think the surgeon can remove it."

"Glad to hear it." As long as the bullet didn't crush the bone, Nate'd probably be all right. Best news he'd had all day.

"What's going on out there?" Nate flicked his eyes toward the window behind closed curtains.

"It ain't pretty." He sighed. "You saw the field this morning. General Cleburne is dead."

"Heard about losing our generals. It didn't need to happen that way."

"Don't I know it." Zach hesitated to tell him too much. "We lost Ben and Sarge."

Nate's eyes glazed. "Hate hearing that."

"They made me a corporal, so you know they're desperate."

"No fooling?" Nate gave a slow smile. "Glad about that. Your first promotion. You'll make officer someday."

His cousin's sincerity eased some of his worry. "We march out tomorrow."

"Nashville?"

Zach nodded.

Nate's eyes flashed. "Haven't we taken enough punishment?"

And then some. With so many wounded staying in Franklin, he knew his days were numbered. This might be his last conversation with Nate. "You concentrate on getting better."

"I will." They clasped hands. "The war may be over for me, but I'll be here for a time. Ask for a furlough to come see me."

"When they just made me a corporal?" Though he wanted nothing more than to stay here with Callie, he shook his head and stood. "I'll be back when I can." He looked at Louisa. "Is Callie in the kitchen?"

"She is. She watched for you all day. Eat a bowl of soup—she made it." She knelt beside Nate and raised her eyes to Zach. "Talk to her."

He couldn't. He'd not tie her to a man in such desperate straits as he. He went into the kitchen where he found her blessedly alone.

Callie turned from the stove, coffee pot in hand. "You came." She placed the pot on the stove. Brown combs swept back beautiful auburn curls to nestle at her ears. A pink dress—she looked real pretty in pink.

"You look … as pretty as a meadow full of daisies." Why'd he say a fool thing like that? Daisies weren't pink.

Her brown eyes sparkled. "I wanted you to think I'm pretty."

"I always have." He touched her face before he could stop himself. "Even when you wore soldiers' garb."

"Truly?"

He looked at her in wonder. "Don't you ever look in the mirror?"

"Not if I can help it."

"I'll buy you one."

She blushed.

He reached for her.

She stepped into his arms and nestled against his chest as if she belonged there. He brushed her warm lips with his. Her arms went around his neck. The kiss deepened as he slid his hands into her hair, the combs pinging onto the floor.

The kitchen door opened. "Callie must have forgotten your coff—" Mrs. Ross halted.

Callie met her hostess's shocked gaze. Dropping her arms to her sides, she stepped away from Zach. She ignored the heat flooding her face. If only Mrs. Ross had waited to barge in—

Barge in? This was her home.

"I'm sorry, Mrs. Ross." She picked up the coffee pot. "I forgot that I came in here to fetch the pot."

"I imagine you did." She put her hands on her hips. "Are you betrothed to this young man?"

Callie shook her head. Had he meant to propose? He'd kissed her with such passion. Which she'd returned. No wonder Mrs. Ross stood there radiating her disapproval.

"Humph. This young woman is under my protection. I'll thank you to remember it and control yourself."

"Yes, ma'am. The fault is mine. Callie is a lady." He shifted his weight from one foot to the other. "You can trust it won't happen again."

Callie's heart dropped. Her dreams withered. He didn't intend to kiss her again. There'd be no proposal of marriage.

"Good. Now, have you eaten yet?"

He shook his head. "I am hungry. Thirsty, too."

Callie picked up a cup.

"You're in luck, then." The hospitable woman poured the dark beverage then Callie gave it to him.

Zach took a long swallow. "Delicious. Much obliged."

"Come in the parlor for a bowl of Callie's soup." She pushed open the door. "A gentleman is parched for my coffee. Join us when you finish your beverage. Remember, I'm right out here." She left without waiting for his reply.

An awkward silence fell between them. She retrieved her combs and set them on the table.

"I didn't mean for that to happen, Callie."

She figured some things were best left unsaid. "Is our corps marching out soon?"

"Tomorrow." He took another long drink as the silence between them thickened. "I came to say goodbye."

"Oh." She crossed her arms, holding onto her shoulders. "You don't have to go. You can quit the army."

He sucked in his breath. "Don't you think I want to quit?" He turned away. Set his empty cup on the table. "We lost a lot of good men. Ben and Sarge are dead."

Her chest ached. "They treated me, a raw recruit, as if my contribution as a soldier mattered."

"They were fine men. Things are … pretty bad for our corps. They made me a corporal. I have duties to my men. I can't abandon them."

A promotion. That's what he'd wanted. "But the army lost too many soldiers to be effective." She placed a hand on his unyielding arm. "Please, don't go to Nashville."

The pain in his green eyes intensified. "I made a promise that I'd see this fight to the end. That means something to me."

Her hand slid off his arm. She retrieved a bowl and spoon from a table against the wall. "You should eat before you go. There's plenty enough to have two bowls."

He stared at her, then looked away. "Much obliged."

Heavy-hearted, Callie led the way to the parlor. She dipped a generous portion and gave the bowl to Zach as others drew him into conversation.

If they kept him talking of battle news for the remainder of his visit, what did it matter? They had nothing more to say to each other.

He ate two servings of soup and then set the empty bowl on a table. He joined her by the doorway to the kitchen. He stepped closer. Gazing into her eyes, he sandwiched both of her hands within his. "Take care of yourself, sweet Callie."

"Keep your head down." How she wished she had the standing as his wife to demand he not go, but she didn't. Then again, not even a wife could muster a man out of the army.

He gave a quick nod before striding for the door.

She memorized every move with an aching heart. He'd march bravely toward battle again tomorrow … as he had so often in the past.

This might be the last time she saw him.

Fingertips to her lips, she returned to the solitude of the kitchen. He'd had the opportunity to declare his feelings. He hadn't. He didn't love her.

CHAPTER THIRTY-FOUR

Callie cringed when ambulances delivered wounded the next day. How long had the poor men been out in the cold? Her heart, already heavy with worry for Zach and the pain of his rejection, grew even heavier.

Mrs. Ross covered her mouth with her hand as attendants pushed her parlor furniture to one side. They tossed hay on the floor. Soon after, eight injured men rested on the hay. Some writhed in pain.

As Callie stared at the wounded, she tried to push away thoughts of the two men she'd shot. She wrung her hands. Two men needed a surgeon because of her. Her body went cold. At least both Federal soldiers had left the battlefield of their own accord.

Her musket lay in the ditch where she left it. She'd never pick up another unless hunting for food.

A soldier grabbed his leg and moaned.

Callie met Louisa's stormy eyes. No doctor had visited their wounded yet. Other than feed them and dress their wounds, all they could do was give them laudanum. The Yankees she'd shot probably fared better than her comrades.

"A surgeon better come today." Louisa grabbed the last medicine bottle and shook it. "Or I'm going out to find one."

"I'll go after we administer the laudanum." From the mutinous look on her sister's face, Callie better not return without a doctor. An injured soldier stifled a groan drawing her gaze to his leg wound. What could they do for those suffering beyond laudanum? Several hospitals had been set up in the town's buildings. She didn't doubt that more patients fit in the courthouse than in a home, but these fellas deserved care also.

Before they'd finished, a doctor arrived.

"I'm Dr. Quintard. I take it these men have yet to receive medical care?" The graying man's gaze swept the parlor.

"Only laudanum to those in this room." Louisa pointed to the hall. "Five more await attention in the bedroom."

"Fine. I will see to them all." His gaze stalled on a man with rust stains on his leg. "It will help if you clean the wounds."

"Of course." Louisa took him by the arm and guided him down the hall. "The men's wounds in here have been washed. Start in here."

Callie marveled that, thanks to her sister's persuasive ways, Nate was among the first to receive attention.

Though her worry for Zach never left her thoughts, Callie was so busy that the days blended together. In addition to duties in the sick room, she helped Mrs. Ross cook meals for ailing soldiers in the courthouse.

Dr. Quintard had removed the bullet from Nate's shoulder, greatly relieving his pain. In the doctor's opinion, the war was over for him. Time would tell how much lasting damage the bullet did in the weeks ahead.

Louisa spent most of her time at her husband's side. Mrs. Ross, a social creature who seemed to crave conversation like others craved food, was often out delivering food and helping neighbors. Her ten-year-old son, Davy, came home only to eat and sleep. Callie had rarely seen him. Wounded even filled the schoolhouse, which made the adventurous Davy happy.

That left a bulk of the care for the wounded in the Ross household on Callie's shoulders. She was grateful to serve her soldiers this way—and grateful for food and shelter. She didn't plan on complaining. Those miserable days of marching in sleet returned to her vividly when it grew so cold that ice formed on the branches, and she prayed for Zach. He didn't have an overcoat ... just a blanket.

It seemed that the terrible battle had done *some* good. The wedge between her and God caused by her pretending to be something she wasn't had disappeared. Her ma would be glad. Now she prayed for Zach's life to be spared every time she thought of him.

A week passed and then another. No word had reached them of a battle in Nashville. If no one had to fight, then their soldiers could come back to Franklin for a long rest.

Her personal sadness was shoved deep inside. Zach didn't love her—at least not the way she craved. That magical night when he sheltered her in his arms might have been in response to her turmoil. Less clear was the reason he kissed her the next day. The surprise of seeing her dressed as a woman again? No matter. He promised not to kiss her again.

And the fact he was still in the army proved he was a man of his word.

Zach's jaw hurt from clenching it so long. His regiment had begun the battle from the extreme right outside Nashville. Then they'd been moved to the left flank atop a hill. Each time he helped the sergeant set up the line. Yet it kept changing, their position growing ever more dangerous for him and his men.

With the battle at Franklin still fresh on everyone's mind, he roamed from group to group with assurances he was far from feeling but were so important to morale. Was this the role he'd aspired to? Leadership in the army was harder than it had appeared from the viewpoint of a rank and file soldier. Being in charge, even at the lowest level, was more difficult than he'd ever imagined. His respect for Ben and Sarge grew by the second.

Orders came to move left. Grimly, he forwarded the order. Then a second order came to move left again. He surveyed his men, his heart racing to find the line was now so thin that they were no more than skirmishers.

They withstood a fierce bombardment from the north and from the west.

Zach kept his ears in tune with the bugler as their situation worsened, listening for the sound of retreat. But it didn't come. He tossed his hat on the snowy hillside. What were the generals waiting for? For all of them to die this time? His men looked around at him for direction. He shook his head.

Movement to the west caught his eye. Hundreds of Federal infantry poured across a creek to their west. Their battered troops couldn't fight them off, that much was certain.

Grabbing his hat, Zach yelled instructions and then followed his comrades in full retreat toward Franklin where Callie waited.

The Federals were still breathing down Zach's neck.

"Every man for himself!" Someone yelled, fueling the frenzied headlong dash.

An abandoned wagon and team stood at the side of the road. Zach unhitched the horses and mounted one of them. He rode straight to the Ross household, arriving well past dark. Cold rain plastered his hair to his head. He glanced around for his comrades, but they were nowhere in sight. Hopefully the bulk of them had made it to Franklin before him.

There wasn't much time to talk with Callie. He'd regretted the way he'd left two weeks ago. Facing the unbelievable numbers of Union soldiers in Nashville had driven one point home—Callie ought to know how he felt before he died.

Mrs. Ross opened the door. "I thought you'd gone to Nashville."

"I did, Mrs. Ross. That fight ended in our retreat." He looked beyond her, past the wounded lying in the parlor to a flurry of pink.

"Zach." Callie threw her arms around his neck. "I worried so about you."

"Callie. My sweet Callie." He hugged her close. "There isn't much time. We're in full retreat."

"Retreat?" Nate leaned against the wall.

Zach slid his hand down Callie's arm to clasp her hand. He held onto her while he strode to his cousin. "You're looking better. Up and walking."

"Just a bit." Nate's face was pale. "Bullet's out. Doc says the war's over for me, but I may be able to use my right arm once my shoulder heals."

"That's good news." Part of his burden lifted. "We're in retreat. Nashville was a disaster. I expect Yankees will be here before long unless this rain holds them up overnight. Look for them here. Maybe tomorrow."

"I'm not much of a threat." Nate looked at his arm. "No soldier in this house is a threat."

"This may become an occupied town, or they may simply pursue us. If Federals tarry, our soldiers will likely become prisoners. You'll be shipped out once you've healed enough to be moved."

Nate rubbed his injured arm. "Reckon we'll have to face whatever comes. I can't walk back to Cageville. Nor can the girls."

"The girls are safe. No one knows they were soldiers. I have a horse outside I can leave with you. If you know a place nearby …"

"My sister, Mrs. Elvira Mills, lives five miles east of here." Mrs. Ross stepped closer. "I can lend you my wagon. Davy can show you where Elvira lives. I'll send along a note of introduction."

"I can make it five miles."

"And I can drive the wagon." Louisa smiled up at him.

Callie glanced from the couple to her hostess. "I think I should stay here until all the patients are well enough to go home or go to another hospital."

"You'd be welcome, dear." Mrs. Ross patted her arm. "And I'd appreciate the assistance."

"I'll want your sister's direction before I leave, but right now I need a private moment with Callie. With your permission."

Mrs. Ross studied him. "Callie? What do you think?"

"I'll speak with him. You can trust him." She led the way to the kitchen then turned. "What is it?"

"I hated the way I left you." He blurted out. He kissed her hand that he was still holding. "You must think I don't care for you."

"Do you?"

The best way was to show her. He leaned down and kissed her upturned lips. "I love you, Callie."

"You do?"

He nodded and kissed her again. "I spent so long fighting my feelings that I didn't know what they were for certain that day I left you."

"Why fight your feelings for me?"

He wrapped his arms around her, wincing as his cheek, still bruised from the butt of a rifle, rested on her head. "Because the army is my career. Though it's a dangerous life, I can't be a quitter." He stuttered over the word. "I'm libel to wind up dead before my time. I don't want to leave my wife a widow."

"Can't you do something else?" She leaned back to meet his gaze with overly bright eyes. "You and Nate can start a new horse farm. Or you can help Pa on our farm."

"Right now, that sounds awful good, but I made a promise." He shook his head. "I'll stay in the army 'til the war ends, one way or the other. It seems pretty certain how this thing will go now." He gazed into her brown eyes, memorizing her features for all time. "I didn't want to … go away … without you knowing how I felt."

A sob caught in her throat. She buried her face against his shoulder.

He gently lifted her head from his shoulder and rubbed the tears from her wet cheeks with his thumbs while his hands cradled her face. "Do you love me?"

"I love you, Zach Pearson." Red-rimmed, puffy eyes stared back at him. "I've loved you since I was a schoolgirl."

"Then I have all I've ever wanted right here." He kissed her once more, a gentle touch that clung to her mouth as if deciding on its own never to leave. He released her reluctantly. "I must go."

She grabbed onto his coat sleeves. "Don't you die. You hear me? Don't you die. Come back to me."

"If I can, I will." He kissed her once more. "Go to Nate and Louisa, once you're no longer needed here."

"If they will have me."

"Your sister will hogtie her husband if he refuses to take care of you."

She smiled through her tears. "Godspeed, Zach Pearson."

CHAPTER THIRTY-FIVE

For the next month, Callie's thoughts were filled with Zach. She could hardly believe he loved her. Her cheeks flushed when remembering his embrace. Yes, he loved her, yet every flake of snow, every cold rain reminded her that his peril wasn't only due to the heartless Yankee general their army pursued through the South. At news gleaned from whispered conversations, Callie's heart turned cold at the atrocities laid at General Sherman's door.

She had to whisper anything that sounded like criticism of Northerners for they now occupied Franklin. She could only be grateful that Louisa and Nate—and two other wounded soldiers well enough to escape—had fled to Mrs. Ross's sister, where they still recuperated.

Within a few days of taking over the town, the Federals had opened the railroad for traffic. Callie stood, arms folded, as their surgeons then examined the Confederate wounded at Mrs. Ross's. They had considered two men recovered enough for prison and sent them away in cars. Zach had been right about the danger to Nate. He'd have been on one of the early trains had he not escaped.

Callie clamped her mouth shut during the surgeons' sporadic visits to check the progress of the wounded. They didn't care about their fellow human beings, or they'd allow the injured to go home. She and Mrs. Ross vented their frustration every time a patient was taken from them. Of the four men left, Callie had little doubt they'd be off to prison when sufficiently healed.

This treatment fueled the flame of resentment inside her for the army, yet she discussed her opinions only with Mrs. Ross, who had warned her that some citizens in this Southern town had Northern sympathies.

The Yankee soldiers treated her courteously. If they knew she'd recently worn Confederate gray and shot two of their soldiers, their attitude would be different. They might send her off to prison.

That day still haunted her. She saw again the rifle pointed at Louisa, the rifle raised to bludgeon Zach, and panic rose to her throat. What could she have done differently?

Nothing. Two Federal soldiers recovered from bullet wounds—one to the hand, the other to the elbow—and Louisa and Zach were alive today because of it.

She kept her eyes lowered when serving the Northern soldiers and doctors who often ate in the Ross home. Their jovial spirits reminded her of countless meals she'd shared with her Southern comrades. Their courtesy toward her and Mrs. Ross gradually thawed the worst of her bitterness. She'd always enjoyed cooking, and their compliments made it a pleasure to prepare meals for them. Their added provisions gave her flour, meat, and other things she hadn't seen in months. The Federals were as grateful for a hot meal, the warmth of a fire, and friendly conversation as any of her comrades had been.

Maybe they weren't so different after all.

Her hostess continued to visit with neighbors despite the Northern occupation. She really wasn't good with patients and left their care to Callie.

Her days were long and filled with activity, yet her mind invariably returned to Zach. The wonder of his love warmed her heart, still so new that her spirit sang even as her throat constricted for his safety. He had to come back for her. It was the only outcome she allowed herself to imagine.

Come back to me, Zach.

Callie donned a warm cloak, borrowed from Mrs. Ross, on a cold day in January. She'd offered to get some groceries for Mrs. Ross. Her errand took her by the field where Zach had fought so heroically … and where so many had died.

She'd been avoiding the area. Today, something drew her here.

Trembling hands dropped her empty basket on the ground at the many grave markers, mute testimony to the tragic number of deaths. The terror of that day rose up again as her mind's eye conjured up the field as she'd last seen it … full of heroic dead. Sarge and Ben were buried here. Sorrow overcame her at the senseless loss. So many good men—and perhaps a few women soldiers—had died here. Nate was shot. Perhaps he would have died if she hadn't been there to bind his wound.

She pressed her palms to her cheeks as realization washed over her—Louisa and Zach would have died if not for her. Callie's body flushed as if with fever. She had saved their lives. That night had convinced her to leave the army, but maybe there had been a purpose for her presence there after all. Zach might be buried in Franklin if she hadn't been there.

Maybe God hadn't been angry with her pretense of being a man and a soldier. Maybe He had used Pa's ultimatum to put her in the right place at the right time.

She stepped onto the grassy slope, the scene of her nightmares. A stoop-shouldered man studied each headstone. The familiar way he walked … she cupped her hand over her mouth. His head used to be held high, his shoulders back. His eyes had twinkled when teasing her and Louisa.

She picked up her skirt and ran to him, afraid to call his name lest the Union soldiers hear. If they found him …

Pa jerked around. He stumbled backward, his face ashen above his beard.

She threw her arms around his shaking frame. "It's me, Pa. Callie."

"Callie. My Callie." His hands cradled the base of her neck.

Tears slid down his cheeks. "I thought I'd never see either of my girls again." He folded her in his arms.

"Pa, the Federals occupy this town." Her gaze darted to the road, blessedly empty of soldiers. "You have to go before they find you."

"Shh. I saw 'em." His arms tightened. "I ain't about to confess to somethin' I don't do no more."

Her hands on his arms, she pushed far enough away to gaze at the broken man Pa had become.

"And I smashed that blasted whiskey jar. Nothing good ever came out of it."

"Truly?" Her breath caught. She searched his worn, lined face. His hair had turned iron gray in the months they'd been gone.

"Yep."

"I missed you, Pa."

He stepped back, his hands on her upper arms as if he feared she'd dash away. "I looked for you and Louisa for months. Every town, big and small, within fifty miles of Cageville. No one had seen you. I came back to the house every now and again to see if you came back … or at least sent a letter to let me know how you got along."

The sorrow on his face smote her. "I'm sorry we run off like that, but I couldn't marry Ezra Culpepper. I just couldn't."

"I know that now. I regret my part in all this. But you gotta know I done what I done 'cuz it was the only way left to me to provide for you." His gaze lowered to a headstone beside him.

"I understand, Pa. Truly. I'm not holding a grudge. I forgave you long ago." She studied his bewildered face. "But how did you find me here?"

He reached inside his brown overcoat and extracted a letter from an inner pocket.

Her letter, the one she'd written before the battle. What pain that must have caused him. "Oh, Pa."

"Got news from a chaplain. Two Shaw brothers went missing

after the battle. Presumed dead. He sent your letter along." His shoulders shook. "Worst day of my life. Worse even than when your Ma died, 'cuz back then I had my daughters."

Tears stung her eyes. "Pa, I'm fine. Louisa and I quit soldiering after the battle." She grasped his cold hand. "She married Nate, who took a bullet in the shoulder. He's healing pretty well. Louisa said he's already able to move it some. They are staying in a home near here, hidden from the Yankees."

"No foolin'? They're married?" His face brightened. "Well, don't that beat all."

"And expecting a blessed event. You'll be a grandfather."

"A grandbaby?" His shoulders straightened. "And I never thought I'd see either of you again."

"I missed you." Her heart lightened to see his dear face again. Having his daughters back with the addition of a son-in-law and the anticipation of a new baby could go a long way toward healing his broken spirit. "I'll take you to Louisa. She'll be so happy to see you."

"Can you really forgive me for driving you away?" His beard trembled. "The war got the best of me, took the best from us. I couldn't take care of you no more. Ezra could. I see I was wrong to force marriage on you."

Tears slid down her cheeks. She had her pa back. "I forgave you before I wrote that letter."

He kissed her cheek. "You've got more of your mother's strength than you know."

"Oh, Pa." Tears gushed as she choked back a sob. "I always felt like the weakest member of the family."

"The strongest ... in all the ways that count."

"Thanks, Pa. Let's get out of this cold." She took his arm. "I'm staying at the home of Mrs. Ross. Without a doubt, she'll offer you a place to stay but be prepared. She'll talk your ear off."

And then he laughed. The most wonderful sound she'd heard in a long, long time.

CHAPTER THIRTY-SIX

It was over. With a heart as heavy as a sack of lead shot, Zach stood in line to sign a parole stating he'd not take up arms against the United States.

Not that he wished to continue fighting until they were all dead, which was worse than surrender.

By a whisker.

After General Lee surrendered in Virginia, Zach had figured it was just a matter of time. He had been and still was as hungry and weather-beaten as any officer or rank and file soldier. They'd chased that scalawag, General Sherman, surveying the carnage he left behind through the cold winter only to surrender to him in the spring.

Not the best way to end the hostilities in his view—Zach would have preferred to surrender to the more honorable Union General Grant. The assassination of President Lincoln had shocked Zach to the core. He'd never dreamed of such a tragic turn of events. He'd never wanted Lincoln's death. It only served to further divide a country that must now find a way to unite once again. What a mess.

Greensboro, North Carolina. The war ended there for him with a second surrender agreement signed by General Joe Johnston as commander of Army of Tennessee on April twenty-sixth, after the United States Government rejected the first.

There'd been no cheering among his comrades. No one gave the Rebel yell they'd perfected over four years of charges, attacks, and retreats. He'd longed for Callie and home, but not this way.

Not returning as a defeated soldier.

Zach didn't raise his eyes as he picked up a pen to sign his parole on May first. It was so hard to breathe that his ribs seemed to squeeze against his lungs. He put the tip on the paper and forced the pen to move across the page. He had no choice but to muster out. He figured that he could join the army again when the situation died down, but did he want to now? After all he'd endured, wasn't that enough to ask of one man?

He stood with Spence, Sam, Johnny, and other comrades one last time the next day as General Joe Johnston gave his farewell address.

"I earnestly exhort you to observe faithfully the terms of pacification agreed upon; and to discharge the obligations of good and peaceful citizens, as well as you have performed the duties of thorough soldiers in the field." The commanding general surveyed the quiet crowd before him. "By such a course, you will best secure the comfort of your families and kindred and restore tranquility to our country."

Our country. They were part of the United States of America once again.

No longer a corporal but a civilian once more, Zach acknowledged the sound advice though his heart struggled to accept the truth. Almost four years of his life given to a cause that failed. He raised his eyes to heaven. At least he hadn't quit.

Birds sang in early May as Callie once more stood on the banks of the Tennessee River. This time, she waited for a ferry to cross with Pa, Louisa, and Nate.

A bee buzzed near her ear, and she stepped back. "The river still looks just as wide." The fresh, green beauty of thriving trees and apple blossoms under a warm sun warred with Callie's memories of that bleak, rainy autumn.

"I can hardly believe we're here again." Louisa, whose side seams had been let out as far as the fabric allowed to give room for the babe growing inside her, stared across the water.

"Crossing it is the only way to get to Cageville." Nate rubbed his upper right arm with his good hand. "And home." He smiled at Louisa.

Memories of that last crossing, when Callie had been a soldier, flooded back. Marching across the wide river with Zach at her side had felt like she walked on water—like Peter had in the Bible. Jesus had saved him when his fears overcame his faith and he began to sink.

She figured Jesus had saved her in much the same way, for she'd left her faith behind when leaving Cageville with bad blood between her and Pa. She hadn't realized the toll a soldier's role would take on her, how it both stole her prayers away and then gave them back on one terrible night that lived in her nightmares.

They'd left Franklin in a previously broken wagon that had been fixed up by Pa. He'd worked at the Franklin livery in exchange for wagon parts. Nate and Louisa had ridden in the back most of the journey.

The war was over. General Lee in Virginia was the first to surrender.

They'd learned yesterday that General Johnston surrendered in North Carolina. The news came as a blow to Callie, even though she'd expected it.

Zach. How she ached for him and the defeat he must feel— the same numbness that invaded her heart. She'd marched with him and their comrades too long not to experience a measure of disbelief, denial, anger, and sorrow at the news.

And he'd been with the army nearly four years.

She hadn't heard from him since he'd left Franklin all those months ago. He had no paper to write her a letter and no money to buy any. Their soldiers hadn't been paid for a long time.

No news had to mean he was alive. He must be alive. He had

to come home to her.

As a boat wide enough to ferry three wagons and teams across the river approached, she lifted a fervent prayer to heaven. *Please bring Zach home to me.*

Callie prepared lunch, too restless for idle hands. It was mid-June and she'd not heard from Zach. Every noise, whether barking dog or passing wagon on the road outside her home, drew her attention. No Zach. She flipped a corn cake in the sizzling skillet, the smell of cornmeal whetting her appetite. She'd spent too many months being hungry to take meals for granted.

Both the war's end and having her back home had renewed Pa's hope for the future. She'd helped him plant several acres with seeds he had hidden away. Not a full crop, but enough to see them through winter. And next summer promised to be even better. Pa worked in the fields in the hot summer sun, content to watch the earth replenish itself after lying fallow so long.

She'd walk over to Louisa's house after lunch. Now heavy with child, Louisa didn't leave the home she and Nate shared with his parents. Her in-laws anticipated their new role as grandparents just as much as Pa. Callie missed Ma more than ever with the new baby coming—a niece or nephew would give her a much-needed distraction if Zach wasn't here six weeks from now. Soldiers had to make their own way home—North Carolina was a far piece to walk.

Nate's right arm had recovered partial movement. It was enough for him to help his parents with their once prosperous horse farm which had only one horse—the one Zach found abandoned on the road outside Franklin. Two months of rest and nourishing hay revived the animal's spirits. All they needed was money to purchase a mare to begin again. They had high hopes for the offspring of their spirited steed—a survivor of a brutal war, just like them.

The town doctor had high hopes that Nate's arm, in time, would recover about half of its former function. Louisa glowed at the prognosis. Nate's arm was already strong enough to hold their babe when it arrived.

Callie's spirits sagged with the rising temperature. She turned the batch of corn cakes out on a plate, awaiting Pa's return from the field. A dog barked in the distance. She wandered into the front room to look out the window. No one.

Restless, she returned to the kitchen. She'd make soup tonight. She picked up a canning jar filled with a dried seasoning mix. She unscrewed the lid and breathed in the aromas of basil, lemon thyme, marjoram, and parsley. She had missed these dried herbs while in the army. The mixture enhanced even plain broth if they had no vegetables to add.

Had Zach made it to Tennessee yet? He must have. She refused to consider that he wasn't making his way back to her.

A footfall on the porch. Had Pa finished in the fields so soon? She wiped her hands on the dishtowel and went to the door.

Zach.

A thinner, older Zach than she'd seen in December but her man. Her Zach. A sob wracked her body, threatening to choke her. She threw herself into his arms. He clasped her to him, his arms as strong and solid as ever.

"I told you I'd come back if I could," he whispered, his voice breaking.

She leaned back in his arms to drink in his expressive green eyes that sparkled with joy. "I prayed enough to get you here."

"I counted on those prayers." He laughed, a rusty sound as if from lack of use.

How long had it been since she'd seen such joy on his face? Had he ever been so happy? Her heart flooded with thankfulness. He was alive, and he was here. He'd come back to her.

His arms tightened around her. He kissed her cheek, her lips, her wet eyes, and then her lips again and again.

His rough beard rubbed against her face—she didn't care. "What … what happened? Did our friends make it?"

"It wasn't pretty." The glow faded from his eyes. "All our friends made it to the end. After we signed … the parole, we headed home. Spence stayed with Johnny and me most of the way. Soon as we got close to Cageville, Johnny headed to see Martha Rose, and I came here."

Her heart ached for all he didn't say. She guessed at the depth of pain signing that document had given him.

"I don't know when I'll be able to talk about the rest, Callie." He rested his forehead against hers. "Maybe never."

More tears spilled down her cheeks at the sorrow on his face.

He wiped them away with gentle fingers. "Let's put that behind us and talk about the future." He went down with one knee resting on the wooden porch.

Heart racing, she almost forgot to breathe.

He reached for her hand. Clasped it to his chest.

His heart thudded against her fingertips.

"Callie Jennings, will you marry me?"

She squealed with pure joy to hear the proposal she'd longed for, dreamed of, for so long. "I *will* marry you, Zach Pearson."

"The thought of marrying you was all that kept me alive this spring." Leaping to his feet, he gave a Rebel yell. "One more Rebel cheer to celebrate my great good fortune to marry the girl I left behind me, the girl of my dreams." He kissed the hand he still held before kissing her lips again, a long kiss filled with promise.

"What about the army?" She raised her eyes slowly.

"I'm no longer a soldier." His eyes lost their luster. "I signed an oath not to take up arms against the Government of the United States."

"But they might need soldiers out West." She'd follow him anywhere, even into danger. Hadn't she proven that? "I'll marry you whether you are a soldier or—"

"Don't know if they'll want me back in their army." He covered her mouth with his lips. "I love you. I'm done with soldiering. Had a stomach full and then some. I'm staying home in Tennessee where I belong."

"I heard a yell. That you, Zach Pearson?" Pa strode up to him, hand extended. "Well, ain't you a sight for sore eyes."

Callie stepped out of Zach's arms.

Zach shook Pa's hand. "I've come to ask for your daughter's hand in marriage, Mr. Porter."

"What?" Pa took off his slouch hat and slapped it against his knee. "If you don't beat all. You know how much trouble you could have saved us?"

Callie couldn't help agreeing as she put her arm around Zach's waist and nestled her head against his shoulder.

"Sorry about that, sir. I think I had a little growing up to do." His arm tightened around her shoulder. "I've mended my ways."

A thousand experiences from her army days flooded back as she glanced from Zach to Pa. "My time as a soldier was meant to be, Pa. I saved Zach's life at Franklin."

"She did." Zach's eyes filled with wonder. "I never thought about it like that. If you hadn't been there that day—"

"Don't think about it." She rubbed the creases in his forehead away with gentle fingers. "I was there. That's all that matters. Come in for dinner, though you may not like what I made."

"What is it?"

"Corn cakes." She sighed. "I imagine you've eaten enough of those to last a lifetime."

"You've been out of the army too long. You ever remember a soldier turning down a home-cooked meal?"

"I guess not." She giggled. "After we eat, we'll visit Nate and Louisa. They're living at your uncle's place. He's been over almost daily asking about you."

"Good ol' Nate." He grinned. "Got a hankerin' to see him, too."

"I reckon we'll be talking to the preacher soon?" Pa folded his arms.

"Let's go now." Zach smiled at Callie. "I'm ready to start my life afresh. With you."

She kissed him right there on the porch, with Pa looking on and grinning.

AUTHOR'S NOTE

When I was searching for my next Civil War story, a friend and fellow Civil War buff told me about a husband and wife who served in the same regiment—she had disguised herself as a man. I had heard that other women served as soldiers. I began researching their story. What I discovered surprised me.

About four hundred women disguised themselves as men to fight for the North or South—and probably more as they only had to sneak away from the army and don a dress to leave the service. Their motives varied. They may have wanted to be near their husband, fiancé, or brother. Some wanted to keep a watchful eye on their men because newspapers reported of drinking and immorality among the soldiers. Some escaped unfortunate family situations. Some needed the pay. Others wanted adventure or to fight the enemy.

Women risked their reputations when joining. If discovered, they were criticized and seen as less than virtuous. Their motives were questioned. This cloud of doubt followed them after the war, for some always doubted their integrity. They often served one to two years before anyone knew they were female. Being wounded in battle usually gave them away. One woman hid her pregnancy until she went into labor while on picket duty.

If caught, they could be discharged, sent home, or imprisoned. It seems to have been at the officer's discretion.

They fought in battles. They were captured and imprisoned. They died in battle. If you'd like to learn more about these brave women, here are a few resources: *Women of the War* by Frank

Moore; *Liar, Temptress, Soldier, Spy* by Karen Abbott; *Women in the Civil War* by Mary Elizabeth Massey; and *I'll Pass for Your Comrade* by Anita Silvey.

I've included some historical figures in this novel. General John Bell "Sam" Hood commanded the Confederate Army of Tennessee in the fall of 1864. General Nathan Bedford Forrest spoke to the men with General Hood. Dr. Quintard was one of the doctors in Franklin. Confederate President Jefferson Davis declared a Day of Prayer on Wednesday, November 16, 1864. General Patrick Cleburne wandered among the gravestones at the Gothic chapel mentioned in the story. Sam R. Watkins, author of *Co. "Aytch"*, was a soldier in the 1st Tennessee Infantry. I loved the authentic way he wrote of his army experiences and wanted to honor his memory by including him.

General Hood's congratulatory written speech read to the men after the Battle of Franklin, the stirring speech given by Sarge after they crossed the Tennessee River, and General Johnston's words after the surrender come from the pages of history.

The 1st Tennessee was tasked with skirmishing ahead of the troops in the Battle of Franklin. They were in the thick of the fighting. Crossing that empty field required courage. History recorded such details as rabbits scampering away, quail landing on the field, and a red sun. If you'd like to learn more about the battle, some resources are: *The Battle of Franklin* by James R. Knight; *Eyewitnesses at the Battle of Franklin* compiled and edited by David R. Logsdon; and *Embrace an Angry Wind* by Wiley Sword.

I stumbled across a Confederate soldier's letter to his wife a couple of years before writing this novel. His grandson shared his letter written in June of 1863, shortly before his death at the Battle of Gettysburg. He knew of Lincoln's Emancipation Proclamation yet assured his wife that he'd slip away in the night and return to her rather than fight for slavery.

Instead, he fought for the rights of their great-great-grandchildren to worship God as they saw fit, not as the federal government mandated. He feared the seizing of their land through taxation or other methods.

He had looked down the road and feared what lay ahead if they lost.

This article stayed with me, influencing my thoughts long after the article was lost. I found it again on http://www.dailyprogress.com/news/confederate-soldier-s-letter-shows-feelings/article_6d9bfaa9-0012-5002-9d54-76bf7e7eef7b.html.

Southern soldiers and citizens suffered greatly, especially in the last two years of the war. Digging deeper to write the novel, their suffering reached out to me across the years, touching me deeply. I hope their story touches you.

Sandra Merville Hart

ACKNOWLEDGMENTS

I have so many people to thank for their encouragement and help in publishing this novel.

Thanks to fellow writer and Civil War buff, Kevin Spencer. When I was searching for a story-line for this novel, Kevin told me that a husband and wife (disguised as a man) served together in a Civil War regiment. Learning more about women on both sides who disguised themselves as men to fight as soldiers sparked the ideas for this novel. Also, thanks to Kevin, his wonderful wife, Charlotte, and his grandson, Caleb, for taking my husband and me on a Franklin tour. We stood beside the Duck River. We climbed Winstead Hill and Spring Hill. We traveled the same roads that the soldiers marched. What an inspiring, information-filled afternoon! You gave me an inside look at the battle. We had a wonderful time. Thank you from the bottom of my heart.

Thanks to Eddie Jones and the wonderful publishing team at Lighthouse Publishing of the Carolinas, including Shonda Savage and my managing editor, Pegg Thomas. Pegg, I've learned so much from you! I've been blessed by your friendship, knowledge, and sense of humor. Thank you for the time you spent pushing me to make my novel better.

Thanks also go to my husband, Chris, who happily accompanies me on my fact-finding trips to museums and battlefields. You're quiet when my mind is racing in a whirlwind of ideas. You're a springboard when I need to bounce ideas off someone. You make research more enjoyable. Thanks for joining me on this wild writing adventure. I love you.

Last but certainly not least, thanks to God, who gives me the story. Lord, I'm humbled to finally understand that You gave me the heart of a writer.